Dear Reader,

Home, family, community and love. These are the values we cherish most in our lives—the ideals that ground us, comfort us, move us. They certainly provide the perfect inspiration around which to build a romance collection that will touch the heart.

And so we are thrilled to have the opportunity to introduce you to the Harlequin Heartwarming collection. Each of these special stories is a wholesome, heartfelt romance imbued with the traditional values so important to you. They are books you can share proudly with friends and family. And the authors featured in this collection are some of the most talented storytellers writing today, including favorites such as Laura Abbot, Roz Denny Fox, Jillian Hart and Irene Hannon. We've selected these stories especially for you based on their overriding qualities of emotion and tenderness, and they center around your favorite themes—children, weddings, second chances, the reunion of families, the quest to find a true home and, of course, sweet romance.

So curl up in your favorite chair, relax and prepare for a heartwarming reading experience!

Sincerely,

The Editors

SHERRY LEWIS

Sherry Lewis's first love has always been books. In fact, she doesn't remember a time in her life when she didn't want to be a novelist. Her first literary success came in seventh grade when she won first place in a junior high school poetry contest and saw the poem published in the school's newspaper. Her first book was published by Harlequin Superromance in January 1995.

She is a self-confessed bookaholic and is firmly convinced she has one of the largest "To Be Read" stacks (actually, an entire room) in the world. She only wishes she had enough time to read them all.

HARLEQUIN HEARTWARMING

Sherry Lewis

New Year, New Love

Harlequin®

TORONTO NEW YORK LONDON
AMSTERDAM PARIS SYDNEY HAMBURG
STOCKHOLM ATHENS TOKYO MILAN MADRID
PRAGUE WARSAW BUDAPEST AUCKLAND

Recycling programs
for this product may
not exist in your area.

ISBN-13: 978-0-373-36422-0

NEW YEAR, NEW LOVE

Copyright © 2011 by Sherry Lewis

This book originally published as A MAN FOR MOM
Copyright © 1999 by Sherry Lewis

For questions and comments about the quality of this book
please contact us at Customer_eCare@Harlequin.ca

® and TM are trademarks of the publisher. Trademarks indicated with
® are registered in the United States Patent and Trademark Office, the
Canadian Trade Marks Office and in other countries.

www.eHarlequin.com

Printed in U.S.A.

New Year, New Love

For my nieces,
Monika and Heidi
Thank you for the joy you bring into my life.

CHAPTER ONE

DARKNESS HAD ALREADY dropped over the city as Sharon Lawrence drove home from work. The clock in her car said five-thirty, but the nearly empty streets—streets usually packed with traffic coming from downtown Denver at this hour—left her feeling out of place. As if someone had ordered a massive evacuation, but she hadn't been told.

She laughed softly at herself and turned up the radio. Thirty-six years old and still letting her imagination run away with her. How many times had her mother warned her about that? Too many.

Braking for a red light, she studied the shops in a strip mall on the corner. One or two stray cars still sat in the icy parking lot, but most of the shops looked deserted. Everyone had plans for New Year's Eve. Everyone, that is, except Sharon.

She hadn't minded staying for the last-minute meeting with the new journalism department head at Arapahoe Community College. Heaven only knew she had nothing else to do tonight. Her daughters, Emilee and Christa, were probably home right now, getting ready to go out on the town with their dates. Sharon's plans were to spend the night with a good book and her cat.

She'd tried to ignore what day it was—not an easy task in light of the party atmosphere that staff members and fellow faculty advisers had carried around all day. To Sharon, the holiday only meant that one year had slipped by and another loomed on the horizon. She hadn't been able to get excited about celebrations and resolutions for years.

She made a face at herself in the rearview mirror and accelerated carefully on the ice-slick streets, turning onto Sycamore a few minutes later. When she saw her best friend's car in front of her house and a dark-colored pickup behind it, she smiled with relief and silently blessed Adelle for pitching in at the last minute and agreeing to meet the contractor.

If not for Adelle, Sharon would have had to cancel the long-awaited appointment to measure the basement of her big old house. She'd been waiting for a month already and she didn't want to start over at the bottom of the contractor's list.

She pulled into the garage and gathered her things from the seat beside her. Inside, she found

Adelle at the dining-room table, scratching Raoul, Sharon's cat, behind one ear and leafing through a magazine. Adelle's long, honey-colored hair curled softly on the shoulders of her silk blouse, and she kicked one slim foot gently as she read.

Sharon dropped her purse, briefcase and sweater on the kitchen counter. "Sorry I'm so late," she said, kicking off her heels and peeling off her suit jacket. "I owe you a huge favor."

Adelle closed the magazine and waved away her apology with one well-manicured hand. "Don't worry about it. Doug and I aren't leaving until eight."

"Did the girls get home?"

"About fifteen minutes ago. They're both upstairs getting ready."

Good. One less thing Sharon had to worry about. "Did they find what they needed at the mall?"

Adelle laughed and pulled Raoul onto her lap. "If they didn't, they bought a lot of stuff they didn't need."

Sharon would have liked to shop with the girls, but the meeting with Dr. Stevenson had thrown the entire afternoon off schedule. "And the contractor's here?"

"Oh, yes," Adelle said with a grin. She shook one hand as if she'd touched something hot. "No wonder you're going to spend your savings fixing up the basement."

"Funny," Sharon said with a laugh. Mr. Malone had to be at least sixty-five, and hardly what Sharon would call "hot." "I'm fixing up the basement because it's hideous down there. It's a huge space, but only the laundry room has walls, and those are only half-finished. And you've seen that atrocious orange and brown linoleum someone glued to the concrete—"

Adelle grimaced. "Yes, I have. But why are you doing it now?"

"Because the girls have been sharing a bedroom their entire lives and now that I can finally afford to do something with the house, I'd like each of them to have their own room."

"Okay, but Emilee's a senior this year. And Christa's only got one year of high school left. Before you know it, you'll be by yourself in this mausoleum."

"Emilee's not going away to college," Sharon told her. "She talked about it for a while, but she's decided to stay here and go to Denver University."

"Really?" Adelle looked surprised. "I thought she wanted to go away. But anyway, that's not the point." Adelle waved her red-tipped hand again. "You should listen to Doug. Sell this place and buy a condo."

Sharon stood and crossed to the kitchen, glancing at Adelle across the breakfast bar. "I don't want to sell. I love this house, and so do the girls. It's home." She pulled two mugs from the cupboard and measured instant cocoa mix into each, then filled the kettle and sat it on the stove.

"I just hope this guy you've hired is reputable. Maybe you should have let Doug check him out before you agreed to anything."

Sharon leaned against the counter and scowled at her friend. "The company comes highly recommended. Honestly, Adelle, I'm perfectly capable of taking care of business without your husband's help."

"Oh, I know you are. Heaven only knows you've been doing it long enough. But if having some workman prowling around your house on New Year's Eve is your idea of a good time, you've got big problems."

"He's not prowling, and tonight's as good a time as any. I'm not going anywhere."

"That's my point," Adelle muttered. "Doesn't it ever bother you that your daughters have social lives and you don't?"

Sharon rolled her eyes in exasperation. "Why should it bother me? I'm perfectly content with my life the way it is. Besides, I'm thrilled that the girls are so popular. I love watching them go out with their friends and get ready for their dates. I was lucky to have any boys interested in me. They have trouble keeping track of all the boys who ask them out." She sighed wistfully. "They're so different from the way I was at their age."

"They're different from the way you are at *this* age, too," Adelle mumbled.

A dull ache started in the back of Sharon's head. She massaged her neck gingerly. "Please don't start with that tonight. I really don't want to do anything tonight but finish the book I've been reading. Even if I wanted a date—which I don't—I don't appeal to men the way you do."

Adelle had beauty, brains and a sense of style that turned heads whenever she walked into a room. Sharon had never felt beautiful. She'd never attracted the opposite sex the way Adelle—and Sharon's daughters—did. She'd had *maybe* two dates all through high school and married the first man who'd ever shown a real interest in her.

Adelle pushed her thick, blond hair away from her face. "You know what you need?"

Sharon had no doubt Adelle planned to tell her.

"You need a man. Someone who'll bring some excitement into your life. Someone who'll get you out of this house once in a while."

Sharon scowled over her shoulder. "I'm not interested."

"You haven't been interested for five years. When are you going to *get* interested?"

"I had a man once, remember?"

"You had Nick," Adelle argued. "I'm not sure he qualifies."

Sharon laughed softly and leaned both elbows on the breakfast bar. "You're still more angry with him than I am."

Adelle gave her head a toss. "Yeah? Well, that's because he hurt you. But that's not the question. The question is, when are you going to start dating again?"

"If the right guy ever comes along—"

"You always say that," Adelle cut in. "Most women in your situation would jump at the chance to meet new men."

"I'm not most women."

"That's for sure." Adelle propped her chin in one hand. "I honestly don't know how you do it alone. Two teenage daughters, a new career and this huge old house to take care of… It's too hard."

"Have you really forgotten what it was like around here when Nick and I were married? My life is much better now than it ever was then. I waited on him hand and foot for fifteen years."

Adelle's expression shifted. "You should have gotten out a lot sooner than you did."

Maybe. Probably. The marriage hadn't been really good after the second year, but Sharon had been determined to stick it out. She'd struggled to hold their lives together until Nick realized just how boring she really was and moved on to greener pastures. A pasture by the name of Tanya, to be exact.

In spite of her own doubts about their marriage, Nick's betrayal and eventual desertion had hurt terribly. And no matter what Adelle said, Sharon had no intention of putting herself at risk for that kind of heartache again.

But she didn't want to let the conversation drift into those waters. She tried steering it back. "I've never understood how you do it *with* a husband. They take up too much time and energy."

"Not all men are like Nick," Adelle argued. "Doug makes my life easier."

"I think that's wonderful," Sharon said honestly. "But I can't even imagine it. Believe me, I don't do anything more now than I did when Nick lived here."

"You went back to school and started a new career," Adelle argued. "You don't call that more?"

Sharon laughed and filled the mugs with boiling water. "Okay. You win that one. But emotionally, there's no difference. I was always alone then. I'm alone now."

Adelle let Raoul jump down, then crossed her legs. "Which brings us back to tonight. You need some fun. Why don't you come with us?"

"With you and Doug? No, thanks."

"Come on. We're just going to a party in Denver."

"A party full of happy couples on New Year's Eve?" The last thing Sharon felt like. "Thanks, Adelle, but I really don't want to."

"I'm sure there'll be other single people there."

"Who?" Sharon asked, handing Adelle a mug and sitting down across from her friend. "Doug's grandmother?"

"No," Adelle said with a laugh. "*She's* got a date. You ought to try it sometime."

"As much as I appreciate your editorial comments about my lifestyle, I really don't need them."

"Maybe you do. If you don't make some changes, you're going to spend the rest of your life alone. Is that what you want?"

The question sent a spiral of panic through Sharon, but she forced it away. "What I want," she said firmly, "is for you to drop this whole subject."

Sighing, Adelle stood and smoothed her hands

over the legs of her wool slacks. "Fine. Stay home if that's what you really want. I'll drink a toast to you and your cat at midnight."

"Raoul and I thank you." Sharon picked up her New Year's Eve date as he strolled past on his way to the lower level. Immediately, a happy rumble started somewhere inside him and worked its way out. He flopped onto her lap and licked her fingertips. "And don't worry. Raoul and I will be fine. Now, go home, give Doug a kiss for me and get into that slinky black dress you just bought. And try not to envy me. I'll be doing exactly what I want tonight," she said as she stood, Raoul in her arms.

Adelle snagged her coat from the back of a chair and hitched her purse onto her shoulder. "Fine," she said, walking to the door with Sharon following. "Delude yourself if you want, but don't expect me to believe you. You're not happy." Without giving Sharon a chance to argue, she stepped outside and closed the door behind her.

Sharon smiled for half a second, then leaned her back against the door. Silence surrounded her, broken only by Raoul's contented purr.

She pushed away from the door, crossed to the kitchen and started stacking dishes in the sink. But she couldn't get excited about housework tonight. Suddenly, her plans seemed a little less appealing than they had just ten minutes before.

Scowling, she paced to the window and stared outside at the snow. Adelle was wrong, she told herself. Completely, unquestionably wrong.

THE INSTANT she heard the door close behind Adelle, seventeen-year-old Emilee Lawrence tugged her sister, Christa, down the stairs to the basement. When Christa looked as if she might say something, Emilee jabbed her with an elbow to keep her quiet.

She didn't speak until they reached the far end of the basement, and even then she kept her voice down. "Did you hear that?"

Christa nodded, but she didn't look even the tiniest bit concerned. "Mom's spending tonight alone. I knew that already."

Emilee sighed heavily. Really, at sixteen, you'd think Christa would get a clue. "So did I. But I *didn't* know she was so miserable about it."

Christa's eyebrows knit in confusion. "She's not miserable. She said she wants to spend to-night alone."

Letting out another sigh, Emilee leaned against a two-by-four and smoothed the fabric of her skirt. "Sometimes you have to listen to what people *don't* say. Mom might think she wants to spend tonight alone, but she doesn't."

"She doesn't?"

"No. She's lonely."

"Lonely? Come on. *Mom?* She's not lonely."

"Of course she is. Think about it. Dad's been married to Tanya for almost five years, and Mom hasn't had one date in all that time. How would *you* feel if you hadn't had a date in five years?"

Christa narrowed her eyes and ran a hand through her short hair. "But Mom doesn't want to date."

Emilee couldn't believe the difference a single year made in their understanding of human nature. How *could* Christa be so dense? "That's what she *says*."

"You think Mom's lying?"

"No. Not lying." Emilee thought for a few seconds, then, "Remember last year when Dad and Tanya decided to take that cruise for Christmas?"

"Well, duh," Christa said with a deep frown. "Of course I remember."

"Remember how we both kept telling Mom we didn't care because we didn't want to go to St. Louis anyway?"

"Yeah. I guess so."

"I don't know about you," Emilee said, "but

I wanted to go. I just said I didn't because, you know, I felt bad that Dad and Tanya didn't want us there."

At last, understanding dawned in Christa's eyes. "Yeah. Me, too." She thought for a few seconds, then shook her head again. "But that's not what Mom's doing. It can't be."

"Why not?"

"Because…" Christa tried for a few seconds to come up with a reason. She couldn't. Her eyes darkened and her lips puckered into a frown. "You really think so?"

Finally. Emilee let out a relieved sigh and worked up a smile. "I *know* so. It's only obvious."

"That's kinda sad." Christa leaned against the concrete wall and crossed one heavily booted foot over the other. "But even if you're right, there's nothing we can do about it—except stay home with her."

"We can't do that," Emilee cried, horrified. "It wouldn't be fair to Jason and Kyle. Besides, Mom wouldn't let us."

"We could pretend that we're sick."

"She'd never believe it." Emilee tossed a lock of hair over one shoulder and frowned at her sister. "Besides, tonight's not the real problem. You heard what Adelle said. If something doesn't change, Mom's going to spend the rest of her life alone."

Christa stooped to pick up Raoul and rubbed one cheek against his fur. "Maybe she needs a boyfriend."

"Mom's not the boyfriend type. She needs a husband."

Both Christa and Raoul stared at her. Christa laughed. "Are you serious?"

Emilee wondered why she hadn't thought of it before. "Sure. We used to do all sorts of things when Mom and Dad were married that we don't do now. Camping. Hiking. Vacations to Walt Disney World…" Okay, it had only been one trip to Florida, but still—

Christa nodded slowly. "And the houseboat we rented every summer on Lake Powell."

"Trips to Yellowstone Park."

Christa's eyes grew dreamy. "Remember that summer we went to Vancouver Island?"

Perfect. Finally, she understood. "Then we're agreed. Mom needs a husband. The trouble is how do we convince her?"

Christa let out a sharp laugh. "I'll let you do that."

"Very funny."

After a few seconds Christa's smile faded and her eyes glittered the way they always did when a plan began to form in her mind. "Maybe we don't have to convince her," she said slowly. "Maybe there's another way."

"Such as?"

Christa pushed away from the wall and ticked off points on her fingers as she talked. "Finding a guy who'll be interested in Mom shouldn't be hard. Right?"

"Right."

"I mean, it's not as if there's anything wrong with her. She's pretty. She's smart. And she's tons of fun."

"Right."

"So, all we have to do is get her together with a few guys. Once they see how great she is, they'll take it from there."

When footsteps creaked on the stairs, Emilee tensed until she realized her mother must be going upstairs to change. Still, she lowered her voice even further before she went on. "There's still one small problem. What guys are we supposed to introduce her to?"

"I don't know." Christa paced a couple of steps away. "It can't be anyone who's stubborn. Dad was *way* too stubborn."

"You're right. And he can't be macho and pushy. You know how Mom hates that."

"He has to like spending time at home. Nobody whose work is more important than his family."

"And faithful," Emilee added. "A one-woman man."

Christa thought for a few seconds. "You know, Matt's parents got divorced last year. His dad's still single."

Brilliant. Matt had been Christa's friend forever. It wouldn't be hard to convince his dad to come over for some reason. "Good. Who else?"

"What about Toni? Did her dad get married again?"

"Yeah, a couple of months ago. It's too bad, too. Toni's dad would have been perfect for Mom."

"I can't think of anybody else right now," Christa whispered. "But we'll come up with a list. There are lots of single guys out there. And it's not as if we have to find her a husband by tomorrow."

A tingle of excitement worked its way from Emilee's stomach to her chest. This was the most perfect plan they'd ever come up with. "Okay. Let's make it our New Year's resolution. By this time next year, we'll find the right guy for Mom."

Christa held out a hand, pinkie finger extended. "Whatever it takes, we'll make sure she's not alone *next* New Year's Eve."

Emilee locked her finger around her sister's

for a pinkie pledge, just like the ones they'd made when they were little. Neither of them had ever broken a pinkie pledge. "It's a deal." She used the serious tone they'd always used for important promises. "By this time next year, we'll have found the perfect man for Mom."

SCARCELY BREATHING, Gabe Malone waited inside the half-finished laundry room until the girls hurried away. Only a thin piece of plasterboard had separated him from them and, considering the topic of their conversation, he'd been reluctant to make any noise until they finished. Obviously, they had no idea he was down here.

He chuckled softly, released the catch on his tape measure and stuffed it into a pocket on his tool belt. Poor Mrs. Lawrence. Gabe hadn't yet met her, but he could just imagine the kind of woman who needed her daughters' help finding a date. Probably a plain Jane with zero personality. Hadn't his dad told him she was an instructor at one of the local community colleges? He added "dowdy" to his list.

Pulling himself back to the moment, he checked his watch and groaned aloud. Nearly six o'clock already, and he still had to shower and change and pick up the roses he'd ordered for his date with Natasha. If he didn't leave now, he might as well call her and cancel their New Year's plans—whatever they were. She wanted to surprise him, and he'd agreed, as long as she let him foot the bill. Now he was eager to find out what she'd arranged.

Natasha was everything Gabe wanted in a woman. Or, more accurately, their relationship was—and had been for the past two months— everything Gabe wanted right now. No pressure. No commitment. No demands.

After dissolving his claustrophobic marriage to Helene two years ago, he'd vowed never to let himself get caught like that again. So far, he'd been successful. The instant a woman started talking commitment, Gabe moved on.

As always, thinking of Helene brought his fifteen-year-old daughter, Tracy, to mind. Before the ink had even dried on the divorce decree, Helene had packed up and moved half a country away to be near her family. For all the contact he had with Tracy now, Oregon might as well have been in another world.

Steering his thoughts away with an ease born of practice, he pulled on his jacket and picked up his toolbox. Thinking about Tracy only upset him, and he didn't want to be upset tonight.

He climbed the stairs resolutely. No matter what his dad had promised when he set up this appointment, no matter what Mrs. Lawrence expected of him, Gabe was leaving.

His thoughts broke off abruptly when he reached the landing. He glanced into the kitchen, hoping to find Mrs. Lawrence or one of her daughters there. The kitchen was empty, but the sound of nearby voices pulled him into the room.

From there, he could see into the dining room, and what he saw surprised him. Instead of the dowdy teacher he'd been expecting, he found himself looking into a pair of deep brown eyes set in the face of a woman about his own age. She wore an oversize pair of sweatpants, a baggy Denver Nuggets sweatshirt and a pair of thick white socks, but despite her questionable fashion choice for the evening, she was a knockout.

If he'd known college instructors looked like that, maybe he would have pursued his education after high school. He couldn't imagine why her daughters thought she needed help finding a man.

Looking away, he reminded himself of his unwritten code of conduct. He had friends in the industry who'd made the mistake of getting involved with clients. He'd watched them go through all sorts of hell, from broken marriages, to lost contracts, to lawsuits. No, Gabe had no business checking out this woman. Not even for an instant.

He tried to focus on Mrs. Lawrence's face, but her hair caught his attention next. Long, dark curls spiraled from a ponytail at the top of her head and brushed the tops of her shoulders. A few wisps had escaped their confines. They framed her face and made her eyes look even larger.

He shifted his gaze to the girls behind her. They were both as fair as their mother was dark. One had short, mussy hair and wore faded jeans and heavy boots. The other had long hair and wore a short skirt and sweater. Even a glance told him the sisters were as different as night and day.

Mrs. Lawrence let out a gasp when she saw Gabe. She put one hand to her chest and laughed nervously. "You startled me. Are you from Malone Construction?"

He pulled himself together quickly, walked into the dining room and extended a hand. "Gabe Malone."

"Oh." She shook his hand and withdrew her own quickly. "I was expecting the other gentleman."

"My father," Gabe said, ignoring an unwelcome flash of awareness at her touch. "He sent me, since I'm the one who'll be doing the work."

The daughters stared at him, one open-mouthed, the other with eyes wide as silver dollars. He smiled at them but their expressions didn't change. He turned his attention back to Mrs. Lawrence. "I haven't finished measuring the basement yet, but it's getting late and I've got plans for this evening. Would you mind if I stop by next week to finish?"

"No, of course not. I don't want to make you late."

"Thanks. It looks like a fairly complicated project—we'll need to rip out what's already there and start almost from the ground up. If we could bring in a whole crew we could probably finish fairly quickly, but I have to be honest with you. We're overbooked as it is. I can probably give you a couple of evenings a week and part of the time on weekends, which means it'll take me a while. If you want to contact another contractor, I'll understand."

"No," she said quickly. "I can't bear the thought of starting over again. Besides, your firm came highly recommended. And I'm not in a real hurry."

"Thanks. I'll give you a call on Monday and set up another appointment."

Mrs. Lawrence draped an arm around the

taller girl's shoulder. "Mr. Malone's the contractor who'll be finishing the basement for us, girls."

"Call me Gabe, please. Mr. Malone always makes me think my father's in the room."

"Gabe, then. And I'm Sharon. Let me give you my number at work. If I'm not in my office, leave a message on my voice mail and I'll get back to you."

While she found a slip of paper and jotted down the number, the girls shifted uncomfortably and shared a wary glance. Gabe nodded to each of them and worked hard to keep his expression bland. He had no intention of telling their mother what they had planned for her. It was none of his business.

Eventually, though, she was bound to find out. And he wondered how she'd react when she did. It might be a kick to watch this little melodrama unfold.

CHAPTER TWO

GABE LEANED BACK in his seat and glanced at Natasha. Candlelight flickered from a glass holder on their table and from others nearby. Soft music and muffled conversation filled the room. The food was excellent and the wine superb, but the astronomical prices had all but wiped out his good mood.

Natasha sent him a provocative smile. "I love this restaurant, Gabe." Her voice came out like the contented purr of a kitten. "Thank you for letting me choose. I'm just glad you weren't so late that we lost our reservations."

Usually, that smile left Gabe slightly off balance and the voice had him ready to do battle with dragons. Tonight, combined with the constant gibes she'd been tossing out all through dinner about arriving late, they left him slightly irritated.

He made an effort to hide his annoyance and took another sip of wine. Giving Natasha free rein to choose tonight's entertainment had been a stupid thing to do. He'd known she had expensive taste. Well, it was a mistake he wouldn't make again.

She lifted her wineglass and studied him over the rim. "Do you know what I'd like to do?"

Gabe hesitated to ask. "What?"

"I'd like to take you shopping."

"Shopping?" Warning bells sounded in the back of his mind. "Why?"

She smiled again, sipped delicately and waved one slim hand toward him. "I saw a suit at Nordstrom the other day, and I know you'd look wonderful in it."

Nordstrom? Gabe wasn't a Nordstrom kind of guy. He glanced at his jacket. "What's wrong with this suit?"

Natasha's eyes widened slightly. "Nothing. Really. It's fine. But…well, it doesn't really accent your shoulders the way it should. And that tie—"

"This is my favorite tie." Tracy had given it to him for Father's Day the year she'd turned twelve. He raised the tie and studied it for a second. "I love this tie."

"Yes, I know." She dabbed her lips with her napkin. "But it is a few years old, and it's really better for more casual occasions. Besides, I doubt it would match the new suit."

He scowled at her. "I'm not buying a new suit."

"How can you say that? You haven't even looked at it."

"I don't need to look at it to know I'm not buying it."

She looked down at the candle, as if she thought that would keep him from noticing her irritation. "Clothes make a statement about a person, Gabe. And yours say the wrong thing."

"And what would be the right thing for my clothes to say?"

She looked up again. "That you're an up-and-coming businessman. If you want to be successful, you need to dress the part."

"I'm a construction worker," he pointed out. "And I *do* dress the part."

She didn't bother to hide her annoyance any longer. "You're not just a construction worker. You'll own your own company someday. There's a big difference."

"I work with my hands," he reminded her, holding one out to show her the scars and calluses. "Why are you so interested in changing me all of a sudden?"

She sighed again. "I'm not trying to change you, Gabe."

"Do I embarrass you? Is that it?"

"No." She glanced at the tables nearest theirs and looked back at him with narrowed eyes.

"I'm trying to help you. The question should be, why are you so determined to hold yourself back by showing up late and dressing like a simple construction worker instead of a successful businessman?"

"I was working," he began, but cut himself off and downed the rest of his wine. He'd apologized and explained earlier. He wasn't going to do it again. "Let's drop the subject."

"Fine. We'll drop the subject."

The way she clamped her lips together told him she definitely wasn't fine. He'd seen that same look many times on Helene's face.

He pushed aside his glass and tried to hide his mounting irritation. "Did you enjoy your dessert?"

Natasha nodded, one jerky movement of her head. "Yes."

Gabe motioned for the waiter and tucked his credit card inside the burgundy leather case with the exorbitant bill. He forced himself to smile as he asked, "Now what?"

Natasha also made a visible effort to pull herself together. She lowered her lashes and smiled again. "Now we're going dancing at the Rooftop."

"The Rooftop?" Gabe sat back in his seat. The Rooftop was one of the most expensive clubs in town.

Natasha narrowed her eyes again. "It's New Year's Eve. I thought you'd enjoy going there."

"Hardly." The harsh word came out before he could stop it. "I'm not made of money, Natasha."

"I realize that," she said with a tight smile, "but I didn't know you were cheap."

"If staying within a budget is cheap, then I guess I am."

"So, what do you want to do? Go home and bring in the New Year?"

He shook his head slowly and made a show of looking at his watch. "Isn't there someplace besides the Rooftop we can go?"

"Not without reservations." She sat back in her seat and linked her hands as she studied him. "You're angry, aren't you? That's why you don't want to go."

"I'm not in the greatest mood," he admitted truthfully.

"Why? Because I'm trying to help you?"

"I don't see how putting myself in debt for one evening's entertainment will help me."

"It's all about image. You need to be seen in the right places. You need to look prosperous."

"You're forgetting one small detail. I'm not prosperous. I'm the second man in a small operation. And my father still runs the business his way. So it could be a long time—if ever—before I am."

She sighed and put one tentative hand over his. "All right. We'll forget the Rooftop. Just come with me on Saturday and look at the suit. If you don't like it, maybe we can pick up some polo shirts."

Gabe longed to pull his hand away, but didn't. "I have to work Saturday."

"Can't you just take an hour off?"

"Not unless it's really important. And a shopping spree doesn't qualify."

"If that's the way you feel," she snapped, "maybe you should just take me home right now."

Gabe nodded. He was past feeling angry. Now he just wanted to put an end to the evening. If he said anything more, he'd only make things worse.

GABE WAITED in the truck until Natasha disappeared inside her apartment, then jerked away from the curb. He replayed their conversation over and over in his mind as he drove along the freeway on his way home. One minute, he wished he hadn't reacted so strongly. The next, anger boiled to the surface again. And by the time he reached his exit, he knew the argument had left him too keyed up to sleep.

Almost automatically, he pulled into the crowded parking lot of Milago's, his favorite after-work hangout. Inside, the jukebox pounded out a country song, smoke stung his eyes and New Year's Eve revelers filled the place to overflowing.

He struggled through the crowd toward the bar where he could see his childhood friend, Jesse, sitting hunched over a bottle at the bar with the remnants of a garlic burger, the house specialty, in front of him.

Smiling for the first time in over an hour, Gabe crossed the narrow room and perched on the stool beside him. Jesse's bushy black eyebrows formed an almost solid ridge over his eyes and a grizzled beard all but hid his pudgy face. He still wore his work clothes—paint-encrusted jeans, paint-dappled work boots and a T-shirt that had started life black, but was now covered with white splotches.

Jesse grinned when he saw him, but his smile faded almost immediately. "What are you doing here? I thought you had a date with what's-her-name."

"I did." Gabe shouted to be heard over the music. "It wasn't going well, so we decided to call it a night."

Jesse nodded as if that didn't surprise him at all. He knew Gabe almost as well as Gabe knew himself. They'd seen each other through the worst parts of their lives.

Not for the first time, Gabe wondered how Natasha would react to Jesse. Even his name—Jesse James MacNamara—would probably set her teeth on edge. But, then, Jesse probably wouldn't like Natasha, either. Gabe motioned for Ringo, the bartender, to bring him a beer.

Jesse took a swig of his beer and managed to keep someone on the other side of him from jostling his arm. "So, when do I get to meet her?"

"After tonight?" Gabe asked. "Probably never."

Jesse lowered his bottle to the bar and wrapped his hands around it. "Why not? You have a fight with her or something?"

Gabe gave a brittle laugh but the sound was swallowed up by a burst of laughter from the crowd. "You could say that."

"She involved with some other guy?"

"No. Nothing like that." Gabe raked his fingers through his hair and took a long drink from his own bottle. The cold beer traced a path to his stomach and brought out a contented sigh. The contentment faded again almost immediately. "It's my fault, I guess. The whole evening was a disaster from start to finish. I was late picking her up, and she didn't let me forget about it all through dinner—which, by the way, was at La Fleur de Lys."

Jesse's eyes widened.

"Then," Gabe went on, "she wanted to go dancing at the Rooftop."

"No kidding? What did you tell her your last name was? Rockefeller?"

"I think that's what she heard," Gabe said, enjoying the sympathetic ear. "All that was bad enough, but when she asked me to go shopping on Saturday, I lost it."

"Shopping? For you or for her?"

"For me." Another shout from the crowd made conversation almost impossible. Gabe waited for the noise to die away. "She found a suit at Nordstrom she wants me to buy."

Jesse's eyes rounded for a second, then narrowed into beady slits. "How long've you been seeing her?"

"A little over two months."

"And she's starting with the shopping thing already?"

"Yep."

"That's a dangerous sign, buddy." Jesse nudged him with an elbow. "She must have decided you're marriage material."

Gabe shook his head quickly. "Not me. I'm not interested in getting married again. Once was enough."

"For me, too. But women never believe it when you tell them that. I think they take it as a challenge. Once they find a man they think can be fixed up, they just start making their list of renovations—"

"Yeah? Well, I don't want to be fixed up. I like myself the way I am."

Jesse grinned at him and rotated toward the crowd on his bar stool. "You look just fine to me."

Gabe barely held back an answering smile and kept his voice purposely gruff. "That's the best argument *for* buying that suit I've heard yet."

"Maybe you should let her do what Nicole wanted me to do," Jesse said, stretching one arm along the bar to grab a handful of roasted peanuts. "Let her take you in for one of those whatchamacallits." He waved the peanuts around as if they might help him find the right word. "One of those makeovers."

"A makeover? Are you serious?"

"Yeah." Jesse patted his round stomach and stretched out the hem of his splotched T-shirt. "*I* don't need one, of course. I wouldn't want to tamper with perfection. But I suppose you could use a little fixing up."

"You just said I look fine the way I am," Gabe reminded him. "I'm doing okay."

"Sure you are." Jesse put one hand on Gabe's

shoulder. "That's why you're sitting at the bar with me on New Year's Eve."

He had a point. Gabe eyed him thoughtfully. "You know what we need to do? We need to start getting out and doing things again. We should plan a fishing trip, or go skiing, or… well, *something*."

"Sounds good to me, but you'll be back together with Natasha before the week's out."

"I doubt it."

"Then you'll have someone new. It's not as if you're ever alone for long."

"I'm not that bad," Gabe protested.

"You're not?" Jesse leaned back on the stool and pretended to be shocked. The music changed to something almost melancholy and the crowd quieted as if by magic. "Tell me, how many women have you broken up with since the divorce?"

"I'm not counting."

"Well, I am. This makes ten. What you need is to find one who's interested in the same kinds of things you are."

"What I need," Gabe corrected, "is to forget about women completely for a while."

Jesse eyed him with obvious disbelief. "You?"

"Yes, me."

"What? You going to spend the rest of your life alone?"

"Maybe."

Jesse tilted back his head and laughed. "Get real, Gabe. This is *me* you're talking to. You could no more spend your life a bachelor than I could dance in the ballet."

Gabe took a handful of peanuts for himself. "Then I suggest you start practicing."

"You've just had a few bad experiences. But not all women are like Helene or Natasha."

Without warning, Sharon Lawrence's image appeared in front of him. Gabe blinked once. Twice. Forced the image aside.

Jesse didn't seem to notice anything. He pulled his wallet from his back pocket and tossed money onto the bar. "I've got twenty bucks that says you'll be back with Natasha or in a new relationship before the end of the week."

Gabe motioned for Ringo to bring them each another beer. "A week, a month, six months. It doesn't matter. I'm through with women for a while."

"Okay, and I say you won't last six months."

"I can do that without batting an eye," Gabe assured him.

"We'll see, buddy. We'll see." Jesse took another handful of peanuts and dropped several into his mouth. "Let's make it interesting— loser pays for a deep-sea fishing trip during the summer."

Gabe pushed away his second beer and stood. He pulled his wallet from his pocket and dropped enough to cover his tab and a tip onto the bar. "Then you'd better start saving your money."

"I might give you the same advice." Jesse stuffed his change into his pocket. "Hold on a second. I'll walk out with you."

"You're not staying to see in the new year?"

"Naw. I'm gonna get my sleep so I can party this summer."

They didn't speak again until they'd stepped outside into the bitter chill of the night. There, Jesse shivered and looked up at the inky clouds in the black sky. "You driving?"

Gabe shook his head. "I've had too much to drink. I think I'll leave the truck here and come after it in the morning. What about you?"

"I walked over. Figured I wouldn't be in any shape to drive by the end of the night." Jesse shivered again as they reached the edge of the parking lot. "You know, buddy, when all's said and done, it must be nice to have a good woman to go home to at the end of the night."

Gabe battled an unexpected surge of loneliness and regret. He stiffened his shoulders and tugged his collar together. Ridiculous. He'd be far better off without a woman in his life. No pressure. No demands. No commitment.

He glanced again at Jesse's retreating figure. Six months, he told himself. He could do that standing on his head.

DODGING STUDENTS as she walked, Sharon argued with herself all the way down the long, windowless corridor. She really shouldn't do this, but questions had been niggling at her all weekend, and after Gabe's call this morning, curiosity had gotten the better of her.

She blamed Adelle for making her so aware of Gabe in the first place. If it hadn't been for her friend's dour predictions, Sharon wouldn't have given the man or his laughing brown eyes a second thought.

When he'd called earlier, they'd made an appointment for Saturday. All she had to do now was find out the skinny on him and put him out of her mind. An adoring wife, half a dozen loving children and maybe even a faithful dog should throw cold water on her overactive imagination.

Luckily, she had a source of information handy. Pauline Horner, one of the senior faculty members, had recommended Malone Construction when Sharon first began looking for a contractor. Pauline and her husband had been friends with Gabe's parents for years. If anyone could help Sharon put an end to these ridiculous thoughts, Pauline could.

Still, she hesitated outside Pauline's office. Maybe she should just forget it. Surely by Saturday she'd have better control over herself. Then again, she couldn't remember when a man had captured her imagination like this. If she had to have Gabe Malone working in her house for the next few months, she'd be smart to nip this problem in the bud.

She knocked resolutely on Pauline's door and stepped inside when the older woman called for her to enter.

"Sharon?" Pauline tugged off her glasses and let them dangle from a chain over her well-padded bosom. "This is a pleasant surprise. I thought you were one of my students."

Sharon's resolve suddenly weakened. "If you're busy, I can come back later."

"Not at all." Pauline motioned across her cluttered desk toward an empty chair. "What can I do for you?"

"Well, I—" Sharon broke off, dismally aware that she had no idea how to bring up the subject without being obvious. She sat, crossed her legs and uncrossed them again immediately. "I thought you'd like to know that I hired Malone Construction to finish my basement."

"You won't be sorry. Harold Malone is as good as they come."

"Actually," Sharon said casually, "his son is going to do the work. Do you know anything about him?" She felt her cheeks flame, and added quickly, "About the quality of his work, I mean."

"Gabriel?" Pauline bobbed her gray head enthusiastically. "Oh, sure. He's very good. He's been working with his dad for years. One of these days, if Harold ever retires, Gabriel will take over the business, I'm sure."

"Good. I just want to make sure I'm getting the best."

"Well, you are. Don't worry about that for a second." Pauline leaned back in her seat as if they'd exhausted the subject.

But now that Sharon had started, she had to keep going. "He's planning to start work this weekend."

"Oh? You're lucky he can get to you so soon. I know they're busy. Harold can't do much of the heavy work himself these days, but Ina— Harold's wife—tells me he hasn't cut the workload at all. I understand he really keeps that boy hopping."

Boy? That's the last word in the dictionary Sharon would use to describe Gabe. Those shoulders... The heat in her cheeks increased.

"Do you think they're too busy to take on the job? I mean, I'm sure Gabe has other obligations besides work…" She let her voice trail away, hoping Pauline would pick up the thread.

"Oh, heavens no." Pauline laughed at the idea. "If Harold takes on an obligation, he'll make sure Gabriel honors it." She paused, and Sharon feared she'd have to prod her again. But Pauline continued. "Between you, me and the fence post, Gabriel needs something to keep him busy."

Sharon squelched a flutter of anticipation. This was exactly what she wanted. Good old-fashioned gossip—for a purely innocent reason, of course. "I'm sure he has family to worry about."

"Well, there's Harold and Ina, of course. And they all get together with Gabriel's sister and her family once a month for dinner. Ina lives for those Sundays…"

He came from a close family. Nice. But that only made him more appealing.

"…but, of course, that wouldn't keep Gabriel from working on your basement. And Ina tells me they're trying to keep him busy. He's been at loose ends since his divorce."

Divorce? *No!* "Oh. But I'm sure he has a girl-friend."

Pauline's face creased in thought. "I don't think there's anybody special. At least no one that I've heard of. To tell you the truth, from what Ina says, I'm worried that he's become a bit of a playboy."

A playboy. Sharon smiled in relief. That would do. With Gabe's chiseled good looks, Sharon could easily believe that. And if she knew nothing else, she knew that she wasn't going to waste time thinking about a man who kept more than one woman on a string.

Pauline looked worried. "Is that a problem?"

"No," Sharon said quickly. "Not at all."

"Gabriel would never let his social life get in the way of work, my dear. Harold wouldn't allow it."

"No, of course not."

"Mind you, women probably find him attractive. He *is* a very good-looking man."

"Is he?" Sharon traced circles on the chair's arm. "I didn't notice."

"You didn't?"

"You know me," Sharon said with a laugh. "I don't pay attention." She stood and managed a cheerful smile. "I'm not interested, Pauline. I just want to make sure I'll get my money's worth on the job, that's all."

"Well, that's good." Pauline settled her glasses on her nose again. "Not that I don't like Gabriel a great deal, but he isn't your type."

"Yes. Well." Sharon moved toward the door, desperate to escape before the conversation went any further. "Thanks for talking to me, Pauline. I won't take up any more of your time."

"Not at all, my dear." Pauline sent her a soothing smile. "I'm sure you'll be very happy with Gabriel's work."

Sharon stepped into the corridor again and closed Pauline's door behind her. She walked slowly through the crowded hallways, assuring herself that what she'd just heard would keep her imagination under control. And she tried desperately to convince herself that it was relief and not disappointment that accompanied her down the hall.

SATURDAY DAWNED cold and windy, and by early afternoon Sharon knew they were in for a major storm. She loaded groceries into the trunk while Christa held the shopping cart to keep the wind from blowing it away. She worked quickly, anxious to get out of the bitter cold, determined to finish this last chore and get home before Gabe arrived.

Christa's offer to help her with the shopping had surprised her. Usually, she shopped alone while the girls went to the mall or a movie with friends. But today, the sixteen-year-old had come to her room while she dressed, and had even offered suggestions about what she wore, her hair and her makeup. It had been a long time since they'd spent time alone together, but after today Sharon planned to do it more often.

"Okay, that's it," she said, hefting the last two bags. "If you'll take the cart back, I'll scrape the windshield and warm up the car."

"Okay." Christa's breath formed soft clouds in the icy air. She backed up a few steps, then stopped. "I, uh…I forgot to tell you, I need to go to that office-supply store on University before we go home, okay?"

Sharon closed the trunk and pulled her keys from her coat pocket. "Why? What do you need?"

"Pens."

"We have dozens of pens at home," Sharon reminded her.

"Not the kind I need. It's for a special project I'm doing for history." A gust of wind whipped past them, tousling Christa's hair.

Sharon shivered and pulled the collar of her coat close. "When is this project due?"

"Monday."

"Monday?" Sharon let out a sigh of frustration. "I thought you'd stopped putting off assignments until the last minute."

"I have. Mrs. Wayman just gave it to us on Friday."

Sharon retrieved the ice scraper from the car and started working on the windshield. "And you need a special pen for it?" Teachers who gave assignments requiring an immediate outlay of cash always irritated her. Not that she couldn't afford a pen, but she didn't want to drive clear across town on icy roads to buy it. "What kind of assignment is it, and what kind of pen do you need?"

"We have to draw a map, and I can't remember what brand of pen it is, but Mrs. Wayman showed it to us. I'll know it when I see it."

Sharon stopped scraping. "Okay, but why don't we just buy it at the OfficeMax on the corner?"

"We can't. They don't have them. But Mrs. Wayman says they have the pens at the store on University because my…um…my friend's dad owns the store."

Confused, Sharon rounded the front of the car and started on the other side of the windshield. "I wish you'd mentioned this sooner. I have to be back to meet the contractor in less than an hour."

"Emilee's home," Christa reminded her. "She can let him in. Besides— Well, the truth is, I told Steve I'd meet him there. We're supposed to work on the project together, and he's helping his dad at the store today." Christa sighed heavily. "It's complicated, Mom. I can't explain it."

Sharon sidestepped slush thrown by a passing car and gave up the argument. They'd had such a lovely time so far, she didn't want to spoil it. "All right, I'll take you there. But I don't want to stay long."

"We won't, Mom. I promise." As Christa turned away with the cart, Sharon could have sworn she saw a flicker of triumph cross her daughter's face. She pondered that while she scraped the rest of the windshield, decided she must be imagining things, and got under way a few minutes later.

While she concentrated on the roads and traffic, Christa sang along to the radio as if she hadn't a care in the world. But when Sharon pulled up in front of the store twenty minutes later and Christa shifted in her seat to face her, something faintly disturbing gleamed in her eyes.

"Aren't you coming in, Mom?"

"I'll just wait in the car and keep the heater going." Sharon pulled a twenty-dollar bill from her wallet and passed it across the seat. "If it costs more than this, don't buy it."

"But... Well, it might take a *little* while. I have to talk to Steve. And I don't want you to get cold out here." She paused, then added quickly, "Besides, don't you want to meet Steve's dad?"

Sharon glanced at the clock on the dash. Half an hour and counting until Gabe arrived. "Not today, Christa."

"Why not? You look great."

Sharon laughed aloud and glanced at her bulky sweater beneath her heavy coat. "I wasn't worried about how I look. I'd just like to get home."

Christa drew a flower on the misty window with her fingertip. "I thought you liked meeting my friends' parents."

"I do," Sharon admitted. "Especially the parents of the boys you're dating." She turned so she could see Christa better. "Is that what this is all about? Has Steve asked you out?"

"No." Christa's eyes widened. "I mean, he's nice and everything, but—"

"But you're not interested."

"No." Christa wiped away her doodles with her sleeve. "Please come in with me."

"All right," Sharon conceded, turning the car toward an empty space in the lot. Maybe this boy was important to Christa. Her denial had seemed almost too hasty. "I'll go in with you, but you did promise to make this quick."

"Thanks, Mom. You won't be sorry."

Sharon followed Christa across the icy parking

lot toward the store. Twice, her feet nearly flew out from under her, but curiosity kept her going. When they stepped inside the heated store, Sharon took a moment to get her bearings.

Christa had other plans. She grabbed Sharon's arm and tugged her over to a tall, thin man with sandy hair and thick glasses who stood behind a long counter lined with glass-enclosed cases of electronic equipment. "Are you Mr. Case?"

He blinked up at them and smiled. "Yes, I am. What can I do for you?"

"I'm Christa Lawrence, Steve's friend, and this is my mom." Christa released Sharon's arm and took a step back, making Sharon feel as if she'd been placed on the display rack.

"Oh." Two bright splotches of red sprang to life on the man's cheeks and he wiped his hands nervously on his pant legs before extending one toward her. "Oh."

Sharon shook it, relieved to find it warm and dry. "It's very nice to meet you."

The poor man jerked his hand away and worked up a timid smile. "Oh. Yes. Same here."

Poor man. He was obviously painfully shy. Sharon tried to set him at ease. "I understand you have a special pen—"

"Don't worry about it, Mom," Christa cut her off. "I'll go find Steve while you two visit."

Visit? Sharon opened her mouth to protest, decided doing so would make her seem unforgivably rude, and snapped it shut again. She watched, helpless, while Christa hurried away and disappeared into the back room.

Obviously, the girl couldn't wait to see Steve. Sharon sent Mr. Case a weak smile. "I'm sure you're busy. Why don't I just find her that pen. If you know what kind it is they need. I'm afraid Christa couldn't remember."

"Pen?" He blinked in obvious confusion.

Sharon frowned. What was wrong with this man? "Maybe I should just ask Christa."

"Oh, but I'm not busy. And I'd like a chance to talk before…" He snorted a laugh and lowered his eyes. "What I mean to say is, we can visit."

Great. She'd have to make small talk until either a customer needed his attention or Christa came back. She made a mental note to discuss this with Christa later and said the only thing she could think of. "You have a nice store."

Another deep flush stained his cheeks. "Thank you."

"Have you been in business long?"

"Two years."

She waited for him to add something to the conversation, but he seemed content to answer her questions. That ought to make the time fly by. "Does your wife work here with you?"

The question seemed to surprise him. "I'm divorced. I thought you knew that."

Why on earth would she know that? Had he taken out an ad in the newspaper?

He propped his hands on his hips and looked around the tiny store as if seeing it for the first time. The flush on his cheeks deepened another shade. One thing for certain, no one would ever accuse *him* of being a playboy. He could barely make himself look at her.

"Well," he said with a stiff laugh. "Here we are. Would you…would you like me to show you around the store?"

For one second Sharon considered answering truthfully. She'd spent half her life teaching her daughters not to lie, no matter what the circumstances. But as she looked at the nervous expression on Mr. Case's face, she couldn't do it. So, she worked up her best smile and told a whopper. "I'd love to."

CHAPTER THREE

EMILEE HAD BEEN WAITING all morning for Christa to get home and report. She figured it was a good sign that they'd been gone so long. Even when they got home, and Christa sent dirty looks in her direction as they carried in groceries, she told herself everything had gone well. Christa could be upset about anything. You never knew with her.

At last, they managed to sneak away to their bedroom. Emilee shut the door behind them and kept her voice down so their mom couldn't overhear. "Well? How'd it go?"

Christa flopped onto her bed and scowled at the ceiling. "She didn't like him. She said he was boring."

"Did he ask her out?"

"No. Mom said he barely spoke at all, except when he was showing her around the store."

"You're kidding?"

Christa raised herself onto one elbow. "Do I look like I'm kidding?"

She didn't. Emilee sighed in frustration.

"It gets worse," Christa said. "She warned me never to do that to her again."

Emilee's stomach knotted. "You didn't tell her, did you?"

"Of course not." Christa flopped backward again. The whole bed bounced. "I'm not stupid, you know."

"Well, that's good." Emilee stepped over a pile of clean clothes Christa hadn't yet put away and sank onto her own bed. "So now what?"

"I think it's pretty obvious," Christa snapped. "We have to think of somebody who's *not* boring."

"Okay. Think."

"*You* think." Christa rolled onto her stomach and sent her another dirty look. "I've wasted the whole day, and I have to get ready for my date tonight."

Emilee glared right back. "You're always thinking of yourself. Just give it ten more minutes. For Mom." That was a nice touch. It seemed to work.

"Fine." Christa covered her eyes with her arm. "We need to find somebody exciting. Who do we know?"

Emilee thought for a minute, but she couldn't come up with anyone. "You know what we need? Someone like…well, like Harrison Ford in *Air Force One*. She loves him in that old movie.

She's made us watch it with her, like, twenty times."

Christa peered at her from beneath her arm. "Good idea. Let's set Mom up with the fake president of the United States from the nineties."

"Don't be stupid. That's not what I mean. I just remember how much she liked the way he protected his wife and daughter in that movie. That's the kind of guy she needs."

Christa let out an irritated sigh. "Where are we going to find a guy like that? I don't think there are any."

"Sure there are. There *have* to be." Emilee ran a hand across her down comforter and wished Christa wouldn't be so negative. "The important thing is not to let ourselves get discouraged. After all, this was only one man, right?"

"Right." Christa didn't sound convinced.

"I mean," Emilee went on, trying to restore Christa's faith in the plan, "we knew we wouldn't find the perfect guy immediately, didn't we?"

"I guess so."

"So, we just keep looking until we find him."

"Okay," Christa said after a moment. "But don't expect me to do what I did today. I know she was getting suspicious, and now she thinks I have a crush on Steve."

"Okay, I promise. Next time, I'll be in charge of getting Mom where she's supposed to be."

It would be better that way, she added silently. *She* wouldn't screw up a perfectly simple assignment the way Christa had. Really. How hard could it be?

GABE SAT ACROSS from his father, watching the minutes tick by on the round-faced clock on the office wall. If he didn't get out of here right now, he'd be late.

Gabe didn't often spend time in the office. He'd much rather work on-site. But every once in a while, his dad would call him in to discuss business.

"Accounts payable are through the roof this time," Harold Malone said, flicking his checkbook with the backs of his fingers. "The statement from Stevens Builders' Supply is nearly a third again as high as it should be."

"We had to buy the materials for the Lawrence job," Gabe reminded him.

"The Lawrence job?" Harold sounded confused, as if he couldn't remember the contract.

"The lady with the old house," Gabe reminded him. "On Sycamore. She wants us to finish her basement. I have an appointment with her at one o'clock."

"Oh, yes." Harold nodded slowly, but Gabe could tell he didn't remember. "Sure."

Not for the first time, Gabe worried about leaving his dad in charge of the office. He loved his father and wouldn't hurt him for the world. But the business was getting to be too much for Harold, and Gabe didn't know how to convince him to retire. Every time the subject came up, the old man resisted, and Gabe didn't have the heart to challenge him. This business was his dad's life. And when he did try to resolve the problem, his mother and his sister, Rosalie, were no help. Three votes against one put Gabe on the losing end of every argument.

"Do you want me to check the invoices against the bill?" Gabe asked. "I can do that tomorrow at home if it would help." It would be a waste of time, but it wouldn't be the first time Gabe had done something unnecessary to make his father happy.

Harold shook his head and pursed his lips. "No. I'll take care of that. It'll give me something to do." He leaned back in his seat and tapped his chin thoughtfully. "We need new contracts."

"Not yet. I've still got several to finish before we're in any position to take on more work. In fact, I've been meaning to talk to you about hiring a couple more guys to help."

"Hiring a couple more guys?" His dad scowled so hard, a fleshy ridge formed between his eyebrows. "Have you seen Derry Kennedy's paycheck?"

"No, but—"

His dad shoved a check across the desk at Gabe. He scanned it quickly and saw that the net figure nearly doubled what they usually paid Derry for two weeks. He lowered the check and met his dad's gaze. "He's been putting in a lot of overtime. We all have. That's why I think we'd be smart to hire a couple more guys."

"Can't afford it," Harold snarled.

"We can't afford to keep paying overtime," Gabe pointed out.

"No, we can't. You'll just have to pick up the pace."

Resentment flashed through Gabe, but he tried to hold it back. "I'm already putting in at least twelve hours every day," he said, struggling to keep his voice level.

"Is it too much for you?"

"It would be too much for anyone," Gabe said.

His dad let out a sharp laugh. "The Malone men have always been hard workers. Just buckle down and do it. We're not slackers in this family."

Gabe battled another flash of resentment. "I

never said I wanted to quit. But there's no way we can meet all the deadlines we currently have unless we bring on more crew." He pulled a sheet of paper from the clipboard on his lap. "I've made up a list of the contracts we have on the books and the deadlines that go with them."

Harold's eyes narrowed as if he thought Gabe had accused him of something. "You don't think I know which contracts we have?"

"I didn't say that." He tried again. "The point is—"

"The point is, you're trying to do my job when you should be out doing your own."

Right. Gabe lowered the list to his lap. He shouldn't be surprised or even disappointed. His dad had shot down every one of his ideas for months. But each time, his frustration level rose, and he honestly wondered if he could hold on until Harold retired—*if* he ever did.

"I've got to get out of here," he muttered. "I'm going to be late."

"What are you bent out of shape about?"

Gabe didn't have time for an argument. "Nothing."

"Good. Don't forget dinner with the family tomorrow."

Gabe stood and snagged his jacket from the back of the chair. "I won't forget," he promised, even though he'd begun to dread going since the divorce. Watching Rosalie with her husband, Jack, always left him strangely ill-at-ease, and their children made him think of his daughter and regret the distance between them. He often brought someone with him to keep his mind off such unpleasant thoughts.

Harold leaned so far back in his chair, the wood creaked. "You'll be bringing a lady friend, I suppose."

"No lady friend. I'll be there alone."

"Alone? What happened to the last lady friend you had?"

"Natasha?"

"If that was her name. I can't keep track anymore."

Gabe shrugged. He knew his parents would like to see him married and settled. But he wouldn't let himself get caught up in that old argument. "Natasha and I aren't seeing each other any longer."

"Why not?"

"Things just didn't work out."

"No?" His dad seemed to look right through Gabe. "What was the problem this time?"

"I don't want to talk about it."

"You never want to talk about it."

No, he didn't. He figured he was entitled to a little privacy.

His dad tapped his fingers on the desk. "Your mother and I thought you were serious about this one."

"Don't get your hopes up," Gabe warned. "I've sworn off women for a while." *Six months, to be exact.*

"Have you?" A smile tugged the corners of Harold's mouth. "Well, then, I guess I can tell you the truth. Your mother didn't like this last woman you were seeing very much."

That didn't surprise Gabe at all. His mother, bless her, hadn't liked any of the women he'd dated since his divorce. And she hadn't really liked Helene. But she'd always hidden her feelings well, and she'd treated Helene like one of the family while they were married.

"You know what you need?" Harold creaked back a bit farther in his chair. "A woman like the one I married. Best woman in the world, your mother."

Gabe stopped just inside the doorway and smiled. "I won't argue with you about that."

"I'm telling you, son. You find a woman who'll keep the home fires burning, and you'll be a happy man."

Gabe was still smiling as he left the room. His parents did seem happy in their marriage. But that didn't mean Gabe wanted what they had.

No. Another marriage for Gabe Malone was simply not in the cards.

STIFLING A YAWN, Gabe poured coffee from his thermos for the third time in an hour. He crossed the basement to one of the windows and sat on the floor, propping his back against the rough, unfinished wall. Music crackled from the radio he always carried on the job. Wind rattled the windows overhead.

Taking a sip, he glanced at the two-by-fours he'd stacked against the far wall and listened to Sharon and her daughters moving around upstairs. An occasional burst of laughter rang down the staircase. Footsteps marched back and forth over his head as they did whatever parents and daughters do on Saturday afternoons.

He should know what they did, he thought with regret. And if Tracy had lived closer, he *would* know.

Someone must have said something funny, because the laughter peeled again. The three women sounded more like friends than mother and daughters. He pushed aside another pang and reminded himself he couldn't do anything about Tracy. The judge hadn't seen fit to grant him custody. Gabe hadn't liked the decision, but he'd learned to live with it—most of the time, anyway.

He could almost hear his father's voice. *Malone men are hard workers. We're not slackers. We don't waste time dreaming.* Thinking about Tracy would only waste time. He couldn't change the way things were, but there were things he *could* control—like finishing this job on time. He'd have to make every minute count to meet the deadline he'd given Sharon earlier, but he could do it. He could, that is, if he didn't sit around all day.

He finished his lukewarm coffee, set the cup and thermos aside and started toward the pile of lumber. Before he'd gone even halfway across the room, Christa bounded down the stairs and burst into the basement like a whirlwind carrying a basket of dirty clothes. She flashed a grin and started toward the laundry room.

Friendly girl. Just like her mother. He smiled back and hefted a two-by-four to his shoulder.

She stopped outside the laundry room, propped the basket on one hip and turned around to face him. "So, how long were you down here the other day, anyway?"

He resisted the urge to tease her. He was here to do a job, not get involved in their family's soap opera. "New Year's Eve? Not long. Why?"

She shifted the basket to her other hip. "Did you hear me and my sister talking?"

Should he tell her? He bought some time by

working the wood into place. "As a matter of fact, I did."

"You *heard?*" She lowered the basket to the floor and closed the distance between them. "Everything?"

"Every word."

"You aren't going to tell my mom, are you?"

He smiled reassurance. "I can't think of any reason why I should."

Relief replaced the panic on her face. "Thanks."

"No problem."

Instead of going away, she trailed her gaze around the room. "Are you going to do this whole thing by yourself?"

"As much as I can."

"Why?"

"We have a small crew, and the rest of the guys are busy with other projects."

"Maybe I could help."

He wiped his forehead with his sleeve and looked at her. "I can't let you help. There are all sorts of rules and regulations, and liability, and insurance. Besides, wouldn't you rather paint your nails or talk on the phone or something?"

"Why? Because I'm a girl?"

Well…yes. But he was smart enough to keep that faux pas to himself. "No. I just thought—" He tried to find a way out of the hole he'd dug for himself. When he couldn't, he decided to put an abrupt end to the conversation. "You'd better get back to your laundry before your mother comes looking for you."

She looked so disappointed, his conscience jabbed him. He took in her frayed pants and bulky sweater, her short-cropped hair and wide brown eyes, and tried to soften the sting of his rejection with a smile. "Have you had any luck finding your mom a boyfriend?"

"No." Her face puckered with worry. "I introduced her to a friend's dad today, but she didn't like him."

"She didn't?" He pulled a handful of nails from his pocket. "What was wrong with him?"

"Too boring."

Gabe's lips twitched, but he didn't let himself smile. "Maybe you should let your mom find her own boyfriend."

"She won't," Christa predicted sadly. "It's not that she doesn't like men. She doesn't think men like her."

"I can't imagine why they wouldn't."

Too late, Gabe realized his mistake. Christa's eyes gleamed with excitement. "Really? Are you married?"

"No, but—"

"Do you have a girlfriend?"

"Not at the moment, but I'm not looking for one, either."

"Why not?"

"Too much work to do." That sounded good. He'd stick with that. "I wouldn't have time to give to a relationship."

Christa nodded slowly. "Mom says guys can only concentrate on one thing at a time."

Gabe turned to face her. "Does she?" That wasn't the most flattering evaluation of his mental abilities he'd ever heard.

"Don't take it personally. She's kind of…" She paused and searched for the right word. "Well, she's…"

A man-hater? One of those women who'd let one bad experience warp her perception? Gabe had met more than enough of them. He shoved aside the uncomfortable thought that he'd done the same thing with women, and told himself that if Sharon thought all men were Neanderthals, it was no wonder she didn't have a man in her life.

But, then, it didn't matter what she thought of him—or of any man, for that matter—he was here to do a job, nothing more. And he'd do a good job, too, even if he *was* a mental midget who couldn't form more than one coherent thought at a time.

He picked up his level from the floor and

checked the board. And he somehow managed to contain his urge to grunt like a caveman. "I hate to break it to you, but guys are perfectly capable of thinking of two things at the same time."

Christa smiled uneasily. "I didn't mean to offend you."

"You didn't."

She looked slightly relieved. "So, do you like doing this kind of work?"

Ugh, he thought. *Man like boards.* Aloud, he said, "Yes, I do. I've always liked working with my hands."

"Is it easy?"

Ugh. Man need easy work. "Not really. If I want to do it right, I need to concentrate."

"Oh." She glanced at the laundry basket and grimaced. "I'd better let you work or Mom will kill me. Besides, I have to do the laundry. I *hate* doing laundry."

On that score, she could be Tracy's clone. Once more putting Tracy out of his mind, Gabe turned back to his boards and nails. He reminded himself that he was here to work. Not to get involved with the family. Not to cross the professional boundary between himself and his clients. Not to make friends with the kids. Not to get caught up in some harebrained matchmaking scheme.

Work.

Ugh.

He worked steadily for what felt like forever, trying not to let all the homey sounds distract him. He ignored the laughter, the constant ringing of the telephone, Sharon's voice calling for Emilee or Christa, and the noise of the vacuum cleaner. And he steadfastly refused to let himself draw comparisons between this and his silent apartment.

By the time he had one wall completely framed, his stomach began to rumble. He glanced at his watch and noted with surprise that two hours had practically flown by. He should have packed a lunch before he left home. Leaving now would break the rhythm he'd established, but hard work always gave him an appetite, and he couldn't ignore his hunger much longer.

He didn't bother tidying up. He'd just hit a drive-through and come straight back. He flipped off the radio and started toward the stairs, but before he could reach them the cell phone in his pocket rang.

Hoping it wasn't his dad calling with yet another job, he pulled the phone from his pocket. "Gabe Malone."

"Gabe?"

Helene. His spirits took a nosedive. "I mailed

you the alimony and child support on the twenty-seventh. If you haven't received them yet—"

"I got the money," she interrupted. "That's not why I'm calling."

"Oh? Then what is it?"

"I have a problem."

Gabe's spirits plummeted even further. Divorced two years, and she still expected him to fix everything for her. "I'm busy, Helene. Can I get back to you later?"

"No." Her voice took on that sharp edge that always made him wary. "This is important."

No surprise there. Helene had always considered her problems—whatever they were—more important than anyone else's. "So is my job," he reminded her. "These people aren't paying me for taking personal phone calls."

"Oh. Well. We certainly don't want to upset anyone."

Wonderful. Just what he wanted. Sarcasm. "No, we don't. Not if you want to keep getting the checks I send."

She let out a heavy sigh. "There are problems other than money, you know."

He ignored the bait. If he took it, they'd end up in an argument. "Look, Helene. It's been wonderful chatting with you, but I need to get back to work."

"Is your job more important than your daughter?"

That caught his attention. "You know it's not. What's wrong with Tracy?"

"Don't worry. She hasn't been hurt or anything."

Relief almost made him dizzy. But it was short lived.

"She's failing in school."

"*Failing,* Helene? That's impossible." Tracy had always been a good student. Helene must be overreacting, as usual. "What did she do, bring home a few *C*'s on her report card?"

"*C's?*" Helene let out a brittle laugh. "I wish her grades were that high. No, Gabe, the highest grade she's getting this term is a *D*."

Gabe couldn't believe that. Not from Tracy. He scowled at the concrete floor. "Have you asked her about it?"

"I've tried. She won't discuss anything with me."

That didn't surprise him. Helene didn't discuss. She attacked.

She took a drink of something and insisted, "You've got to do it."

He smiled slowly. Maybe this was his chance to get involved in Tracy's life again. "All right. Put her on."

"She's not here. I waited to call until she'd

left for the library—*if* that's where she went. I don't know where she goes anymore. I don't even think she goes to school half the time."

"She's been skipping school?" he asked.

"I don't know. Probably." Helene's voice grew shrill, the way it always did when something upset her. "Why else would her grades drop so suddenly?"

He could think of several reasons. "Is she feeling all right? I mean, she's not sick or anything, is she?"

"No, she's not sick. She's just…" She broke off and floundered for the right word. "She's just being obnoxious. I'm telling you, Gabe, I'm at my wit's end with her."

"I'll talk to her," he promised, wishing that Helene had spoken to him sooner.

"You'll *talk* to her." The sarcasm came back.

"What else can I do from a distance of thirteen hundred miles?"

"You could try being her father."

"I *am* her father, Helene. As good a father as I can be under the circumstances."

"Oh, please. Except for the checks you send once a month, you've practically forgotten she even exists."

The accusation stung. He paced away from the door, but when static cut into their connection he stepped back again. "That's not true, and you know it."

"Do I?"

"What do you expect me to do?" he demanded. "I can't be there for her. You took care of that by moving half a country away."

"You could try calling her once in a while. Obviously, you have access to a telephone—"

He tried to head her off before she could gather steam. "Helene, I don't have time for this. I have work to do."

"Well, *I* have an unhappy teenager who's failing in school."

"She wasn't an unhappy teenager when she lived here," he snapped, even though he knew that wasn't entirely true. Their constant arguing had been affecting Tracy for a long time. He paced as far as the static would let him, then pivoted toward the stairs again. "Maybe you should stop blaming me for this and start trying to figure out what's really going on. Is there a boy involved?"

Helene made a noise of disgust. "Of course you would think that."

"She's a teenage girl. It's a decent theory."

"If she were dating, I would know about it."

"How? You just said you don't know where she goes anymore. Do you know anything about her?" He regretted it as soon as he said it.

The ice in her glass clinked as he heard her lift it. A second later, she let out a soft, satisfied sigh. "I know she needs her father to call her once in a while. Or are *you* too busy dating to be bothered?"

"Yeah, 'cause that's what I do, hop from woman to woman." He could tell the moment the words left his mouth that his voice had come out too loud. To make matters worse, he heard someone behind him.

He wheeled around to find Sharon standing inside the open doorway.

The heat of embarrassment crept up Gabe's neck into his face. He tried to smile, but his lips froze in something closer to a grimace. *Way to go, Malone. This ought to really impress her.*

He didn't waste time analyzing why he cared. Before he could say or do anything, she pivoted and started back up the stairs.

That finally galvanized him to action. He trailed her to the bottom of the stairs and called after her. "Sharon? Wait. I'm almost through here. What did you need?"

She turned back to face him, and he imagined the red in her face matched the color in his own. "It can wait."

"No." He shook his head quickly and tried to get the urgency out of his voice. "No, just give me half a minute and I'll be with you."

She ignored him and hurried up the stairs.

Sighing in frustration, he turned his attention back to the phone. "I need to go, Helene. I'll call Tracy this evening." Without giving her a chance to argue, he disconnected and stuffed the phone into his pocket. And he made a valiant attempt as he climbed the stairs to look serious and professional—not at all like the player Sharon must think he was.

SHARON STIFFENED when she heard Gabe coming up the stairs. She adjusted the hem of her sweater and tried to look natural, but his words echoed through her mind relentlessly.

She didn't like jumping to conclusions, but his conversation seemed to bear out what Pauline had told her. At least she wouldn't have to worry about finding him attractive anymore. If that didn't turn her off, nothing would.

He stopped in front of her and propped his hands on his tool belt. Her gaze settled on the muscles in his arms. She looked away quickly, only to find herself staring at the tuft of dark hair revealed by the open buttons on his plaid shirt.

Obviously, she couldn't look *there*. She glanced at the light fixture overhead, decided she must look ridiculous and settled her gaze on her hands.

"Sorry about what you heard down there," he said. "I—"

"Don't be." She forced herself to look at him and felt her cheeks grow warm. "I'm sorry I walked in on your conversation."

His lips curved gently. "You don't need to apologize to me. It's your house. I was talking to my—"

"You don't have to explain to me," she said firmly. "I just wanted to let you know my schedule in case you want to work on the basement sometime other than evenings and weekends."

"Great." Something she couldn't identify flickered through his deep brown eyes. He pulled a notebook and pen from his shirt pocket. "I can use every extra hour I can work into my schedule."

She breathed a sigh of relief. If she could stay focused on business, she'd be fine. "This semester, I'm off all day Wednesday and every other Friday afternoon. And I'm usually through with classes and home by six on the other nights."

He scribbled a note and glanced at her again. "If it's all right, then, I'll plan to be here early on Wednesday and stay all day."

"That's fine." She casually brushed a lock of hair over her shoulder and forced herself to meet his gaze again. Her mouth dried and her breath caught in her throat. She decided to end the conversation before he tried to explain his phone call again.

Half hoping Gabe would take the hint and go back to work, she reached for the heavy bag of sugar she'd left on the counter.

Before she could lift it, he stepped in front of her and plucked it out of her reach. "Let me get that for you. Where to?"

She blinked in surprise. "I have a plastic container for it in the garage."

"Okay. Show me where."

"You really don't have to. I'm used to doing it myself."

"No problem. My mother would have my hide if I let you carry something this heavy." His eyes met hers again and the kindness she saw there surprised her.

She felt herself relax slightly. "And how would your mother know?"

He laughed, a warm, easy laugh that unlocked something else inside her. "Oh, she'd know. Believe me. She's got radar for that sort of thing."

Her earlier uneasiness all but vanished. She stepped past him to open the garage door. "I wouldn't want to get you in trouble with your mother."

He stepped through and waited for her to direct him. She motioned toward the row of plastic containers lining the front of the garage. "Over there. I use those to store flour and sugar—all the things I can buy in bulk. It's cheaper that way."

He raised an eyebrow, but she couldn't tell whether he thought she sounded miserly or frugal. She flushed again, embarrassed at the way she was rambling, and bit her tongue to stop herself.

He emptied the sugar into the container and settled the lid in place again. To her surprise, he let his gaze travel over her little stash of food. "Rice, macaroni, egg noodles. You know, that's a really good idea—if you have the room to store everything. My apartment's too small." He stopped, laughed softly and turned a self-mocking gaze on her. "Who am I kidding? I never cook, anyway. Other than dinner at my mother's once a month, I can't remember the last time I had a home-cooked meal."

Sharon didn't know how to respond to what he'd said. If Nick had said something like that, he'd have been trying to wrangle an invitation, but she saw no guile in Gabe's eyes. What she did see moved her. He looked almost wistful.

He laughed again and turned away from the bins. "Sorry. I didn't mean to take up so much of your time."

"You didn't," she assured him. "I appreciate the help."

"Yeah…well." He averted his gaze again. "I'd better get going."

"Of course." She watched him hurry across the garage as if he couldn't put distance between them fast enough. Leaning against the wall, she listened to him start his truck.

If Gabe Malone had the heart of a playboy, she thought with a smile, she'd eat her hat.

THAT EVENING, Gabe tossed his jacket over the back of the couch and left the bag holding the burger and fries he'd bought for dinner on the coffee table. After over twelve hours on the job, he was more tired than hungry, but he knew better than to skip a meal. He'd only regret it in the morning.

He grimaced at the bag of fast food. Whatever Sharon had been cooking for dinner had smelled a lot better than this. He'd definitely had his fill of fast food, but he hated sitting alone in restaurants, and he was too tired to cook for himself.

Stretching to work the knots out of his back, he found the remote control and turned on the television. He'd never liked silence and had long ago gotten into the habit of letting the television or radio play when he was alone. It didn't matter what filled the silence—just as long as something did. When the local news filled the screen, he glanced at his watch and groaned. How had it gotten so late?

Luckily, Oregon was one hour behind Colorado. He might still reach Tracy tonight. He hoped he could. He didn't want to miss this chance to close the rift between them. He hurried to the bedroom and changed into sweatpants and a sweatshirt. Back in the living room, he picked up the cordless phone, sat down on the couch and started to dial.

While the phone rang, he fortified himself with a couple of fries. Tracy answered almost immediately, making him swallow quickly to clear his mouth. "Tracy, it's Dad."

"Oh, hi." The coolness he'd learned to expect filled her voice and doused some of his anticipation.

"Did your mom tell you she called me?"

"Yes."

"Then you know why I'm calling."

"Yes."

"She says you're having trouble in school this year. Is that true?"

"Yeah, I guess."

"Do you want to talk about it?"

"Not really."

He couldn't help comparing this conversation

with the byplay between Sharon and her daughters. No comparison. But, then, Sharon had the luxury of being with her kids all the time. "Your mother says the highest grade you got last semester was a *D*. Is that true?"

"No, but I did get two of them."

Not good, but not quite as bad as Helene made it sound. "That's not like you, Tracy. What's the trouble?"

She let out a soft sigh. "I don't know."

"Well, something must be bothering you. You usually get good grades without even trying."

"Yeah, I know."

"Well?" He waited, wanting feedback but getting only silence. "Are you having trouble with friends?"

"No."

"A boy?"

"No."

"Are things okay between you and your mom?"

"Yeah, I guess. Is that the only reason you called? To yell at me about my grades?"

"I'm not yelling," he pointed out reasonably. "I haven't even raised my voice. But I am worried about your grades."

"You don't need to worry. I'm fine. School's fine. Mom and I are fine." She paused briefly.

"Is that all, Dad? Because I'm right in the middle of a book—"

Gabe held back a sigh of frustration. Shoved the hurt aside. Told himself he couldn't force her to talk to him. "Well, then, I'll let you get back to it."

"Okay."

"I love you, Trace."

She hesitated for no longer than a heartbeat, but it was enough to send a shaft of insecurity through him. "Yeah. I love you, too."

He disconnected and stared at the phone for a few seconds, then dropped it on the couch and leaned his head against the cushions. Maybe she'd just been distracted. Then again, maybe the physical distance between them had eroded their relationship even further than he'd thought. She'd turned down his invitation to visit during the summer, pleading other commitments. Gabe had told himself repeatedly that, at her age, he shouldn't expect her to leave her friends and stop all her activities just for a visit with her dad. But that hadn't taken away an ounce of his disappointment.

He'd dreamed once or twice about moving to Oregon so he could see her for an evening or on the weekends, but he couldn't leave the business. And it was a cinch Helene wouldn't bring Tracy back to Denver. She'd made that clear when she moved away.

Scowling, he picked up his burger. It had grown cold and looked anything but appetizing. He dropped it back onto the coffee table with a grimace. What little appetite he'd had before had disappeared.

He flicked channels on the television for several minutes, but he couldn't rid himself of a nagging discontent.

Maybe he should head over to Milago's. A garlic burger and a beer just might make everything look brighter again. A little music. A few laughs. Sure. That's exactly what he needed.

On the other hand, he was in no mood to see Jesse or talk about the bet they'd made.

In the end, he did the only thing a man who's sworn to remain single for six months *can* do. He turned off the television and went to bed.

CHAPTER FOUR

A WEEK LATER, just in from her Saturday-night date with Jason, Emilee crept up the stairs and down the dimly lit hallway toward her bedroom. She paused as she passed her mother's room and listened carefully to make sure she was inside, then flipped off the hall light. She needed to talk to Christa, but she didn't want their mom to hear.

She slipped into the bedroom, closing the door soundlessly behind her. "Christa?"

No answer.

She made her way carefully through the clutter on Christa's side of the room toward her sister's bed. "Christa? Are you awake?"

"No."

Emilee moved a little closer. She stubbed her toe on something hard and let out a soft yelp.

"Will you be quiet?" Christa mumbled. "I'm trying to sleep."

Emilee dropped onto the foot of her bed. "It's not my fault. You left your boots in the middle of the floor."

"They're on my side." Christa rolled onto her back. "What are you doing, anyway?"

"We need to talk."

"It's after midnight."

"So?"

"So I don't want to talk." Christa yanked the covers over her head.

"We *have* to," Emilee insisted. She grabbed one of Christa's feet and jiggled it. "We have to plan."

"Plan what?" The covers muffled Christa's voice.

"Our New Year's resolution—remember?"

Christa grumbled for a second or two, then sat up and leaned against the headboard. "Okay. Fine. What do you want?"

"I've figured out who we should set Mom up with."

That brought Christa fully awake. "Who?"

Emilee smiled. This was the best idea she'd had yet. "You know that guy who works at the bookstore? The cute one Mom talks to sometimes?"

"Yeah. But he's married, isn't he?"

"I don't think so. I remember hearing him say something about his ex-wife once."

Christa shifted on the bed, bouncing Emilee in the process. "How can we find out? I mean, we can't just ask him."

"We can if we're smart. We'll bring it up in casual conversation."

"Won't he get suspicious?"

"No. Trust me."

Christa laughed. "Yeah. Right. Remember, I thought I was being smart when I took Mom to meet Steve's dad, and that was a disaster."

Emilee made a noise of agreement, though she just knew she could handle it better than Christa had.

Christa tugged the covers up to her neck. "Is he exciting?"

"I think so. I heard him say something about bungee jumping once."

Christa snorted a laugh. "Bungee jumping? Get real, Emilee. Mom would never do something like that."

"She might. You never know."

"*I* know. Can you imagine Mom bungee jumping?" She laughed again—rudely.

Emilee rolled her eyes in frustration. "Well? Do you have any other suggestions?"

"Isn't there somebody exciting and single at Mom's work?"

"At the college? If there was, don't you think he'd have asked her out by now?"

"Maybe. Probably." Christa bent her legs and rested her chin on her knees. "I guess you're right. Maybe the guy at the bookstore is our best bet. But you know, I was thinking…" She broke off and shook her head quickly. "No, he wouldn't be right for Mom."

"Who?"

"Gabe."

Emilee stared at her. "Gabe? The construction guy?"

"Yeah. He's really nice. Besides, he knows all about the plan."

Emilee's stomach knotted. "He does? How?"

"He overheard us."

"Are you sure?"

"Yep. He told me so."

Emilee couldn't believe it. Christa acted as if it was no big deal. "When did he tell you?"

"Last week."

"Why didn't you tell me?"

"Because he promised he wouldn't say anything to Mom."

"You believed him?"

"He hasn't told her, has he? I mean, if he had, we'd know."

She was right about that. But it didn't make Emilee feel a whole lot better. "I don't like this. You should have told me."

Christa stretched out on the bed again. "Relax, Em. He's cool. We can trust him."

"You'd better be right," Emilee warned. "But you *are* right about one thing—he's not Mom's type. He's too rugged looking. So let's concentrate on getting her to take us to the mall."

"That'll be easy," Christa said, yawning. "Now go to bed and let me get some sleep. I'm tired."

"So am I." Emilee crossed to the clean side of the room and undressed by moonlight.

And she crossed her fingers for luck. Maybe this time they'd come up with a winner.

SHARON KNEW she was being foolish. Every instinct she had told her so. But she had to admit that she was looking forward to Gabe's arrival.

She tried to concentrate on counting scoops of coffee into the filter. Instead, she found herself straining for the sound of his truck. She told herself to think about the exam she planned to give her advanced-journalism students during the upcoming week. Instead, she glanced at her reflection in the window, to check her hair and makeup.

Foolish. She was acting like Emilee or Christa before one of their dates. She filled the carafe with water and told herself to get a grip. Gabe had been friendly, but never flirtatious. She had no business letting her thoughts get so out of control. And she certainly didn't want the girls to guess how just the sight of him made her heart leap. She'd never hear the end of it.

Resolving again to put him out of her mind, she dropped a slice of bread into the toaster. Before it had time to pop up, Christa bounced down the stairs into the kitchen. Sleep had formed spikes with her short hair, and her Winnie the Pooh slippers scuffed gently against the carpet.

She stopped at the bottom of the stairs and gaped at Sharon, rubbed her eyes with her fists and stared again. "Why are you all dressed up?"

Sharon scowled at her and picked up the morning newspaper from the counter. "I'm not all dressed up. I'm just dressed."

"Your hair's done and you have makeup on."

"For heaven's sake, Christa. You're making it sound as if I never comb my hair or do my face."

"Well, you don't," Christa pointed out. "At least not this early on a Sunday morning." She took a couple of steps closer. "You're wearing lipstick, aren't you?"

"I may have put some on. I don't remember." Sharon spread a small amount of margarine on her toast and juggled it, her coffee and the newspaper as she walked into the living room.

Christa waited until she'd made herself comfortable on the couch, then dropped onto the floor beside her. "Are you going somewhere today?"

Sharon shrugged and handed Christa the comics. "Maybe. And maybe I'll just stay here."

"Can we go to the mall?"

The one request guaranteed to make Sharon wary. She enjoyed helping the girls pick out the right outfit or pair of shoes, but their shopping excursions always left dents in Sharon's budget. "Why do you need to go to the mall? You just went a couple of weeks ago."

"Because." Christa yawned again and spread the comics on the floor in front of her. "Because…um…I need a new pair of jeans?"

"Really? You *need* them?"

Christa nodded and tried to look solemn. "Yeah. I really do."

"I thought you had plenty of jeans."

"I don't have the right ones."

"You poor thing."

"Yeah." Christa tried to look picked on. "It's really tough on me." Her voice caught and she wiped away an imaginary tear. "I just feel so horrible. It's really bad for my self-esteem."

"I'll bet it is." Sharon feigned concern. "And I suppose it's affecting your grades, too."

"Definitely. I got an *A*-minus on a test last week."

"An *A*-minus?" Sharon put one hand to her chest and gasped. "Tell me it isn't so."

Christa laughed and ducked her head. "Okay, so I don't need the jeans. But can we go to the mall, anyway?"

"Why? You're not planning to introduce me to some friend's dad again, are you?"

Sharon had meant the question as a joke, but Christa's eyes widened as if she'd been accused of something horrible. "No."

Sharon ran a hand across Christa's sleep-mussed hair to reassure her. "Don't worry, I'm not upset with you. But Mr. Case was very hard to talk to. I thought he was going to collapse every time he said two words to me. If you promise there won't be a repeat performance this week, I might consider taking you to the mall later."

Christa looked pleased. Too pleased. "Okay. Can we get a pretzel while we're there?"

"Have I ever not bought you a pretzel at the mall?"

"Never."

"Then I'm not likely to start changing my ways now, am I?"

Christa's grin widened. "No. Can we go to

the bookstore, too? I've finished all the books I have."

Sharon liked that idea. A trip to the bookstore always put her in a good mood. If anything could make her stop thinking about Gabe, that would. "Absolutely."

"I'll even make breakfast so you have enough energy to do some serious book browsing."

Another flicker of caution worked its way through Sharon. Usually, she had to do some serious persuading to get help from Christa in the kitchen. "You're volunteering to make breakfast?"

"Yep. And Emilee can do the dishes."

"I can do *what?*" Emilee's groggy voice sounded behind them.

Sharon shifted to see her better. "Christa's offered to make breakfast, and she's volunteered you to do the dishes afterward."

"Dishes?" Emilee groaned and shuffled across the room toward one of the wingback chairs. "I hate doing dishes."

Christa stretched her arms above her head and sent Emilee a pointed glance. "I didn't think you'd mind. Mom's taking us to the bookstore."

Emilee's eyes widened slightly. "Really? All right. I'll do the dishes, then."

A trip to the bookstore usually didn't pry a

reaction like that from Emilee. Sharon wondered briefly if they had some other reason for wanting this trip to the mall, but she shook off her suspicions with a silent laugh. She was letting her imagination run completely away from her. After all, what ulterior motive could the girls possibly have for wanting to go to the bookstore?

Two hours later, standing in the middle of the Outdoor Recreation section of the bookstore, Sharon asked herself the same question. But this time with growing trepidation.

Since walking into the store fifteen minutes ago, Emilee and Christa had tagged after one of the booksellers relentlessly. They'd peppered him with questions about every outdoor activity Sharon could imagine—and some she'd never thought of.

No doubt about it, the girls were behaving strangely. Were they hoping to go on some camping trip? Maybe they were trying to get Sharon interested. Certainly, each time she tried to steal away to one of the fiction sections, Emilee or Christa would draw her into a conversation about the outdoors. It was, she thought grimly, odd behavior for two usually independent teenagers. If she didn't know better, she'd swear one of them had a crush on the salesclerk.

That thought brought her up short. *Did* she know better? Sharon studied him carefully. She knew him by sight. He'd helped her on more than one occasion, and they'd even had a couple of short conversations while she'd waited for Christa and Emilee to pick out their books. But why would one of the girls find him attractive? He had to be at least twice their age.

She listened halfheartedly to his monologue on skydiving—she was obviously wrong about the camping—and tried to decide which of her daughters showed the most interest. Christa had already asked about bungee jumping and rappelling. Emilee about hang gliding and river rafting. Sharon tried to pay attention to what he was saying.

"I was about your age the first time I went skydiving. I gave myself the trip for my high-school graduation—"

Skydiving. Just the thought of it made Sharon slightly nauseated. She preferred to keep both feet firmly planted on terra firma.

"—after that first fall, I was hooked for life. You aren't really aware of the ground as you fall—"

Sharon's stomach gave a lurch. *She'd* be aware of the ground, she thought.

Brett—the clerk's name according to the badge on his chest—caught her eye. "So, tell me. Do you share your daughters' interest in adventure?"

Sharon took an involuntary step backward as if she thought he might try to haul her into a plane if she stood too close. "No. I'd rather read a good mystery."

Amusement lit his eyes. "Well, they must have gotten it from somewhere. Maybe you have a latent interest you haven't tapped into yet."

Not likely. "To tell you the truth, I never realized until today they were interested in any of these things."

"You ought to try bungee jumping," Christa urged. "I'll bet you'd like it. In fact, maybe we could all go—"

Sharon let out a nervous laugh and took another step away. "Not me. I have no desire to fling myself from a bridge while attached to a rubber band."

Brett pulled a thick volume from the shelf and handed it to Emilee. "You'd like skydiving. There's nothing like the freedom of a free fall. The silence is incredible."

"There wouldn't be any silence if I went," Sharon assured him. "I'd be too busy screaming."

He looked disappointed. "If you're ever interested in trying, I can put you in touch with the right people."

Christa's eager gaze darted to Sharon's. Emilee

managed a more nonchalant look. "Does your wife do all these things with you?"

"Oh, I'm not married. It takes a special kind of woman to put up with all the stuff I like to do."

Emilee's smile grew. "Well, there are special women out there."

Sharon's maternal instincts screamed to full alert. No way would she let Emilee get involved with someone so much older and more experienced. Belatedly, she realized Emilee was saying something about her.

Before she could tune back into the conversation, a page came over the PA system.

Brett sent them a rueful smile. "That's for me. I guess I'd better pay attention to some other customers." He softened his smile when he turned it on Sharon. "But, hey, it's been nice talking to you. And I'm serious about helping you hook up with the right people if you decide to try any of this stuff."

Sharon waited until he'd disappeared around the corner, then turned to face Emilee and Christa. "Are you two really interested in trying these things?"

Emilee flicked her gaze away. "I don't know."

"You've got to admit one thing," Christa said.

"This kind of stuff isn't boring. And neither are the people who do it. Look at Brett—"

"I don't want to look at Brett." Sharon kept her voice low so nobody could overhear her. "I want to know why you're suddenly so interested in this stuff. Does it have something to do with a boy?"

Christa looked shocked. "A boy? No."

"You're not trying to impress some guy by jumping out of airplanes?"

Emilee ticked her tongue against the roof of her mouth. "Really, Mom—"

If she wouldn't confess, Sharon would have to ask. "Do you have a crush on Brett?"

Emilee's face paled. "A crush? Me?" She shoved the book Brett had handed her back onto the shelf. "Geez, Mom, that's sick. He's old enough to be our *father*." She grabbed Christa's arm and tugged her away. "We're going to look at the romances."

More confused than ever, Sharon rested one arm on a shelf for support and watched them walk away.

GABE STOOD BACK and admired the pile of old linoleum against the concrete wall. Not bad for a man working alone, if he did say so himself. He could have cheerfully wrung the neck of whoever laid that ugly orange-and-brown floor covering. He'd had a tough time prying it off the concrete. But the room looked a lot better now.

Even with the trouble he'd had, it had been a productive day. Sharon and the girls had vacated the house shortly after he'd arrived, so there'd been nothing to take his attention off the job. No laughter. No deep brown eyes or softly curling hair. Even better, his dad had left him alone all morning.

So far, with the sporadic hours his other commitments and Sharon's work schedule forced him to keep, he'd been running behind. He should have finished this task at least a week ago, but every time he turned around he ran into another snag.

If it wasn't his father adding something to his workload, it was something in the construction of the house. If not that, an unexpected inspection or trouble with equipment on one of the other contracts put him behind. And, of course, when Sharon was around, he had trouble concentrating. But if he had more days like this one he might actually finish on schedule.

Whistling softly to a tune on the radio, he grabbed a broom and began to sweep up the loose dirt and dried glue. Within seconds, a cloud of grit surrounded him and settled in his hair, nose and mouth. At the same time, the phone in his pocket gave off a staccato ring.

He should have known it was too good to be true. Trying to clear his mouth of the dirt, he answered with a muffled, "Gabe Malone."

"Malone Construction?" The man on the other end sounded angry.

"Yes, what can I do for you?"

"Myron Ball here."

Gabe searched his memory, but he didn't recognize the name. He propped the broom against a two-by-four and said again, "What can I do for you?"

"You can tell me when you're planning to show up. My wife and I have been waiting for you all morning."

"I'm sorry. Do we have an appointment?"

"You're damn right we do. You were supposed to be here at ten o'clock."

Gabe glanced at his watch with dismay. Almost twelve-thirty. It didn't take a brain surgeon to figure out what had happened. "When you made the appointment, did you speak with my father?"

"How am I supposed to know?"

Gabe made a vain effort to keep frustration with his father from coming out in his voice. "I apologize for the mix-up, Mr. Ball. My dad and

I must have gotten our wires crossed. Why don't we make another appointment right now?"

"Another appointment? You mean you're not coming today?"

"I'm in the middle of a job right now, but I can work you in on Monday." He pulled a notebook from his pocket and found the stub of a pencil in his toolbox. "Why don't you tell me where you're located?"

"I already told the other guy, and he promised to have someone here at ten o'clock sharp." Mr. Ball's voice rose a few decibels. "What kind of outfit are you?"

"A good one," Gabe assured him, but he didn't think he'd made much of an impression. Even he could hear the lack of conviction in his voice.

"You assured me you could add a bed-room onto our house by the end of March. How am I supposed to believe you can do that when you don't even show up for your first appointment?"

Gabe tried to keep his mounting irritation in check. "Look, Mr. Ball, it was an honest mis-take—"

Mr. Ball cut him off. "All I want to know is whether or not you can finish the job on time."

"I can't answer that until I take a look at what's involved. We've already got several jobs lined up."

"Don't give me that. You already told me it would be no problem."

"Like I said before, Mr. Ball, I wasn't the one you talked with. And my father—"

"Your father promised me you could do the job." Mr. Ball's voice climbed a notch. "You know, you people came highly recommended to me, but I'm beginning to have second thoughts."

"I've apologized for the misunderstanding," he said as patiently as he could. "And I'll try to get there today. Beyond that…" He left the rest unsaid. Myron could fill in the blanks himself.

Mr. Ball rattled off a Boulder address and added, "Can you be here by one o'clock?"

Gabe glanced at his watch. "I'm too far away. How about one-thirty?"

"One o'clock," Myron demanded, "or you can forget it."

"I'll see what I can do." Gabe disconnected and stuffed the phone back into his pocket. They didn't need the contract, but there'd be trouble if he didn't follow through. Yanking out the phone again, he punched in the office number, let it ring once and hung up again.

He wouldn't accomplish anything by talking to his dad. If his dad even remembered making the appointment, he'd also believe he'd told Gabe about it. And that would officially make this mess Gabe's fault. Unfortunately, that was becoming less and less unusual.

Out of frustration he slammed his hand against a two-by-four. Pain tore up his arm but it didn't lessen the horrible sense of futility. He couldn't leave Sharon with this debris in her basement. She couldn't even get to the laundry room without stepping over piles of rubbish. He'd just have to send someone else to Boulder before one o'clock.

Knowing he'd set the match to another powder keg by doing so, he dialed Derry Kennedy's number and arranged for him to check out the job. But this, he told himself savagely, was the last straw.

He couldn't ignore the problem with his dad any longer. He couldn't stand by and watch the company's reputation go down the tubes. Malone Construction was known for its excellent work, its reliability and its professionalism, but they couldn't afford to coast along on a good name alone. His dad's mistakes were going to cost the firm dearly.

Gabe was caught in the middle of an impossible situation—hurt his father or put his ability to earn a livelihood and support his daughter in jeopardy. The trouble was, both options left a bad taste in his mouth.

GABE PACED outside his father's office, trying to decide how to tell his dad about Myron Ball without offending him. He knew Harold would be angry when he found out Gabe had authorized overtime for Derry yesterday, but he figured he might as well come clean right away. Putting it off would only make matters worse.

The sun had already started to set, but he could see his breath forming soft clouds as he walked. Even though he was aware of the cold, his nerves kept him warm.

Before he could decide exactly what he wanted to say, the office door opened and his dad filled the doorway. "What's going on out here?" Though Harold still had much of the bulk Gabe remembered from his childhood, he looked old.

Gabe stopped in his tracks and laughed self-consciously. "Nothing. Just thinking."

"Why don't you think in here? It's warmer." Harold stepped aside to give him room to get through the door.

"Maybe I will." Gabe closed the distance between them and climbed the stairs, but he had trouble meeting his dad's gaze as he passed him to get inside.

Harold led him into the office and sat behind the desk. "So, what's on your mind?"

Gabe took his usual chair in front of the

desk and cocked an ankle across his knee. "I need to talk to you about a problem I ran into yesterday."

"Oh?" Harold pushed aside a stack of files and rested his arms on the desk. "With the Lawrence basement?"

"No. That's coming along okay, but I could use some more time on it." He resisted the urge to skirt the issue and forced himself to plunge in. "I got a call from a man named Myron Ball." He watched his dad's face carefully for some sign of recognition. There wasn't any.

Harold leaned back in his chair. "Who's that?"

"He said he had an appointment with me and he was pretty upset when I didn't show up."

"You forgot?" Harold's face clouded. "Didn't you write it down?"

"I didn't know about it. I wasn't the one who talked to him."

"So you're saying *I* did?"

"It must have been you, Dad." Gabe kept his voice gentle as he added, "You and I are the only ones you've authorized to schedule appointments."

Harold gripped the armrests on his chair and lifted his gaze to the ceiling. The muscles in his jaw worked, his shoulders stiffened and he blinked rapidly—all signs that Gabe had upset him. "I've never forgotten an appointment in my life," he said at last.

"It could happen to anyone," Gabe assured him. "We have more contracts on the books than we've ever had. And we're shorthanded..."

"Whether we're shorthanded or not, the reputation of this company was built on my good name. We're known for being reliable and for doing quality work. I wouldn't do anything to jeopardize that."

"I know—"

"If I made an appointment with someone—" Harold cut him off "—you can be sure I told you about it."

Gabe had anticipated that argument. "You didn't tell me, Dad. You might as well know, I had to call Derry in to go over there."

"You did what?"

"It was the only thing I could do. If I hadn't, we would have lost the contract for sure."

Harold's face reddened. "You're determined to bankrupt us, aren't you?"

"Not at all. But I didn't come here to argue with you about that. We have to find some way to make sure it doesn't happen again."

"Keep better track," his dad said sharply.

Gabe ignored that and gestured toward the stacks of files on the desk and file cabinet. "Actually, I think we should hire someone to come in a couple of times a week to help with all this backlog."

That was a mistake. Harold shot to his feet and glared down at him. "I'm perfectly capable of taking care of my own business." His voice was taut with anger. "I don't need someone coming in here and messing up my system."

Gabe stood to face him, still hoping he could convince his father to listen to reason. "We wouldn't hire someone to take over, just to help out. You could teach them your system."

"You think this is easy?" Harold waved his hand, a gesture that took in the entire crowded office. "You think just anybody can figure it out?"

"No, but—"

"You're right, 'no.' And I'm not going to waste valuable time trying to teach it to someone else. If you spent half as much time doing the work you have lined up as you do trying to change things around here, we wouldn't have a problem."

Gabe kept a firm hand on his rising temper. "You can't run the business the way you did thirty years ago, Dad. It's gotten too big."

"And who's responsible for that?" Harold demanded, thumping himself on the chest with his palm.

"I'm not saying you haven't done an incredible job up to this point—"

"Then what *are* you saying?"

"I'm saying you're pushing yourself too hard. You don't need to do it all yourself anymore. You should be working half the hours you do now."

Harold's face stiffened even more. "I didn't realize you were so anxious to have me out of the way."

"I'm not. I just hate to see you pushing yourself so hard. Dad, you're almost seventy years old. You and Mom should be relaxing, traveling, enjoying life."

"I *am* enjoying life," his dad argued, but his tone sounded slightly less chilly. "*This* is what I enjoy."

Some of Gabe's certainty faded, but he pushed on. "What about Mom? She's been waiting most of her life for you to slow down a little and spend time with her."

"If your mother isn't complaining," Harold said, "I don't know why you are."

Gabe didn't answer right away. With his dad just a few feet away, looking injured beneath the anger, he couldn't bring himself to voice his deepest concerns aloud. No matter how much he had riding on the company, his father had more. Harold had started the business with very little money and a whole lot of work, and Gabe had no right to force him to give it up—no matter what happened.

He rubbed his temples with his fingertips and tried to work the tension from his neck. "Forget I said anything. I haven't been myself lately."

Harold's anger evaporated and concern took its place. "What's wrong?"

He had a list to choose from, but he picked the most important. "Just a little problem with Tracy."

"Tracy?" The older man dropped into his seat again. "She isn't sick, is she?"

"No. Nothing like that." Briefly, Gabe told him about Helene's phone call and his own conversation with Tracy. "I'm afraid I'm losing her, Dad. Things haven't been the same between us since the divorce."

"Well, of course they haven't." Harold sent him an exasperated look. "You can't expect them to be, can you?"

"I suppose not, but—"

"I'm not saying I think you and Helene should have stayed together. I don't. Your marriage was rocky for a long time, and everyone around you could see it. But even so, breaking up the family is bound to upset Tracy."

"Yes, I know, but—"

"But you think she should be over it by now?"

Gabe smiled sheepishly. "Something like that."

"She's a kid, Gabe. Believe me, kids don't see things the same way adults do." He sent Gabe a half smile and added, "I ought to know. I have a couple of kids of my own."

Gabe laughed softly. "So I've heard."

His dad seemed to relax a little more. "Give her time, son. And while you're waiting, make sure she knows you're still around for her. She's probably scared to death that you'll forget about her."

"She knows I could never forget about her," Gabe argued, but honesty forced him to admit that he could have done more than he had to set Tracy's mind at ease.

"All I know," Harold said, leaning back in his chair with a groan, "is that your mother sends her something at least once a month just to make sure she knows we're still here."

That was news to Gabe. His mother had never mentioned it to him. "What kinds of things?"

His dad shrugged casually. "Cards, usually. Just a note that says we're still thinking about her. You know the kind I mean."

"Yeah," Gabe said thoughtfully. "I do."

"I could ask your mother to pick up a few for you next time she goes to the store."

Gabe shook his head quickly. "I think this is

something I'd better take care of myself." He stood and turned toward the door, then looked back at his dad with a grateful smile. "Thanks, Dad."

"For what?"

Gabe didn't know how to answer that without embarrassing them both, so he just waved a vague hand. "For everything." But his step was lighter as he left the office, and so was his heart for the first time in days.

CHAPTER FIVE

SHARON LEANED BACK in her chair and rubbed her eyes. She'd been grading tests steadily since Emilee and Christa left for school, but she hadn't made much progress. She couldn't concentrate with Gabe working downstairs and concern for the girls running constantly through her head.

The blast of an electric saw sounded from the basement and mingled with the music coming from Gabe's radio. Even with the poor reception he got in the basement, she could recognize this morning's choice—country-western. The last time he'd been here, he'd listened to rock. And the time before, oldies. Obviously, he was a man of many moods.

She picked up her coffee and carried it toward the bay window, thinking about her moody daughters. They'd seemed fine since their trip to the bookstore over the weekend. Neither of them had mentioned Brett again. But Sharon couldn't relax.

Raoul stepped in front of her and flopped onto his back so she could scratch his belly.

She set aside her coffee and complied. "What's the matter with those girls of yours?" she asked him.

He ignored her and rolled over so she could scratch one side.

"I'm serious, Raoul. I'm worried about them."

He blinked up at her, let out a muffled *murff,* and rolled onto his other side.

"Fine. Don't tell me, then." She finished scratching the cat and moved to stand by the window. Raoul wound himself through her legs and stared up at her. *Murff.*

"Well, *something's* wrong," she insisted.

His purr started up, a heavy, squeaky rumble that sounded like a rusty motor.

"I know you don't believe me," she said, folding her arms against the chill that seeped in through the glass. "But I know those girls, and I know something's wrong."

He stood on his hind legs and propped his front paws against the legs of her jeans. *Murowww.*

She scooped him up and scratched behind his ears. He leaned into her hand and purred louder.

"Maybe you're right. Maybe I'm just imagining it." Frowning, she turned away from the window. But she couldn't make herself grade another paper. She couldn't think.

Gabe pounded nails into boards. Her head pounded in rhythm. No wonder she couldn't concentrate. She longed for a hot bath filled with scented bubbles, candles surrounding the tub, and a good novel. But the thought of taking a bath with Gabe in the house made her uncomfortable.

Not that she worried he'd come looking for her while she was relaxing—he'd been working on her basement off and on for nearly two weeks and had managed to completely resist her charms so far—but she still couldn't stop thinking about him. And those thoughts came at the oddest times. During class. While she fixed dinner. She kept waiting for him to do or say something macho and obnoxious. Something *playboyish* that would make her dislike him; instead, she found him more attractive every day.

But this kind of thinking was ridiculous. She needed to get him off her mind for a little while. Maybe she should see if Adelle wanted to meet for lunch. A couple of hours not listening to Gabe working, not watching him haul boxes of supplies down the stairs, not listening to him whistle to the songs on the radio might do her a world of good.

She'd clear the walks and driveway first, then call Adelle. She was eager to try the used snowblower she'd bought last week. It should make the job much quicker.

After bundling up to face the weather, she stepped outside into the garage. But there, she stopped in her tracks and stared at the mounds of snow blocking the driveway. She hadn't realized how heavily it had been snowing. She wondered if her little snowblower would be able to churn through it.

Well, there was only one way to find out. She spent a few minutes studying the owners' manual, plugged the cord into the electrical outlet and tried to start the machine. The motor clicked a couple of times, but it didn't turn over. She gave it another try, and a third. Still nothing. Not even a sputter.

She stepped away from the machine and studied it as if she'd be able to see the problem from a distance. But, predictably—since she knew next to nothing about mechanical things—distance didn't help. Scowling, she moved closer again and bent to depress the throttle once more just as the garage door opened behind her.

Gabe smiled when he saw her and shrugged into his jacket. "Trouble?"

His smile sent tingling warmth rushing through her, but she tried not to let him see her reaction. "A little, but I'm sure I'll get it going."

"Have you ever had trouble with it before?"

"This is the first time I've tried to use it." She propped her hands on her hips and glared at the machine, as if *that* might get it running.

Gabe hunkered down beside it. "Mind if I take a look?"

Did she mind? Was he kidding? His thigh brushed her shin briefly, but she stepped away, motioning him closer. "Be my guest. Please."

He tried starting the machine, unplugged the power cord and tinkered with something on the motor. Still no luck. Scowling slightly, he pulled a rubber cap off the spark plug and inspected it.

Sharon found herself watching the play of his shoulders beneath his jacket and the surprising dexterity of his large hands as he poked and prodded inside the motor.

After several minutes, he shook his head in resignation. "You've got a problem here I can't fix."

"Do you have any idea what it is?"

"Could be the carburetor. Or the starter motor. Either way, you're going to have to take it somewhere for repairs—unless you know how to work on motors yourself."

She shook her head quickly. "I'm not much of a mechanic."

He sent her a lopsided smile that made her

heart stutter. "Let me help you get it to a shop. There's a good one I use that's not far from here. We can take it in my truck."

Out of long habit, she shook her head. She was used to relying on herself and the idea of accepting help made her nervous. "I don't want to put you out."

"You won't be. It'll be much easier to let me take it in the truck, than to stuff it into your trunk. Besides—" he shifted his gaze to the driveway "—your car's pretty low to the ground. You'd probably get stuck somewhere on the side of the road."

That convinced her. "Thank you. It's very nice of you to help."

He smiled again. "I told you about my mother—"

She laughed softly. "Oh, yes. Well, I wouldn't want to get you in trouble." She hurried inside and grabbed her purse. By the time she came back through the garage, he'd loaded the machine in the truck and cleared a few feet of snow from the driveway.

When she saw what he'd done, she stopped in her tracks. "You don't need to do that," she protested lamely.

"I don't mind. Of course, if you'd rather do it—"

"I wouldn't," she admitted.

He grinned again. "Call it a favor. I'll be glad

to finish when we come back." He left the shovel in the garage and led her through the snow to the truck. "I hope you don't mind if I stop somewhere while we're out for something to eat."

"No," she assured him quickly. "Of course I don't mind."

"What about you?" he asked as he opened the truck's door for her. "Have you had lunch yet?"

"No, I haven't."

"Well, then, we ought to get lunch together. How about the Blue Iguana?"

"The Blue Iguana?" She loved the restaurant, but she'd assumed they'd pick up burgers at some fast-food joint, not share a real meal together inside a restaurant.

"It's nearby, isn't it?"

"Yes. Only a few blocks away."

"But is the Blue Iguana okay with you? Or would you rather eat somewhere else?"

Was he real? So seldom during her years with Nick had he deferred to her choice about anything that she'd forgotten what it felt like to be consulted. Slowly, she released the death grip she had on her coat collar and smiled. "The Blue Iguana sounds great. It's one of my favorite restaurants."

"Really?" That smile crossed his face again,

then disappeared. "Maybe it's not a good idea after all. I'm not exactly dressed to go out."

Sharon looked at his clothes. "You look fine to me. The Blue Iguana's pretty casual."

He seemed surprised. "You don't mind being seen with someone in old work clothes?"

The question caught her off guard. "Why should I?"

He studied her with an intensity that made her stomach flutter. She stuffed her hands into the pockets of her coat and told herself to grow up. She was a woman, for heaven's sake, not a teenager. She could ride in the cute guy's truck and even have lunch with him without losing her cool. She could ignore the butterflies in her stomach and the sudden, incessant pounding of her heart. She could even spend an hour in his company without dreaming of a future with him.

At least, that's what she told herself.

WITH GABE ONLY half a step behind her, Sharon followed the restaurant hostess to a window booth. Outside, the wind tossed bits of snow against the window. Inside, heated air took away some of the chill, and the spicy scent of food and Mexican folk music on the loudspeakers helped her relax.

So far, she hadn't been nearly as uncomfortable

as she'd expected. Gabe had chatted easily about the weather, a news report they'd heard over the radio and his work on the basement. By the time they'd dropped off the snowblower and pulled into the restaurant's parking lot, she'd put her earlier discomfort firmly behind her, and she intended to keep it there.

As they settled into seats across the table from each other, she reminded herself once again for good measure. This was lunch—nothing more. Two adults, both of whom needed to eat, sitting at the same table.

Gabe pulled two menus from a rack near the window and handed one to Sharon. "It smells good in here, doesn't it?"

Sharon nodded. "Yes it does. I love their food."

"Do you know what you want, or do you need a minute to look at the menu?"

"Oh, I know what I want," she said with a smile. "Everything they serve is good, but I have my favorite."

"And what is that?"

"Cheese enchiladas made with flour tortillas." Sharon let her smile relax a bit further and waved her hand as if he'd offered an argument. "I know. They're full of fat and cholesterol, but they're *wonderful*."

Gabe laughed softly and rested one arm along

the back of the bench. "So are the smothered burritos."

"Your favorites?"

"I order them every time," he admitted. "Does that make me sound boring?"

"If it does," she said, "I'm boring, too."

Gabe looked at his menu. "Maybe I should order something different, like a tostada or a taco." He cocked an eyebrow at her. "Or I could really live it up and order a combination plate."

Sharon put one hand to her chest in mock horror. "Don't you think a combination plate is a bit extreme? I'd hate for you to go overboard."

Gabe's lips curved in a lazy smile. "Okay. I'll play it safe. Two smothered burritos, one soft-shell taco. Now, what about you? Are you going to take a risk?"

She shook her head quickly. "Not me. One cheese enchilada is all I'll be able to eat."

"Only one?" He looked genuinely shocked.

"Yes, but usually I order three just so I can take the leftovers home. Emilee and Christa tease me about it all the time."

"So, you come here a lot?"

"Fairly often. Probably more often than we should."

He leaned back while their server put tortilla

chips and salsa on the table, then recited both orders for the young man.

"We'd like separate checks," Sharon added when he'd finished.

Gabe glanced quickly at her, then back at the waiter who hovered near Gabe's shoulder as if he needed Gabe to confirm her request. Gabe nodded and returned his attention to Sharon, continuing their conversation as if they hadn't been interrupted. "Have you lived in the area long?"

"About ten years," she said, then added, "My ex-husband and I bought the house together. It's a big old thing, and it needs lots of work, but the girls and I love it."

He nodded thoughtfully. "How long have you been divorced?"

"Five years."

"It's been two for me." His expression altered subtly.

Sharon wondered what had happened to his marriage, but she wouldn't let herself ask. Instead, she spent a few seconds adjusting her sweater over her lap. She glanced up again and caught Gabe watching her.

He worked up another smile, but this one lacked that appeal that had thrown her for such a loop at home. "You and your daughters seem to have a good relationship."

"I suppose we do."

"You suppose? I hear you laughing together a lot." The eyebrow arched again and teased an answering smile from her.

"All right," she conceded. "Yes. We're close."

"I could tell. It must be nice." He sounded almost wistful. "I wish I had that kind of relationship with my daughter."

"*You* have a daughter?" She tempered the surprise in her voice with another smile. "I'm sorry. I didn't realize you were a father."

"I am. Her name's Tracy. She's fifteen, and she lives in Oregon with her mother."

"You aren't close to your daughter?"

"Unfortunately, no." He ran his fingers through his hair and looked out the window. "Too much distance."

"That shouldn't make any difference."

Gabe snapped his gaze back to hers. "It's not easy maintaining a relationship long-distance, no matter who it's with. And with kids, it's especially hard."

"I'm sorry," she said quickly. "I shouldn't have said anything. But I do know how much Emilee and Christa miss their dad, and how glad they are to hear from him when he calls."

Gabe looked interested. "Does he call them often?"

"About once a month, but it's still not enough.

I wish I could make him understand how much they need him, but he only seems interested in his new life."

"Maybe he's afraid to call more often than that," Gabe said with a shrug.

"Why would he be afraid to call?"

"I'd say that depends on whether or not the two of you get along. I'd call Tracy a lot more often if I didn't have to fight with Helene every time I try."

"Tracy doesn't have a cell phone?"

"She does, but Helene tears a strip out of me when I call that number because of the charges to her account, even when I offer to pay for them. No matter what I say it always ends in an argument." He scooped salsa onto a chip. "In fact, I was yelling at my ex-wife when you came downstairs the other day."

So it hadn't been a current girlfriend. The news shouldn't please her but it did. An awkward smile tugged at her lips. She bit it back, but not soon enough.

"I guess you're wondering about what you overheard."

"No." She jerked back in her seat, nearly overturning her water glass as she did.

"You're not even curious?"

"Not in the slightest."

That brought a laugh from him. He stopped

as their server approached carrying hot plates of food. When he'd walked away again, Gabe said softly, "You're not a very good liar. You know that, don't you?"

"So I've been told."

He laughed again, softer this time. Kinder. "Well, just for the record, I don't date *that* much. I don't even know why I said that to her."

"You don't have to explain anything to me."

"I'd like to. Believe me, I was as embarrassed as you were by that argument." He took a bracing swig of Tecata and shifted in his seat. "Actually, we were talking about some problems Tracy's been having and I asked whether there were boys involved. Helene said she'd know if there were—I accused her of not knowing anything about Tracy, and the whole thing disintegrated from there."

That sounded as unreasonable and ridiculous as some of the arguments she'd had with Nick.

"So you see," he said, forking a bite of burrito and chile verde, "I'm not exactly a player, even though I tried to convince my ex-wife that I am. I'm not that kind of guy."

She nearly dropped her fork. "I didn't for one minute think—"

"You never know," he said with a teasing smile. "Some women think all men are dogs."

"I don't happen to be one of those women."

"Anyway, I had no business bringing that into your home. I should have ended the conversation when I realized she wanted to argue."

"If you can do that, you're superhuman. Even after five years, I find myself arguing with Nick. And the strange thing is, they're *old* arguments about things that don't even matter anymore."

Gabe took a bite of his taco and chewed slowly. "That sounds fun."

"Oh, believe me, it is." Sharon went on, more than a little surprised by her willingness to discuss something so personal, "Nick's remarried. He's got a new family. What happened between us is so irrelevant to either of our lives, I don't know why we get caught up in it every time we talk."

"I know what you mean."

She took a bite of enchilada. "The trouble is, once you have children, the other parent is always a part of your life. You can't get rid of them."

"No matter how much you might want to." His smile faded, and he studied her with an expression she'd never seen on his face before. "So, why is it you've never married again?"

The question caught Sharon off guard. She lowered her fork to the table. "I'm not interested in getting married again."

"Why not?"

She decided to turn the tables on him. "Why aren't you married again?"

He shrugged as if he didn't mind the question. "I'm not good at the whole family scene. Dinner at six. Meat loaf every Monday. Falling asleep to some late-night talk show."

"When you put it that way, it does sound boring. But it doesn't have to be that way, you know."

"You haven't answered my question. Why aren't you interested?"

"Because I lost part of myself in my marriage to Nick, and I'm not willing to do that again. I don't want to take the risk until I really know who I am and what I want."

Gabe held her gaze. "It doesn't have to be that way, either."

"Maybe not," she said doubtfully.

He studied her for a moment. "After five years alone, do you know who you are?"

"I'm getting closer."

He laughed and lifted his glass. "Here's to figuring out who you are and what you really want."

She lifted her own glass to meet his, amazed at how easily she could talk to him. She could almost believe his claim that he wasn't a playboy.

As she lowered her glass, the cell phone in

her purse let out a muffled ring. Instinct told her to ignore it. She didn't want anyone or anything to interrupt the moment. But Gabe would wonder why she didn't answer. Besides, only a few people had her cell number, and two of them were in school.

She answered, fully expecting to hear Adelle's voice on the other end. Instead, a strange man's voice greeted her.

He identified himself as Norman Taylor, the nurse at the high school, and said, "Your daughter, Emilee, is in my office. She says she's sprained her ankle and needs you to come and get her."

The glow she'd been feeling faded. "How badly is she hurt?"

"I don't think it's anything major." His comment sounded unfinished, as if there should have been a "but" after it.

She supplied it. "But—"

Mr. Taylor hesitated for an instant. "But I don't think she's telling me the truth."

"You think it's worse than she says?"

"No. I don't think she sprained it at all."

Disbelief and anger succeeded in ruining Sharon's mood completely. "If you think that, you don't know Emilee very well. She would never do something like that."

Gabe flicked a curious glance at her, then went back to pretending not to listen.

"Nevertheless," Mr. Taylor said, "I'd bet my reputation she's faking this injury. I wonder if she should talk to the school psychologist."

"Psychologist? That's outrageous. Emilee's never been in any sort of trouble before."

"Perhaps not, but trouble always starts somewhere, doesn't it?"

Sharon couldn't believe her ears. She forced her voice lower. "I'll tell you what, Mr. Taylor. I'll come and get Emilee and I'll take her to the doctor. If you're wrong, I expect you to apologize to Emilee and to me." Without giving him a chance to speak again, she broke their connection and stuffed the phone back into her purse.

"Trouble?" Gabe's voice reached her through the red haze of maternal anger.

"I'm sorry," she said, gathering her purse and coat and sliding to the edge of the booth. "I need to get to the high school. Emilee's hurt."

"Badly?"

"The school nurse says not. In fact, he accused her of faking the injury."

Gabe pulled his wallet from his back pocket and removed several bills, which reminded Sharon she needed to pay for her share. She started to dig for her wallet, but Gabe tossed enough onto the table to pay for both meals. "I'll cover it for now," he said, placing one hand on the small of her back and steering her toward the door. "We can work it out later. Right now, we need to take care of Emilee."

We. To her surprise, she liked the way that sounded. It had been forever since she'd had someone with her during a crisis, and she found Gabe's presence comforting. Her common sense told her to rely on herself the way she always did. But every other part of her wanted to accept what he offered. A shoulder if she needed one to cry on. A listening ear. Friendship.

For the first time in a long time, Sharon silenced the logic and listened to her heart.

EMILEE LAY BACK on the narrow cot in the nurse's station and smiled up at the ceiling. Her mom would be here soon, and so far everything had gone according to plan. Last night, she and Christa had agreed to find someone who could make their mom laugh. Emilee figured Mr. Taylor could do that. He was always joking around with the kids at school.

She couldn't believe her luck. Imagine, Mr. Taylor, of all people, single. Divorced. Thank goodness, Emilee had mentioned The Plan to her friend Brittany who knew all about Mr. Taylor because he was a friend of her dad's. According to Brittany, Mr. Taylor had two kids in high school and one who'd graduated already, which meant he must be about the same age as Emilee's mom. And that made him a perfect candidate. Not too old. Not too young. Just right.

Okay, so his hair was thinning and he had a paunch. And his nose was kind of big. Maybe he wasn't Brad Pitt, but he wasn't *bad* looking. Not really. And Brittany said he was nice. Not too macho. Not shy and boring.

As if her thoughts had conjured him, Mr. Taylor pushed open the door and peeked inside to check on her. "Any swelling yet?"

Emilee glanced at her ankle and tried to look injured. "Maybe. Yes, I think a little. It feels puffy."

"Pain?"

"Lots. It's throbbing." Throbbing sounded good. He couldn't ignore throbbing. "Did you call my mom?"

He nodded. "She's on her way."

She tried not to grin. "I knew she'd come. And I'm sure she'll want to talk to you about it. You know, in case it's broken or something. She's a really good mom. Very concerned about us."

He didn't look impressed, but Emilee didn't let that discourage her. Once he saw her mom, *that* would change.

As if on cue, the familiar rhythm of her

mother's footsteps sounded in the corridor. Emilee worked up a groan just as her mother stepped into the doorway behind Mr. Taylor.

Her mom hurried past him into the room. "Emilee? Are you all right?"

"I'm okay. But my ankle hurts." Emilee watched through narrowed eyes, waiting for the moment when they'd take their first good look at each other.

To her dismay, her mother ignored Mr. Taylor completely and settled on the edge of the bed. She ran her hand across Emilee's forehead. "What happened?"

"I twisted it on my way down the stairs." Emilee kept her story simple. No added frills. Those would only trip her up.

"Did you fall? Are you hurt anywhere else?"

Emilee should have thought of that. A bumped knee would have been a nice touch. But she couldn't afford to change her story now. She shook her head sadly. "No, just my ankle."

Her mother tossed a look over her shoulder at Mr. Taylor. Emilee knew that look. It wasn't her mom's friendliest one. She held out a hand to help Emilee stand. "I'm taking you to the doctor."

"The doctor?" She wasn't supposed to do *that*. "It's just a sprain, Mom."

"Yes, I know." Her mom wrapped an arm around her waist. "Do you think you can walk to the car?"

"Probably." Emilee tried to look uncertain. "But don't you think you and Mr. Taylor should talk before we go? You know…in case there's something special we should do?"

"Mr. Taylor has already offered his suggestions." Her mom's voice sounded tight and angry. Not good.

"But—" Emilee held back a sigh of exasperation and tried again. "I mean, am I supposed to keep my foot elevated? What should I take for the pain?" She glanced at Mr. Taylor helplessly. "Did you tell her that already?"

Sharon kept moving toward the door. "It's a sprain, Emilee. I know how to deal with it. Besides, Gabe Malone's waiting in the office for us, and I don't want to keep him too long."

Nothing her mother could have said would have surprised her more. Emilee stopped short, remembered she was supposed to need help and forced herself to keep limping. "What's he doing here?"

"He helped me take the snowblower to the shop. He was with me when Mr. Taylor called." Her mom's voice sounded different. And did Emilee only imagine it, or was she blushing?

No. She hadn't imagined it. Her mom's face had turned red.

Emilee didn't like that. Gabe was a total hunk, but she and Christa already decided he was completely wrong for their mother. She limped a bit farther and saw him pacing the length of the office. To her surprise, he looked worried.

He caught sight of them and started forward to help. Dumbfounded, Emilee stopped walking. He was worried about *her*. Totally cool.

She smiled slowly and beefed up her limp a little. Maybe it hadn't brought her mom and Mr. Taylor together, but who knew what might happen now?

CHAPTER SIX

GABE WISHED he'd taken the time to clear the walks before he and Sharon left the house. He trailed her, carrying Emilee's backpack and books, and watched her help the teenager slowly along the narrow path leading toward the garage. Beneath the snow, ice made their progress treacherous.

The wind had picked up again, and now it flung bits of snow, needle-sharp, into his face. He hunched farther into his coat and waited while Emilee, favoring first one foot, then the other, climbed the two short steps to the door. He didn't want to upset Sharon, but he thought the school nurse just might be right.

He didn't have to be a brain surgeon to figure out why Emilee wanted her mom at school. Norman the nurse must be single. But why would Emilee try to line her mother up with that geek? He wasn't Sharon's type at all. He was too short. Too dumpy. Too…nerdy.

He forced the whole subject out of his head. He didn't care who they found for her. The guy could be Attila the Hun, for all Gabe cared. Still, you'd think the girls would have better taste than that.

Grim-faced, he watched Sharon climb the steps. She certainly was easy to talk to. He'd found himself telling her more about himself than he'd intended and he might have said even more if they hadn't been interrupted. Sharon was different from any woman he'd ever known. Her reaction to his work clothes told him that. But neither of those things changed his mind about avoiding women. Besides, he had the bet with Jesse to consider.

He forced himself to look away, but from the corner of his eye, he saw Emilee turn and notice the way he'd been watching her mother.

She grinned at him.

He scowled and followed them into the living room. He had to nip this in the bud—he didn't want Emilee or her sister getting any big ideas about him.

Sharon helped Emilee settle onto the couch, tossed her coat over the back of a chair and hurried away, muttering something about pillows. He didn't watch her leave, but let his gaze travel around the room. Two wingback chairs, each covered in pale blue, flanked the living-room window. Throw pillows in a light plaid of blue, yellow and beige matched the almost-colorless carpeting and couch. Nice.

He held out the backpack and books. "Where do you want me to put these?"

Emilee shifted her weight on the couch to see him better. "Anywhere. So, you and Mom were together when I called?"

He nodded warily. "We took the snowblower to the shop and then stopped for lunch."

Emilee's eyes widened in surprise. "Lunch? Where?"

"The Blue Iguana."

"Really?"

"It was on the way."

Emilee nodded thoughtfully. Too thoughtfully, to Gabe's way of thinking. Before the girl could say anything else, Sharon came into the room carrying two pillows covered in crisp white cases. She settled one behind Emilee's back and the other beneath the foot Emilee favored most often, then stepped back and propped her hands on her hips.

Gabe decided now might be as good a time as any to leave. "I think I'll finish the walks—"

Sharon whipped around to face him. "But you didn't get to finish your lunch. I'll fix you a sandwich before you start working again."

He decided not to turn down the offer. "All right, but let me give you a hand with it."

"Not on your life. I've already put you out enough. I'll just get Emilee an ice pack and call Dr. Hartvigsen—"

Panic darted across Emilee's face. "I told you I don't need to go to the doctor."

"I'm calling him, anyway," Sharon insisted.

"Mom—" Emilee's voice changed to a whine Gabe recognized only too well. The same tone Tracy used when she wanted to wheedle something out of him. "I don't *want* to go to the doctor. My ankle will be better in a couple of days."

Gabe would bet money on it.

Sharon sighed and perched on the arm of the couch near her daughter's feet. "I know it's probably nothing serious," she conceded, "but I want that nurse at your school to know you're really hurt."

That obviously caught Emilee by surprise. "What do you mean?"

"He doesn't believe you've sprained your ankle," Sharon told her. "And he had the nerve to suggest you might need to see the school psychologist."

"But I *did* sprain it," Emilee insisted. She looked so frantic, Gabe had to turn away to hide his smile. He'd give almost anything to see the look on her face when the doctor examined her.

"I know you did." Sharon unfolded a thick

afghan and settled it over Emilee's lap. "You wouldn't lie about something like that."

Sharon left the room again. Gabe felt Emilee watching him as he slipped out of his coat. Sensed her assessing him as he settled into the chair. Caught the slight smile on her lips as he met her gaze again. He could almost see her mind working.

She leaned back on her pillow but she didn't look away. "My mom's nice, don't you think?"

How in the world was he supposed to answer that? Anything other than an absolute no would encourage the plan he saw taking shape right before his eyes. He nodded warily.

"She's divorced, you know."

"Yes," he said carefully. "I know." He nodded toward her feet. "How's your ankle?"

"Sore. You'll like your lunch. She's a great cook."

"I have no doubt." He wondered if Sharon could hear them, but when he heard her voice coming softly from the other room and realized she was on the telephone, he relaxed slightly. "Which ankle did you hurt again? Left or right?"

Emilee's eyes narrowed almost imperceptibly. "Left. See that picture over there?" She nodded toward a framed photograph of a river running through a forest of autumn colors. "My mom took that."

"Very nice. How did you get hurt?"

"Walking down the stairs." Emilee glanced around for another of her mother's selling points. "You ought to see our yard in the spring and summer. We have flowers everywhere. Mom loves to garden."

"I have hay fever," Gabe lied. "Funny. Your ankle doesn't look swollen from here."

"Well, it is." Emilee scowled slightly, then brightened again when she caught sight of Raoul stretching his way into the room. "She's really good with animals."

"I'm allergic." Another lie, but a necessary one.

He rubbed one hand across his chin. "I wonder why that nurse at your school thought you were faking the sprain."

Emilee shrugged. "I don't know. Do you have a girlfriend?"

He deepened his scowl. "No, and I don't want one, either." Poor Sharon. With this girl plotting against her, she didn't stand a chance. Neither would he if he didn't stop her right here and now. He propped his arms on his knees, held her gaze steadily and lowered his voice. "I'm *not* the guy you're looking for."

"How do you know?"

"I know."

"Well, *I* know you think my mom's pretty. I can tell."

"That's not the point."

"Don't you like her?"

"Of course I *like* her," Gabe said. "But we're completely wrong for each other. Even if I was interested in finding another girlfriend—which I'm not—it would never work."

"Why not?"

"Because…" He quickly replayed the list of undesirable qualities he'd overheard on New Year's Eve. "Because I'm stubborn. Very stubborn."

"So's she."

"And I'm pushy."

"I think you're nice."

Simple words, but they touched him deeply. He didn't want Emilee to know that, though. He growled just to show her how wrong she was.

She ignored him. "Mom must like you if she went to lunch with you."

"That was nothing," he assured her, surprised by how untrue the words sounded.

"For *my* mom?" Emilee shook her head. "You don't know her. She's never done anything like that before."

An unmistakable wave of pleasure washed over him. He pushed it away. "We're friends," he whispered. "Nothing more." Then more firmly, "She's a client of mine."

Emilee didn't even look slightly discouraged. To make matters worse, Sharon's footsteps started moving toward them. He narrowed his gaze and lowered his voice even further. "You'd better get rid of any ideas you might have about me and your mother if you want me to keep my mouth shut."

Emilee scowled at him.

"She's coming," he warned. "Do we have a deal, or not?"

Emilee leaned against her pillow and let out a long, pathetic sigh. "Oh, all right. It's a deal."

Satisfied, Gabe sat back in the chair and once again reminded himself of his long-standing rule against mixing business and pleasure. But when Sharon rounded the corner holding a plate of food and a glass of soda, when she drew nearer and the light scent of her perfume wrapped itself around him, he wondered, just for a second, if he'd made a mistake.

SHARON FLIPPED through a magazine in the waiting room of Dr. Hartvigsen's office and tried to ignore Emilee's obvious agitation in the plush seat beside her. Sunlight streamed through a window on one side of the waiting room. Someone sneezed. Someone else sniffled. A little boy hacked a cough too close to Sharon's chair.

"Let's just get out of here," Emilee whispered. "I don't need to see the doctor. I'm fine. My ankle's fine."

Sharon shook her head firmly. Emilee had said the same thing at least two dozen times since breakfast. "It's *not* fine. You limped around the house all night last night."

"But it feels better this morning."

Sharon closed the magazine, keeping her finger between the pages to mark her place. "Good. And *I'll* feel better after the doctor looks at it."

Emilee rolled her eyes in exasperation. "Mom—"

"Don't argue with me, Emilee." She wasn't in any mood for an argument. Not with Emilee. Norman Taylor was another matter entirely. She couldn't wait to wave the doctor's diagnosis under his nose. "You know, I had to take the morning away from classes to bring you here."

"That's the whole point, Mom. You didn't need to take time off work. I mean, it's not as if I've never had a sprained ankle before. Besides, it doesn't hurt nearly as much as it did yesterday."

"This may not be your first sprain," Sharon

said, "but it *is* the first time you've ever been accused of lying about it."

"Is that what you're upset about?"

Sharon rested the magazine on her lap. "Yes, that's what I'm upset about."

"And that's why you made me come here?"

"Yes," Sharon admitted. "I'm not going to sit back and do nothing while that nurse at the school accuses you of lying."

Emilee shrugged casually. "If I don't care what he said, why should you?"

"Because I'm your mother, and because you don't lie."

A slow flush crept up Emilee's cheeks. She glanced down at her fingernails for a few seconds. "I've got a history test this morning that I don't want to miss. And I used an ankle wrap. It'll be fine."

"If Dr. Hartvigsen says it's okay for you to walk on it, I'll take you to school as soon as we're through here." She thought that might make Emilee a bit happier.

It didn't. Emilee let out another heavy sigh and muttered something under her breath Sharon couldn't quite hear.

Before Sharon could figure out what she'd said, Dr. Hartvigsen's nurse poked her head into the waiting room. "Emilee Lawrence?"

Emilee stood quickly and started toward the

nurse. Sharon set the magazine aside and started after her, but Emilee held up a hand to stop her. "It's okay, Mom. You don't need to come in with me."

Sharon's step faltered. She'd always gone with the girls for regular checkups, and they'd always wanted her with them when they were sick or hurt. But at seventeen, she supposed Emilee might imagine herself too old to need her mother around. "All right. I'll wait here. But I want to talk to the doctor after he's examined you."

Emilee's eyes widened as if Sharon had offended her. "Why? Don't you trust me?"

The question knocked Sharon completely for a loop. "Of course I trust you. That has nothing to do with it."

Something flickered in Emilee's eyes. Worry? Panic? Fear?

Sharon caught her breath and wondered if Emilee was trying to hide something. All the concerns she'd managed to put behind her for the past few days came back again.

She returned to her seat in the waiting room and tried to read several short articles, but the words seemed to swim on the glossy pages. She set the magazine aside and picked up another one with lots of pictures.

After what felt like forever, the nurse reappeared in the doorway. "Mrs. Lawrence? Dr. Hartvigsen can see you now."

Relieved, she followed the nurse to the doctor's office at the end of the corridor. Dr. Hartvigsen motioned her toward one of the empty leather chairs. "Have a seat, Sharon."

She sat and propped her purse beside her feet on the floor. "Thanks for taking the time to talk with me."

"It's quite all right." He frowned slightly and scratched just above one ear. "I've had a look at Emilee's ankle."

"How bad is it?"

His frown deepened. "Not bad at all."

"But she *does* have a sprain?"

Dr. Hartvigsen smoothed his fringe of graying hair with one hand. "To be perfectly honest, Sharon, I don't think there's anything wrong with Emilee's ankle."

Sharon stared at him in disbelief. Her mood took a plunge. She didn't want Emilee to be hurt, but she didn't want Norman Taylor to be right, either. "Are you sure?"

"There's no swelling, and I can't find any evidence of a sprain." He linked his hands over his round stomach. "I hate to say this, but I think she's pretending."

If Dr. Hartvigsen hadn't been treating the girls for as long as she could remember, or if he'd ever been wrong before, she might have argued. Motherly instinct told her to argue anyway. Common sense held her back.

Dr. Hartvigsen's eyebrows knit in concern. "Is she having trouble at school?"

"No." The word sounded far more definite than it should have. Sharon ran her hands across the legs of her slacks and tried again. "None that I'm aware of."

The doctor let out a sigh. "Well, maybe it's nothing to worry about. Maybe it's just a test she's trying to avoid or trouble with some of the kids at school."

"I wish I could believe that," Sharon admitted. "But Emilee didn't want to stay home. In fact, she practically begged me to let her go to school this morning."

"Really?" He seemed as confused as Sharon. "Well, then, maybe I'm missing something. You can always get a second opinion."

Sharon shook her head slowly. "No. I believe you. In fact, that's exactly what the school nurse thought. I brought Emilee here this morning so you could prove him wrong. It's just not like her to do something like this."

Sharon leaned down and retrieved her purse from the floor. "I know you're busy, Doctor. I won't keep you any longer. Thanks for talking to me."

He stood and came around from behind his desk, clapped a gentle hand on her shoulder and steered her toward the door. "Hopefully it's not a big problem. After all, Emilee *is* seventeen. That's a rough age. Believe me. My wife and I raised three daughters of our own. All sorts of things go on inside them. They think they're adults, but emotionally…" He let his voice trail away and shook his head in resignation.

Sharon tried to smile, and failed.

Dr. Hartvigsen patted her shoulder again. "Have you been unusually busy at work or distracted by anything?"

She shook her head without conviction.

"Sometimes kids this age do things as a cry for attention," the doctor said. "Maybe it's nothing more than that."

Maybe. Sharon just didn't know.

"Of course," the doctor went on, "there are professionals who could give you better advice than I can."

Professionals. Analysts. Psychiatrists. Sharon didn't like the way that sounded. She steeled herself to face Emilee again now that she knew the truth. Or maybe more appropriately, now that she realized she had no idea what was going on with her own daughter.

She'd never had trouble with her kids before. *Never.* And she didn't intend to start now. If

Emilee had a problem, Sharon would get to the bottom of it. If Emilee needed attention, Sharon would give it.

One thing was certain. She wouldn't give up until she'd resolved the problem.

GABE WOULD NEVER admit it aloud, but the strain of keeping his bet with Jesse was beginning to wear on him. Lunch with Sharon the day before had left him even more acutely aware of her.

She was very attractive and one of the nicest women he'd ever met. He could talk with her easily about any subject—even the ones he usually avoided. But she was a client. He couldn't lose sight of that.

He never should have made that stupid bet in the first place.

He lugged his toolbox through the garage and knocked on the door. And he told himself firmly he wouldn't let her get to him tonight, no matter what she said or did. No matter how she looked. He'd just have to be strong. He could do it. He *could* resist.

She opened the door a moment later and stood there, bathed in the soft light of the landing. Her dark hair framed her face and caught the glow of the lamp. But she didn't smile the way she usually did when she saw him. And when he looked closer, he could see something unsettled lurking in her eyes.

Touched by her vulnerability, he shifted his toolbox to the other hand. "Are you okay?"

"I'm fine," she said as she stepped aside to let him enter. "No, I take that back. I'm not fine at all. I went to Emilee's school after work to apologize to Mr. Taylor. I'm still a little upset by our conversation."

"Norman the nurse?"

She laughed, and some of the tension seemed to leave her. "Norman the nerd is more like it."

"What did he say?" He caught himself and added quickly, "You don't have to tell me. It's none of my business."

"It's okay. I don't mind. In fact, maybe talking about it will help."

He was pleased to hear that. "Okay, then. Talk away." He left the toolbox by the door and followed her into the dining room, looking at anything but her.

She sat at the table and motioned him toward a chair. "Both of the girls are out with friends tonight. I've been scouring the kitchen trying to work off some of this anger. To tell you the truth, I'm not sure who I'm most angry with— Mr. Taylor or Emilee."

"Why Emilee?"

"Because she *was* faking. Dr. Hartvigsen couldn't find anything wrong with her ankle. I've been trying and trying to think of a reason why she'd do something like this, but I just can't."

Gabe sat slowly, aware that he held the information she wanted, yet hesitating to give it to her. "Emilee seems like a pretty steady girl," he said. "I'm sure it's nothing serious."

"I wish I could believe you. One part of me wants desperately to believe you, but the other part tells me I need to be realistic." She dropped her hands to her lap and studied them for a moment. "I am upset with Emilee, but do you know what makes me angriest?"

Did he *want* to know?

She told him anyway. "Mr. Taylor."

He raised one eyebrow. "Why?"

"Do you know what he thinks is wrong?"

Gabe shook his head slowly.

"He thinks Emilee's acting out because she doesn't have a father figure. No, wait, because her real father doesn't live with us anymore." She shot to her feet and paced toward the bay window, then whirled back to face him. "I told him I've been divorced five years. I asked him why she'd suddenly start acting out now. Do you know what he said?"

Gabe couldn't even begin to guess.

"He said she talked about the divorce almost constantly when she first came into his office. About how hard I work to make ends meet, how much I have to do around the house, how I never get out and do anything anymore."

Subtlety obviously wasn't one of Emilee's strengths. Gabe lowered his gaze and tried not to let her see the smile that tugged at his lips. "Maybe he misunderstood her."

"I don't think he did." Anger flashed in her eyes. "She even told him how much time I have to spend in the garden every spring and summer and said I need help around the house. And the worst part was, I could tell he felt *sorry* for me. He told me to call Parents Without Partners."

Bad move, Emilee. Very bad move. Gabe tried to think of some way to ease Sharon's worry without breaking his promise to the girls. He stood and rounded the table. "I don't think Emilee expected him to have that reaction."

"I wouldn't have thought so either before today." Sharon kneaded her forehead with her fingertips. "I just can't believe she's upset because her dad's not here. Things are so much better now than they were before."

"Maybe she's worried about you," Gabe suggested. "Maybe she'd like to see you find someone who'd make you happy."

"I *am* happy," she snapped.

In spite of her obvious distress, Gabe chuckled. "Anyone who saw you right now wouldn't think so."

She scowled at him, but she couldn't maintain it. Slowly, a smile replaced the frown and her eyes lost some of their anger. "Well, okay," she admitted grudgingly. "I'm not ecstatic right this minute—"

Without taking time to think it through, Gabe put an arm around her shoulder and gave her a gentle squeeze. "I'm sure you have nothing to worry about with Emilee."

Immediately, the mood shifted. At least his did. Warmth spiraled all the way up his arm to his chest. His fingertips tingled. For a moment, they both froze.

Then she met his gaze and held it. He swallowed convulsively and tried to look away. His mouth dried. His pulse roared in his ears. It would be so easy to pull her close and hold her. To kiss her.

But it would also be so wrong. Somehow, he managed to release her.

"Maybe you're right." She took a step away and brushed back a lock of hair. Gabe noticed her fingers trembling slightly. "Thanks for the listening ear, but I'd better let you get to work. I know you have a lot to do."

"Yeah." His voice came out thick. He cleared

his throat and tried again. "Yeah, it's, uh…" He checked his watch and nodded. "It's getting late."

"If you'd like to get in some extra time on the basement, I'll be working at home all day tomorrow." She flushed slightly and added, "I need some time to think."

"Thanks. An extra day would help." He turned away, ignoring the urge to pull her into his arms again, and snatched up his toolbox from beside the back door. Obviously, he wasn't quite as strong as he'd thought he was.

CHAPTER SEVEN

TIRED, ACHING, SORE and frustrated, Gabe pulled into Milago's parking lot and hurried to get inside and out of the cold. He'd have a garlic burger and a beer, then go home to his empty apartment and the memory of having his arm around Sharon, which he hadn't been able to put out of his mind all evening.

He wanted to kick himself for holding back the truth about Emilee. There was, after all, a perfectly harmless explanation for what she'd done. He could have set Sharon's mind at ease and maybe even made her laugh. Instead, he'd opted to leave her in turmoil. First thing tomorrow, he vowed silently, he'd talk to those girls about their ridiculous scheme and convince them to tell their mother everything. Then he could stop feeling as though he'd lied to her.

He found Jesse sitting at the bar again. Jesse smiled as Gabe hitched himself onto a stool. "Long time no see, buddy. What's going on?"

"I've been working." Gabe made little effort to keep his irritation under control. He never should have taken that bet with Jesse, he said to himself for the umpteenth time.

Jesse's eyebrows formed a solid ridge over his eyes. "*Just* working?"

"Just working." Gabe started to order a beer then changed his mind and ordered a whiskey soda.

Jesse flashed an annoying grin. "Hitting the hard stuff, eh? That's not like you."

"It's like me tonight," Gabe said with a growl. "Do you mind?"

"I don't mind at all. Knock yourself out." Jesse let a silence lapse between them for a moment, but not long enough. "I guess this means you're winning the bet so far."

"You'd better believe it."

"And you're doing okay?"

"I'm doing fine."

"You're not even tempted?"

"Not in the slightest." Gabe took a drink, grimaced when the whiskey burned a path to his stomach and told another lie. "In fact, I've never been better."

"Glad to hear it." Jesse turned his beer bottle around in his hands. "Guess you won't have any trouble making it the next five months, either."

"Piece of cake." Gabe swiveled on the stool to look out at the dance floor. A dozen couples swayed to a slow country song. Women leaned their cheeks on their partners' shoulders while the men held the women close. Gabe swiveled back again and focused on a jar of pickled eggs behind the bar.

Chuckling, Jesse nudged him with an elbow. "Piece of cake, huh?"

"Okay," Gabe snarled. "So it's not that easy."

"You want to call off the bet?"

"No." Pride answered before common sense could prevail.

"You really think you can make it another five months?"

"With my hands tied behind my back." Gabe signaled Ringo to bring him another drink. One more wouldn't hurt.

Jesse added another beer to the order, turned around on his stool and propped both elbows on the bar behind him. "So, how are you coming on that basement?"

"Slow. I only get to work on it a few hours each week, and you know what it's like when you're dealing with old buildings. There's been one setback after another." He could hear the tension in his voice, but he seemed powerless to change it. Anything connected to Sharon seemed to bring it out lately.

Jesse rubbed his face with his palm and glanced at him from the corner of his eye. "What kind of setbacks?"

Gabe glared at him. "What is this? Twenty Questions?"

Jesse pulled back sharply. "Conversation, buddy. That's all."

Gabe suddenly felt like a jerk. "Sorry. Just ignore me tonight. I'm not myself."

"So, what's bugging you?"

"Nothing." He sent Jesse a thin smile and amended, "Everything."

"Helene giving you problems again?"

"Not really. But it's been over a week since I talked to Tracy. I tried to call last night, but she wasn't home. You're lucky your kids still live nearby. At least you get to see them once in a while."

"Don't kid yourself. They might live only ten miles away, but it still isn't easy when they get to be teenagers. Half the time, I think they're glad to see me. The other half, they act like I'm trying to ruin their social lives by asking them to spend time with me." He looked away for a second. "I try not to let it bug me. Remember how we used to feel about spending time with our parents? It hasn't been *that* long since we were teenagers."

"Some days it feels like it's been forever. But you're right. I guess I need to try to put myself in Tracy's place." Gabe settled more comfortably on the bar stool.

"That's not the only thing bothering you, is it?"

Gabe didn't answer right away.

"There's a woman, isn't there?" Jesse spun around on his stool and pounded the bar with his fist. "I *knew* it."

"You're wrong."

"No, I'm not. I know you too well. You can't lie to me."

"Okay, so there is someone."

Jesse brayed a triumphant laugh. "All right! Who is she?"

"It's not what you think," Gabe cautioned. "This one's not like the others." He rubbed his forehead a bit harder. "She's all wrong for me, but I can't stop thinking about her."

"Wrong for you how?"

"She's…domestic. You know the type. Likes to spend her evenings at home. Thinks a big evening is watching the movie of the week on TV. She's got a couple of kids—"

"Oh, yeah," Jesse said with a grin. "She sounds like a real loser."

"That's not what I mean," Gabe protested. "There's nothing wrong with that for some guys. But I'm no good at that kind of life. You know that as well as I do."

Jesse's smile faded. "All I know is that after Helene, you're afraid."

Gabe glared at him. "Afraid of what?"

"Afraid of letting any woman see the real you."

"I've got news for you, buddy. This *is* the real me."

"Hey," Jesse warned, "this is me you're talking to, remember? Nobody knows you better." He shifted on the bar stool to lean closer. "Tell me about her."

Gabe turned his glass in his hands for a few seconds, trying to decide what to say. "She's a journalism instructor at the community college."

One of Jesse's eyebrows winged upward, but he didn't interrupt.

"She's intelligent—obviously. Loves her kids. I think she'd do anything for them. She's been divorced for five years."

Jesse let out a low whistle. "That's a long time."

Gabe shrugged that away. "She's different, you know? She's easy to talk to. I find myself telling her things I usually don't tell women I get involved with."

"And that's a problem?"

Gabe shrugged again. He didn't know anymore.

"Are you attracted to her?"

Gabe laughed. "You could say that."

"So? Maybe I'm missing something, but I don't see the problem here."

"Apart from the fact she's a client—which is a problem itself—she's the wrong kind of woman for me," Gabe said again. "And I'm all wrong for her."

Jesse clapped a hand to his shoulder. "Ever since Helene walked out on you, you've been a hit-and-run kind of guy. Leave 'em before they get too close."

Gabe couldn't deny that.

"I don't think her being a client is an insurmountable obstacle. Sounds to me like the real problem is, you've finally met a woman you don't want to treat that way."

"I don't need you to play devil's advocate. I know how I've been acting the past couple of years."

Jesse shrugged his argument away. "So, what's the problem?"

"I, uh, I've been lying to her."

"*You?* About what?"

"Her kids are trying to find her a husband. I overheard them making plans on New Year's Eve, but I haven't told her."

Jesse laughed, but when he saw the scowl on Gabe's face he sobered. "Come on, man, I thought it was something important."

"It is important," Gabe insisted. He filled

Jesse in on the problem with Emilee and added, "So, now she's worried about her daughter, convinced there's some big problem. She's at home right now, pacing the floors, trying to figure out what's wrong."

"That'll all come out in the wash, bud. Just let the kids know you're interested and they'll call off their big scheme. Their mom won't ever have to find out."

"I'm not telling the kids," Gabe said as his stomach tied itself in knots. "I'm not going to make them think there's a chance for something permanent between me and their mom. You don't do that with kids."

"You're still trying to convince yourself there's no chance?"

"I *know* there's no chance. We might have a few good months together, but then what? She'd want to get married. I don't."

Jesse polished off his beer and stood, smoothing his pant legs as he did. "All right. If you say so."

"I do."

"Well, I don't know what you're going to do about it, but I'll tell you what *I'm* going to do."

"What?"

"I'm going to start calling around and find a

real nice outfit to take us fishing this summer. I have a feeling I'm going to be having myself a free trip."

GABE LOWERED his hammer to the floor and rubbed his forehead as if that might help ease the pounding inside. His tongue stuck to his mouth as if he'd swallowed an entire bag of cotton balls and tasted worse. Far worse. Every time he let his eyes stray to the sunlight streaming in through the basement windows, pain shot through his head. His stomach rolled. And the noise—

He'd lost track of time last night after Jesse left Milago's and the bartender had kept refilling his glass. So far this morning, nothing had made him feel better. Not the breakfast he'd forced himself to choke down. Not the endless glasses of water he'd gulped before leaving home. Not the sunglasses he'd been wearing in a desperate attempt to block out the light. The only thing that didn't cause him pain was the scent of freshly baked bread drifting downstairs from Sharon's kitchen.

He dug into his toolbox, wondering if by some odd chance he'd dropped a bottle of pain reliever in there. Wrenches clinked heavily against screwdrivers and sockets as he searched, sending shafts of pain from his head to his neck. Not surprisingly, he couldn't find anything but tools, a couple of wadded receipts and a key to something.

Swearing under his breath, he stood carefully and let out a sigh. Even that hurt. He couldn't afford to lose an entire day's work, so that left him with no choice but to swallow his pride and ask Sharon if she had something for a headache. If she took one look at his eyes, she'd probably figure out exactly what was wrong with him. So he'd keep his sunglasses on.

Classical music met him as he neared the top of the stairs. The high-pitched violins sent shock waves through his head. He clenched his teeth and forced a smile.

He found Sharon on the dining-room floor surrounded by stacks of papers. She glanced up at the sound of his footsteps, rocked up onto her knees and stretched to reach the volume control on the stereo. Blessedly, the music cut off midscreech.

"I hate to bother you, but I wonder if you have any pain reliever." His speech sounded slurred, but only because his tongue kept sticking to the roof of his mouth. "I've got a headache that just won't quit."

Compassion flitted across her face. She stood quickly. "Of course. In the kitchen. I'll get it."

He trailed her into the kitchen, intrigued by the scent she wore that filled the space between them. Light. Clean. Flowery, but not too sweet. He inhaled deeply and savored the mingled scents of perfume and bread for a moment—so much nicer than wood shavings and dust. He let his breath out again slowly.

She handed him a small white bottle, crossed to the sink and filled a glass with water. So far, so good. He'd take the pills and get back to work. And he'd put Sharon, her flowers, music, perfume—*and* her bread out of his mind. He shook three tablets into his palm, shoved them into his mouth and reached for the glass she held toward him.

When his fingers brushed hers, that same tingle he'd felt yesterday swept up his arm. He jerked the glass away, spilling some of the water in the process. Cursing himself silently, he downed the pills and gulped the rest of the water, then glanced at the mess he'd made on the floor. "I'm sorry. Let me—"

She'd already pulled a couple of paper towels from a roll on the counter and bent to mop up the water. He used the opportunity to put the glass on the counter and get out of the kitchen. Being near her was too…dangerous.

"I hope the pills help," she called after him.

He turned toward her again and let himself study her face. "I'm sure they will."

Her lips curved into a gentle smile. "You know what would probably help even more?"

He shook his head carefully, wincing a little even at that small movement.

"You should put something in your stomach. Have you had lunch?"

"Not yet."

She glanced at the bread maker. "Fresh bread will be ready in a few minutes. Would you like some?"

He'd be smart to say no. But the sound of her voice soothed him, and for this one moment, it turned out, he didn't want to be smart. No matter what he'd said to Jesse, he didn't want to leave her just yet. "I'd love some."

She pulled a knife from one of the drawers and left it beside the cutting board. "Putting food in your stomach is the very best thing for a hangover."

She knew. Of course.

Embarrassed, he averted his gaze. "I don't usually drink on a work night."

She grinned and leaned against the counter. "It's a good thing. You don't carry your hangovers very well."

"I look that bad, huh?"

"No." Her eyes darkened for a second, but

she turned away quickly. "You don't look bad at all." She pulled the bread from the machine and worked it out of the metal container. "Do you want butter, or do you want it dry?"

"Dry. Please."

She nodded him toward the dining-room table. "Have a seat. I'll bring it over to you."

He shook his head and waved a hand in front of himself. "I don't want to track dirt onto your carpet."

She gave him a slow, amused once-over, put the bread on a small plate and set it on the counter. "All right. Let me get you a stool." She rounded the end of the counter and carried a stool from the breakfast nook.

Gabe reached toward it, intending to lift it for her. Their fingers brushed a second time, and this time he saw awareness to match his own in the depths of her eyes.

She glanced away quickly, relinquished her hold on the stool and crossed into the kitchen. "Coffee?" Did he only imagine it, or did her voice sound strained?

He shook his head. "No, thanks. Even the thought of coffee isn't sitting well this morning."

"I'll bet it isn't. How about some more water?"

"Yes. Please." He tried to take his eyes off

her but found he couldn't, no matter how hard he tried.

She picked up the knife and sliced more bread. "So, were you celebrating something or drowning your sorrows last night?"

"Neither."

Her eyes locked on to his and she drew a deep breath.

Slowly, deliberately, he stood and pulled her to him. "I was trying not to think about you."

His pulse seemed to take on a life of its own. His mind stopped thinking. Slowly, giving her plenty of time to pull away, he lowered his lips toward hers. Even knowing he shouldn't be doing this made no difference.

She didn't move. Didn't blink. Before he could stop himself, his lips brushed hers and she moaned softly. She melted against him… and then the telephone rang and shattered the moment.

She pulled away quickly and flicked her gaze toward the telephone. The second ring galvanized her to action. She hurried away from him without a second glance and grabbed the receiver as if it had saved her life.

Gabe stood there, unable to move, unwilling to believe she'd walked away. Finally, when he realized she'd settled into the call, he picked up the bread and water and carried them back to the basement.

One kiss. That's all he'd wanted. And he'd gotten it. So why this almost unbearable disappointment?

WITH HER MIND REELING, Sharon clutched the telephone and tried to make sense of Adelle's excited words.

What had she done? How had she let her attraction to him get so far out of hand? And what would happen now? Neither of them wanted a serious relationship, and she had Emilee and Christa to think of. She couldn't just bring a man she was casually seeing into their lives.

Not that she even thought she could be casual about Gabe. Her feelings were too strong already. Until Gabe walked into her life this had all been easy. No romantic feelings, no problem. But now...

"Are you even listening to me?" Adelle cut into her thoughts.

"I'm sorry, Adelle. I guess I'm a little distracted today."

"A little? This is the most important news of my life, and you didn't hear a word I said."

"Tell me again. I promise I'll pay attention."

"My doctor just called half an hour ago. I'm pregnant."

"Pregnant?" That brought Sharon back to reality quickly. Adelle and Doug had been trying for years to have a baby. "I'm so thrilled for you. How far along are you?"

"Two months. The baby's due in August. Can you believe it? I'm going to be a mother."

"And you'll be a great one. How did Doug react?"

"I haven't been able to reach him yet. But I couldn't wait to tell you."

"The girls and I will give you a baby shower when your due date gets closer," Sharon promised. "And you know you'll have three willing babysitters whenever you need them."

"Babysitters." Adelle sighed, then let out a yelp. "Sharon, I don't have any idea what to do. I'm going to need your help."

Sharon laughed, remembering the near panic she'd felt when she'd learned about Emilee's impending birth. "Of course I'll help you, Adelle. You know that. We'll go shopping and spend every penny we have buying things for the baby."

"Promise?"

"Absolutely. Have I ever let you down before?"

"Never." Adelle covered the mouthpiece of her telephone for a second, then came back on the line. "I'll have to call you later. Someone's just come into my office."

When they'd disconnected, Sharon pulled a piece of bread toward her and ate it slowly. The taste filled her mouth, warm and fresh and comforting. Excitement and contentment warred within her, alternately filling her with a strange lethargy, then making her head reel with thoughts and plans, hopes and dreams.

She hadn't felt like this since long before her marriage ended. She'd been sleepwalking for years, only half-alive. Suddenly, she knew she wanted more. She wanted to keep this feeling, this heightened awareness of the world around her.

So maybe the next move should be hers. Maybe it was finally time to take a risk.

GABE PAID FOR A SODA and carried it toward an empty table in the mall's crowded food court. He'd spent his entire Saturday evening searching for the right gift for Tracy, but he hadn't found anything. Correction—he'd found a thousand things, but he had no idea which of them might be right.

He didn't know what styles of clothes she liked, what kind of music she listened to or even what kinds of books she read. And that made him wonder what kind of father he really was.

He'd wanted to get her something special—something more than a simple card like his parents sent, something that showed her he'd put some thought into buying it. But now he wondered if he should take the easier route and stop by the card shop on his way back to the truck.

Settling into one of the uncomfortable wrought-iron chairs behind a small metal table, he let his gaze drift across the crowds of people. Groups of teenagers milled around in front of the theater. Mothers and daughters laughed together as they walked in front of him.

Sharon wouldn't have this problem, he thought. She knew exactly what Emilee and Christa liked. She knew what teenagers in general liked, which meant she'd probably have no trouble picking out something for Tracy even though they'd never met.

He thought about calling her and asking for help, but he shoved aside the idea immediately. Another job had consumed his entire day, but had also given him a chance to think. He'd gone too far with that kiss yesterday afternoon. He didn't want to push his luck.

Taking a long drink of soda, he tried to relax. He'd never win his bet with Jesse if he kept thinking about Sharon. The bet wasn't the important thing—except that it would cost him dearly if he had to pay for the entire fishing trip. No, what *was* important was why he'd made the bet in the first place. He didn't want to get involved with any woman for a while. He needed a clear head to sort through his problems with Tracy—not to mention dealing with his dad on a daily basis.

"Gabe?"

The sound of his name brought him around sharply, and face-to-face with Emilee and a young man who gazed at her with an expression so soft it made Gabe think of a young pup. He tried not to look amused. "What are you doing here?"

"Jason and I are on our way to a movie. What about you?"

"I'm shopping for my daughter."

"Is it her birthday?"

"No." He motioned for them to join him. "I just thought I'd send her something to show her I'm thinking of her."

"Cool." Emilee sat across from him and waited until Jason took a seat. "What did you get her?"

"Nothing yet," Gabe admitted. "I'm having trouble finding the right thing. Any suggestions?"

"How old is she?"

"Fifteen."

"Clothes." She nodded firmly, as if that settled everything. "Girls that age always like new stuff to wear."

Gabe shook his head slowly. "I haven't seen her in almost a year. I don't even know what she likes, what size she takes or what she needs."

"Don't buy her something she needs," Emilee protested. "Buy her something just for fun."

"That's the trouble." Gabe propped his chin in his hand. "I haven't paid attention to what's in style and what's not."

Emilee laughed. "So buy her something from a chain store. That way she can exchange it if you get the wrong thing. That's what my dad does."

She made it sound so simple.

Gabe took another sip. "I don't suppose you have time to give me your opinion?"

Emilee glanced at Jason who shrugged indifferently. "It's fine with me," the boy said. "If we miss the movie, we can always go to the next showing."

Relief and gratitude brought a smile to Gabe's lips. "If you'll help me, I'll pay for your tickets."

"Fine with me," Jason said again.

Emilee stood and tugged on Gabe's arm. "All right, then, let's get to work. What is she like?"

Gabe tossed his cup into the trash and matched her pace as they left the food court. "She's a little quieter than you and Christa. And she doesn't go out a lot with friends—at least she didn't when she lived with me. In fact, she and I are nearly opposites, which is probably another reason I'm having such a hard time finding a gift." And another reason he had such a hard time talking to her.

"So, she's like my mom." Emilee ducked past a group of people, then stopped to wait for Jason to catch up.

Gabe's step faltered. Was Tracy like Sharon? He didn't know if he would have made that comparison. But now that Emilee had, he thought she might be right. Funny, he'd always believed two people so different couldn't really be close, but Sharon and her daughters certainly proved that theory wrong.

He slowed his pace and stared at his reflection in a store window as the thought replayed again. Had he been letting *that* affect his relationship with Tracy? Had he put some of the strain between them? He didn't like thinking that at all.

When Emilee realized he was lagging behind, she stopped again. "What's wrong?"

"Nothing," he assured her quickly. "Where are you taking me?"

She named a store and added, "I saw a pair of jeans in there the other day that would be perfect. In fact, I want a pair to start college in the fall—if they're still in style."

"Sounds good to me." He picked up his pace again. "Where are you planning to go to college?"

"Probably Denver University."

Did he just imagine the flash of disappointment he saw on her face? No, there it was again. "Isn't that where you want to go?"

"Not really. The University of Utah has a better nursing school, and that's really what I want to study. But Mom wants me to stay here."

Gabe took in the dejected slump of her shoulders. "Does she know how you feel?"

She shrugged.

"Why don't you tell her? I've been around you enough to know she wants you to be happy."

"It wouldn't do any good."

"Sure it would." He could say that without hesitation. "Admittedly, I don't know your mom real well yet, but I'm sure she wants you to get the best education you can. And I'll bet she has no idea how disappointed you are." He tucked his hands into his pockets to avoid the urge to give her a fatherly hug. "She's as concerned about your happiness as you are about hers."

Emilee smiled slowly.

"And speaking of *that*," he said with a playful scowl, "we need to talk."

"About what?"

"About the scheme you and Christa have up your sleeves. You've got your mom worried."

Emilee's smile faded. "I know."

"Don't you think it's time to tell her why you faked that sprained ankle?"

"No." Emilee took Jason's hand as if she needed moral support.

"Well, I do," Gabe said sternly. "She's convinced something's troubling you, and worried sick because you aren't willing to talk to her about it."

"There *is* something troubling me," Emilee said over her shoulder as she wound through a couple of benches and some potted plants. "I don't want her to be lonely anymore."

"I know, but—"

She wheeled around to face him. "I'm not going to tell her, Gabe. Not yet. And you promised you wouldn't tell her, either—remember?"

How could he forget?

"Besides, it's not as if we're doing something bad."

He thought about Jesse's assurance that it would all come out in the wash. Maybe he was overreacting, but he sure hated keeping his mouth shut while he watched Sharon worry. "Just promise me you'll tell her eventually."

"Of course we'll tell her." Emilee tossed a lock of hair over her shoulder and rolled her eyes at him. "Just not yet. Now, do you want to see those jeans or not?"

"I want to see them."

"Good. They're really cool. I just know your daughter will love 'em."

Clapping one hand to Jason's shoulder, he nodded for Emilee to lead on. And he pushed aside the flicker of apprehension that Emilee's promise hadn't quite taken away. As long as the girls planned to tell Sharon the truth, he could relax and concentrate on fixing things between himself and Tracy. And he couldn't do that with Sharon on his mind all the time.

The best thing he could do for everyone concerned was to put her completely out of his mind. He just wished it wasn't so hard to do.

GABE TRIED WITHOUT success to follow the conversation taking place across his parents' cavernous living room. He had hoped to start a discussion about his father's retirement, but was reluctant to spoil the jovial mood his family shared tonight or ruin his niece's birthday dinner.

He linked his hands behind his head and

pushed back in his mother's recliner. Rosalie laughed at something Jack said, his father's deep chuckle blended with his mother's. Three of Rosalie and Jack's kids huddled together in front of the TV, sharing control panels for a video game. For the first time in memory, the picture of domestic bliss raised a flicker of longing. He refused to let Sharon's image form and thought of his daughter instead. Tracy belonged here, too. She was as much a part of the family as the rest of them. Maybe he'd call her when he got home.

Rosalie glanced at him and frowned when she saw the look on his face. While Jack launched into a new story, she crossed the room and perched on the arm of his chair. "What are you sulking about tonight, big brother?"

"I'm not sulking," he said with a slight smile. "I'm thinking."

"About what? Problems with your latest girl-friend?"

Sharon's smile danced in front of him. He blinked it away. He didn't want her to guess how close she'd come to the truth. He squared his shoulders and raised an eyebrow. "There isn't any latest girlfriend."

"What?" Rosalie rocked backward so far, he thought she'd fall off her perch. "You're kidding, right?"

He looked at her.

"You're serious?"

"Is that such a shock?"

"To be honest, yes."

He pushed aside a flicker of mild resentment. He might not like the reputation, but he'd earned it.

Rosalie motioned toward the small knot of people on the other side of the room—Jack parked in the middle of the couch, his mother beside him, his father tinkering with something on the floor. "Why don't you come over and join the rest of us instead of sitting over here by yourself."

"I'm really tired tonight. And I don't want to spoil the mood."

She sobered instantly. "Dad's still working you like a plow horse?"

He immediately regretted tossing out the description a few weeks earlier during an argument over dinner, but he wouldn't lie. "You know Dad," he said, lowering his voice. "He'll never change."

"Is he still forgetting things?"

Gabe hesitated for only a moment. If he sugarcoated the truth now, she'd never believe him when he tried to discuss it with her later. "He's getting worse."

Her dark eyes clouded. "That's just so hard to

believe about Dad. He's always been so on top of things."

"He still has his moments," Gabe assured her. "But it's starting to affect the business. We're going to have to talk to Mom, sis."

"We can't do that. You know how it will upset her."

"It'll upset her a lot more if they lose everything they own."

Rosalie studied him with guarded eyes. "You don't really think that could happen, do you?"

"It might. It probably will, unless we do something."

"Oh, Gabe." Her shoulders slumped and she looked exactly as she had at eight years old when they'd had to put their dog to sleep. She'd been allowed to cry. Gabe had been expected to keep his feelings hidden, just as he forced himself to do now. Malone men didn't cry—about anything.

"How can we tell him he has to leave the business," Rosalie whispered. "Look at him."

Another burst of laughter from across the room only added to his guilt. "I look at him every day, sis. I'm the one who has to deal with his lapses in memory and the dissatisfied customers and appointments scheduled on top of each other."

"I just can't stand the thought of hurting him."

"I don't like it any more than you do," he assured her. "But it's getting out of hand."

Her deep brown eyes flicked over his face, silently begging him to say it was all a joke. "You're serious, aren't you?"

"Dead serious."

She glanced away, swallowed convulsively, then pulled herself together. "I still think we ought to wait."

"For what?" His voice came out too loud. He softened it again. "For the business to collapse?"

"No, of course not. But maybe he'll step down on his own."

"He's not going to step down, sis."

She turned a challenging stare on him. "How do you know?"

"Because he has no idea how bad he is."

"How do *I* know he's as bad as you say?"

To his dismay, his mother caught that last bit. "What are you two arguing about?"

Rosalie darted a warning glance at him. "Nothing, Mom. Gabe's just trying to tell me he doesn't have a girlfriend, and I don't believe him."

Always the clown, Jack rocked back in his seat. "What? Are you kidding? What happened?

Have you dated every single woman in Denver already?"

Very funny. Normally, Gabe would laugh at Jack's comments. Not tonight. "I don't happen to be dating anyone at the moment. It's no big deal."

"But it *is* a big deal," Jack argued.

Gabe's mother put a warning hand on Jack's arm. "Don't tease him."

"I'm not teasing him," Jack protested. "I'm interested in what's going on, that's all."

The conversation with Rosalie had left Gabe on edge. "I wish you'd tell me why you find my personal life so fascinating."

"Because you *have* one," Jack said with a laugh. "The most interesting thing that ever happens to me is when one of the kids gets sick."

"At least you're allowed to know when they *get* sick. I wish I could know even *that* much about Tracy."

"Gabriel," his mother warned softly, "that's enough."

He glanced at the kids. "Sorry," he muttered, "but he doesn't know what he has."

"Ignore Gabe," his dad advised, getting to his feet and adjusting his belt over his waist. "He's just feeling overworked. But like I keep telling him, you've got to put in if you want to take out."

Gabe bit back the reply that rose to his lips, but he wondered just how long his dad expected him to keep making deposits before he could take his first withdrawal.

"And speaking of the business," Harold said. "I forgot to tell you this earlier, but I'm moving you off the Lawrence job."

"You're *what?*" Gabe shot to his feet. "Why are you doing that?"

"Because I have another job lined up for you. Derry can finish the Lawrence contract."

"No." Gabe searched frantically for a reason his dad would accept for his refusal. "I'm right in the middle of it—"

"It's nothing Derry can't handle. I need you on the other job."

"Give Derry the other job."

His dad scowled at him. "I've already told him to take over on the Lawrence project. He'll start Monday."

Gabe struggled to pull himself together. But he'd reached the end of his rope. "I'd rather stay on the Lawrence project myself. I know where I am with it. I'd like to finish it."

"Nonsense." Harold lowered himself onto the couch with a groan. "You'll go where you're needed."

Twenty years of bouncing from job to job at his father's command rose up together and frayed the slim hold he had on his temper. He might as well be seventeen years old again, for all the respect his father showed him. "Maybe you should find someone else for both projects," he said, his voice ominously low. "I quit."

He snatched his coat from the arm of the chair and headed for the door.

His mother followed him, her eyes dark with concern. "Gabriel. Come back and talk with your father. Work out this misunderstanding between you. He needs you. Harold, talk to him."

His father grunted a refusal.

Gabe turned to face her, angry with himself for hurting her but unwilling to humble himself yet again. "He doesn't need me, Mom. He never has. He doesn't need anyone but himself."

CHAPTER EIGHT

HUMMING SOFTLY, Sharon cracked half a dozen eggs into a bowl, added milk and a dash of paprika, and stirred the whole thing with a fork. She loved Saturday mornings. She loved fixing the girls a leisurely breakfast instead of tossing toast at them as they raced out the door for school. Savoring her morning coffee instead of gulping it as she drove through rush-hour traffic to work. Waking slowly and watching the sun light the room instead of dressing in the dark.

This morning, with Gabe about to arrive any minute, the world seemed especially fine. Even with an overnight snowstorm, the late January sunlight and the steady drip of melting icicles held the promise of spring. And Sharon felt like a kid on Christmas morning.

Another last-minute meeting had forced her to leave a message with his father on Wednesday, telling him not to come until today. And now, the thought of seeing him again after a week made her nervous. But she'd made the decision to move forward, and she couldn't wait to see him again.

For the first time in her life, quiet bothered her. She missed the crackling of his radio, the buzz of his saw, the pounding of his hammer. She missed the sound of his voice and the tread of his step on the stairs.

As she reached for her coffee, a plaintive yowl pulled her attention toward the bay window where Raoul batted his paws against the glass, trying to catch a falling icicle. Laughing softly, Sharon picked him up and scratched his belly.

"You don't want to go outside, boy. There's still snow on the ground. You don't like wet feet, remember?"

Somewhere nearby, someone started a snow-blower and shattered the peaceful morning. Sharon set Raoul on the floor and made a mental note to check with the repair shop about her snowblower. She rinsed her hands and forced herself to stop dreaming.

She whisked the eggs and called to the girls. "Emilee, Christa, breakfast will be ready in a minute."

Almost immediately, Christa thundered down the stairs and bounced into the room. "Morning, Mom." She pulled a pitcher of orange juice from the refrigerator and nodded toward the front of the house. "How'd you manage that?"

"Manage what? The snow? I didn't ask for it."

"No." Christa grinned and shook her head as if Sharon had said something funny. "How'd you get Gabe to do our driveway and sidewalks?"

Sharon paused midwhisk. "Gabe?"

"Yeah. He's out there with a snowblower."

With difficulty, Sharon kept her gaze riveted on the pan and whisked the eggs again—casually. "Are you sure it's him?"

"I'm pretty sure." Christa poured juice into her glass and took a drink. "I can't see his face, but his truck is parked in front of the house."

Sharon forced herself not to race outside. "He must have picked up the snowblower from the repair shop. I guess I should find out how much I owe him."

"I'm sure he'll come inside when he's through."

Sharon didn't think she could wait that long. "I think it would be more polite for me to go outside. Don't you?"

Christa looked at her strangely. "I guess so."

"Will you take over the eggs for me? I'll be back in a minute." She snatched her coat from the hook by the back door and slipped into it as she stepped into the garage. With her heart in her throat, she pushed the button to raise the automatic door and waited while it creaked slowly upward.

Sure enough, he'd already cleared the driveway and disappeared around the corner near the front door. Sharon crossed the garage and waited for him to come back.

The instant she saw him, her stomach flipped. And when he glanced up and noticed her for the first time, she felt like a schoolgirl with a crush. She didn't entirely mind the feeling.

He cut the motor, and the sudden silence seemed out of place. "I stopped in to pick up a sander I'd left at Ray's, and he mentioned you hadn't picked up the snowblower yet. I figured you might need it today." His voice, deep and rich, carried easily across the distance between them.

"Yes. Thank you. I was going to give him a call after breakfast." Sharon took a careful step onto the driveway and lost herself in the pull of his eyes. "How much do I owe you?"

"I've got the invoice in the truck. It wasn't much, really." He shoved his hands into the pockets of his jacket and stepped around the snowblower toward her.

Her pulse stuttered as he moved closer. "I'll give you a check, if that's okay."

"Sure. That's fine." His voice sounded normal. Obviously, he wasn't overwhelmed by the sight of her.

She looked away and studied his handiwork.

"It's nice of you to bring it back, but you really didn't need to clear away the snow, too."

He moved a few steps closer. Close enough to bring back the memory of his kiss. "It's no big deal," he said with a shrug. "When I was a kid, my mother used to send me out to shovel the neighbors' walks. I guess old habits die hard."

Well, *that* certainly made her feel special. Just like the elderly couple down the street. "I hate to keep you from your work. The girls and I can finish this."

"It'll only take me a few more minutes," he said. "Besides, it's the least I can do after that hangover remedy you gave me the other day."

Satisfaction rushed over her. At least he hadn't completely forgotten. "You needed it."

"I certainly did." He looked away quickly. "How did your meeting go on Wednesday?"

Was he purposely changing the subject? "Fine. Long. I'm sorry I had to cancel our appointment. I know you're busy with other projects—"

"No matter. It's been a crazy week, anyway." He looked down and let a few seconds lapse. "Actually I wanted to bring the snowblower so I could tell you I'm not with the company any longer. My dad'll be sending one of the other crew members to finish your basement."

"Oh." Her stomach knotted, and she could have sworn a shadow dropped over the sun. She searched his face for a clue about his feelings, but she couldn't read his expression.

She lifted her chin and forced a shaky smile. "That's fine. Will he be coming today?"

Still gazing out over the snowy yard, Gabe shook his head. "I don't know what my dad's told him to do."

She struggled to keep the disappointment from her voice. "What about you? What will you do now?"

He shrugged nonchalantly. "Temporary jobs for the time being." He glanced at her quickly, then away again. "Actually, this is a good thing. It'll give me a chance to focus on what's really important, like my relationship with Tracy."

As opposed to any relationship Sharon might have imagined developing between them. Apparently, she'd read more into their kiss than he had. One kiss, she told herself sternly, in the throes of a hangover didn't mean anything. And she'd obviously been a fool to think it did.

She stuffed her hands into her pockets and turned toward the house. "I'd better go back. I'm in the middle of fixing breakfast. Just bring me the receipt for the snowblower when you're finished." She took a step away, and tossed the next line over her shoulder. "And thanks again for the help."

To her dismay, Gabe looked at her then. Really

looked at her. "Sharon, about what happened the other day—"

She cut him off. "There's no need to explain." She didn't want to hear what he had to say. She knew from her experience with Nick that explanations meant nothing. It didn't matter *why* he didn't want to be with her, it only mattered that he didn't. "It was a fluke. You were hungover. I understand."

Without waiting for an answer, she hurried through the garage and closed the door firmly between them.

Inside, she tried to buy a few minutes to compose herself before she had to face Emilee and Christa. She wiped her feet on the mat and slipped out of her jacket. But as she started to hang it on the hook, the girls plowed into the doorway.

"Is it Gabe?" Christa asked.

"Yes, it is."

"Maybe we should invite him to have breakfast with us," Emilee suggested. "I mean, since he's doing the walks and everything."

"Don't bother. He's not staying." Sharon forced herself to sound nonchalant, even though her heart felt like lead and her lips like clay. "In fact, someone else will be working on the basement from now on."

Christa's smile collapsed in disappointment. "Why?"

"Because he has other jobs to do." Sharon motioned for them to let her through the door. "What's all the fuss about Gabe, anyway?"

Emilee stepped aside to let her pass. "I don't know. He's nice, I guess."

"He's a contractor I hired to work on the basement," Sharon said, more as a reminder to herself than the girls. "That's all he is."

"Yeah, but—"

"But nothing." Sharon sent each of them the sternest scowl she could manage. "For heaven's sake. What's gotten into you two? You need to get dressed, Emilee. Christa, I'd like you to set the table. And I'd like both of you to help me rearrange the living-room furniture this morning."

Emilee stared at her, unmoving. "What's the matter?"

"Nothing's the matter. I just want to clean the house. It certainly needs it."

"Yeah, but you only rearrange furniture when something's upset you," Christa said.

"Nothing's upset me," Sharon snapped. "I'm fine. I just want to clean the house."

"Okay," Emilee said slowly. "But Matt called while you were outside. He invited Christa and me to go tubing."

"Tubing?" No. She didn't want to be alone to think. She grasped at the only excuse she could find. "It's freezing outside."

"It's not *that* bad," Christa argued. "Besides, we're just going over to the school. If we get cold, we can be home in five minutes."

"I need your help around the house this morning."

Christa pulled three glasses from the cupboard and carried them to the table. "Can't we help when we get home?"

Sharon started to shake her head again, then stopped herself. What kind of mother was she? How could she use her children like that? If she told them the truth, they'd stay, but that was out of the question. "All right. I suppose you can go—as long as you're careful and you *promise* to help when you get home."

Grinning, Christa dropped onto a chair and leaned her elbows on the table. "Do you want to come along?"

"Tubing with you and Matt?" Sharon started to shake her head, then thought better of it. "It's been a long time since I—"

"Come on, Mom. Emilee and Jason will be there. And so will Brittany and Tyler."

"That's a great idea," Emilee said from the bottom of the stairs. "Come with us."

Getting out in the fresh air just might help. A

little exercise might release some of this heart-ache. At least, it would help her stop thinking about Gabe. Besides, it had been a long time since she'd done anything like this with the girls. Maybe she should go along. Maybe she should concentrate on her own daughters and work on whatever had made Emilee fake that sprained ankle. She didn't want a repeat of that. And she *had* promised herself she'd start living. Okay, so she'd fling herself down a hill instead of into Gabe's arms.

"Maybe I will give it a try."

Emilee's lips curved into a satisfied smile. "You will?"

Christa ducked her head. "You'll love it. I know you will."

"You won't be sorry," Emilee promised. "We'll have a great time." She hurried up the stairs to change.

They both seemed unusually pleased, and Sharon couldn't figure out why for a minute or two. But, as she carried the eggs to the table, she realized they could probably sense that something was wrong. And they thought tubing would help her feel better.

She smiled softly and brushed a kiss to the top of Christa's head. "Thank you, sweetheart."

"For what?"

"For worrying about me." Sharon moved to

her seat and settled a napkin on her lap. "I'm lucky to have daughters like you and Emilee, but there's really nothing to worry about. As long as I know you two love me, I don't need anything else."

She reminded herself sternly that she'd been telling herself this for years. And she'd been doing fine. So why did she feel she was lying to her daughters today?

As SHARON TRUDGED uphill behind Emilee and Christa an hour later, she had second thoughts. Tubing? What had gotten into her? She'd never enjoyed careening out of control down a hillside. She must be more desperate than she thought.

Well, she'd try to have a good time, no matter what it took. She wouldn't allow a single thought about Gabe or the persistent ache in her heart to ruin the morning for the girls.

She recognized Matt and Jason immediately, and Brittany—short and more petite than Emilee and Christa. The stocky young man standing at her side must be Tyler.

She didn't recognize the stick of a boy who tossed armfuls of powdered snow at everyone or the tall man standing to one side of the kids. "Who else is here?"

Emilee glanced at the top of the hill. "That's Matt's dad and his little brother."

Sharon studied the group a little closer. "Is Matt's mother here, too?"

"Uh-uh," Christa told her. "Matt's parents are divorced."

Matt and Jason spied them coming and loped downhill toward Christa and Emilee. Sharon trudged through the powder behind them, breathless. When she reached the top of the slope at last, Christa grabbed her hand and tugged her toward Matt's dad without even giving her a chance to catch her breath.

"Mom, this is Matt's dad. Bob Cummings."

Déjà vu. They might have been in that stuffy little office-supply store again. Except that Matt's father didn't look shy, he didn't blush and he didn't turn away from Sharon's gaze.

He smiled slowly and studied her for so long and with such intensity, she had to force herself to stand still. Finally, he held out a hand sheathed in a bulky glove. "Nice to meet you."

She shook his hand briefly. At least, she intended for the contact to be brief. Apparently, Bob didn't. She tugged her hand away, nearly losing her own glove in the process. Somehow, she managed to keep her smile in place—an artificial one, but a smile nonetheless. "It's nice to meet you, too."

Christa grinned. "You two have a lot in common, you know."

"Oh?" Bob perked up. "Do you like collecting coins, too?"

Sharon shook her head slowly. "No."

"Do you bowl?" Bob looked hopeful.

"No. Sorry."

"You're both divorced," Christa announced.

Sharon studied her daughter's wide grin. *That's* what Christa thought they had in common? Divorce?

Bob stepped a little closer. "How long has it been for you?"

"How long has what been?"

"How long have you been divorced?"

"Oh." She stomped her feet, trying to get them warm again. "Five years."

"It's just been six months for me." Bob sighed and looked out over the slope. "I'm still not used to it."

"It comes with time," she assured him.

"Six months," he said again, rocking back on his heels.

Sharon worked up a sympathetic smile and took a step away. The last thing in the world she wanted was to stand outside in bitterly cold weather discussing the sordid details of his divorce.

She looked around for Christa or Emilee, but they'd already started downhill on one of the bulging inner tubes. Jason, Brittany and Tyler huddled at the top of the slope a few feet away. Matt's brother tossed an armful of snow straight into Sharon's face, brayed a laugh and raced away.

Bob didn't seem to notice. "I don't get to see a lot of the boys anymore. Two weekends a month, that's all."

Apparently, he didn't believe in disciplining his son on those weekends. Sharon wiped her face, scooped snow out of the neck of her coat and took another few steps toward the kids.

Bob matched her pace. "I really wanted a joint-custody agreement. I think that would have been more fair, if you know what I mean. Just because Donna's their mother, that doesn't mean she should have them all the time."

"Yes, well, nothing about divorce is fair, really. Everyone loses. Especially the children." She watched Emilee and Christa reach the bottom of the hill and roll off the tube.

Bob's son raced up from behind and threw more snow down the back of her neck. Bob smiled indulgently, as if he thought the kid's antics were cute.

Sharon put some more distance between them.

Bob trailed after her as if they were stuck together. "You know," he said, nodding toward the bottom of the hill, "Matt really likes Christa."

"Christa likes him, too," Sharon assured him. "We all do. He's a good kid."

Bob rubbed his skinny face with one gloved hand. "No, I mean he really *likes* her."

Sharon gaped at him. She wasn't about to discuss her daughter's feelings with Bob. "They're very young," she said hesitantly.

Bob squinted into the sun with his whole face, watching as another inner tube reached the bottom of the slope and kids toppled into the snow. "I'd like to see Matt end up with someone like Christa."

"They're still in high school."

"Matt's mother and I met in high school."

And look how that ended, Sharon wanted to say. "Christa isn't ready to be in a serious relationship with anyone," she said instead. "She still has to finish high school. And she's planning to go to college, of course."

"College? Really?" He sounded shocked.

"Of course. Matt's planning to go, isn't he?"

Bob shrugged. "Yes. Of course. But I didn't realize Christa was thinking of going."

"She is, thank goodness. It's so hard to make a decent living these days without an education, and by the time these kids hit the workforce, it will be even harder."

Bob's lips tightened. "You may be right. Of

course, it isn't as important for girls as it is for boys."

Sharon's mouth fell open—literally. She stared at him for a long moment, trying to convince herself he wasn't serious. He *couldn't* be serious.

He didn't even crack a smile.

"You don't mean that," she said hopefully.

"It's true. Men are traditionally the bread-winners."

"Except in families where men aren't around to win the bread," she reminded him. "Or where the man can't earn enough. Or where the woman *wants* a career."

Bob studied her as if she'd just crawled out from beneath a rock. "You're one of those, aren't you?"

"One of what?"

"You're a feminist, right?"

She'd never heard that label attached to her before, and hearing it now almost made her laugh. Almost. "I just believe that everyone—men and women alike—have the right to choose the lifestyle that works best for them."

Bob folded his arms and gazed out toward the horizon. "If you ask me, that's what's wrong with women today." He turned his gaze to her. "In fact, that's what's wrong with our whole economy."

Sharon felt as if she'd stepped into a time warp. "You think that because women are doing something besides having babies and cleaning house they're destroying the economy?"

"You can argue with me if you want, but you can't deny that we've got a real unemployment problem in this country."

"Yes, but that's because machines and computers do the things people used to do. Like lighting street lamps and directing traffic and… and a million other things."

"It's because women are taking jobs away from men." His icy gaze sent a chill up her spine. "And that's not the only problem. They're so busy trying to wear the pants in the family, they don't pay attention to their children anymore."

"I don't suppose it's ever occurred to you that *fathers* should pay attention to the children, too."

His scowl darkened. His son threw more snow on her. "I knew it. I knew it. You're some sort of bra-burning, card-carrying feminist."

"Bra-burning?" Sharon laughed. The sound echoed across the empty field and made Christa, Emilee and their friends turn to look at them. "You're about forty-five years behind the times, aren't you?"

"All I know," Bob said, propping his hands

on his hips, "is that women like you are slowly destroying this country."

Sharon took a steadying breath, but it didn't do a thing to calm her. She had a thousand arguments she could have hit him with, but she recognized that nothing she could say would change his mind. And he definitely wasn't worth ruining the morning for the kids.

She held up both hands as a signal for him to stay put. "I'll tell you what, Bob. Since we obviously disagree completely, why don't you stay on this side of the hill and I'll stand over there." She gestured toward the far side of the slope. "That way, we don't have to speak to each other."

"Suits me." He flicked an angry glare at her. "I just wish they'd warned me about you."

No more than Sharon wished somebody had warned her about him. She pivoted away, caught his son in the act of scooping up another armful of snow and leveled him with a glance. "Don't even think about it."

The kid hesitated, glanced at his father, and dropped the snow to the ground. Smart choice.

Seething, Sharon crossed the top of the hill. Tyler chased a squealing Brittany with a handful of snow. Christa and Matt climbed the hill together backward, shouting encouragement to

Emilee and Jason who flew down the slope on the second inner tube.

Sure, at their age having boys around was fun. But what happened to guys when they grew up? She couldn't think of one fun thing about the conversation she'd just had with Bob. As for Gabe, he wasn't interested in having fun—not with her, at any rate.

Adelle's prediction that Sharon would end up old and alone echoed in her memory. But right now, right at this moment, spending the rest of her life alone didn't sound bad at all.

EMILEE GRIPPED A MUG of cocoa in both hands and shifted uncomfortably to make more room in the crowded corner booth.

Matt passed a vanilla cola to Christa, but he spoke to Emilee. "What did your mom say to my dad today, anyway?"

"The question is, what did your dad say to my mom?"

He shrugged and dropped his arm onto Christa's shoulder. "Whatever it was, they sure didn't get along."

That was an understatement. Emilee leaned her head against the back of the booth and stared at the framed pictures on the opposite wall. Buddy Holly, Elvis Presley, Ricky Nelson. Lots of other people she didn't recognize. Usually, she liked coming to the Sock Hop. Tonight, the loud jukebox, the crowds, the cluttered walls, the gum-popping waitress who'd served them all made her nervous.

She hadn't expected that finding a man for her mother would be this hard. She certainly hadn't expected her mom to fight with every man they found.

Christa scooped chili with a fry and popped it into her mouth. "I thought Mom would like Matt's dad."

"I thought she'd like Mr. Taylor at the school, too," Emilee reminded her.

Matt wedged several fries into his mouth, dripping chili on the table in the process. "Maybe she really *doesn't* want to meet men."

That was the stupidest thing Emilee had ever heard. "Of course she does. She just doesn't know she does."

Christa laced her hands together on the table. "She didn't like Steve's dad. She didn't like Mr. Taylor. And she didn't like Mr. Cummings—"

"We're not giving up," Emilee warned. "The Valentine's Day dance is in two weeks, and I'm *not* leaving her home alone while we both go out."

Matt stopped chewing and stared at her. "What

if you don't find someone before Valentine's Day?"

"Well, then, Christa and I will just stay home."

His eyes flew wide. "You can't do that."

"Why not?"

"Well… Because." He glanced at Christa and turned a deep shade of red. "Because I want Christa to go to the dance with me."

Christa beamed. "You do?"

"Well… Yeah."

"She can't go," Emilee said decisively. "Not unless we find someone for Mom before then."

Christa kicked her under the table.

Emilee refrained from returning the favor. "I won't go, either. Not unless we can make sure Mom's not alone."

"And just how do you plan to explain why we're both staying home?"

"I'll think of something," Emilee assured her.

"She's not going to care if she's home alone," Christa insisted. "She hates Valentine's Day."

Sometimes Christa could be so dense. "She hates it because she's alone. And because Dad never did anything special for Valentine's Day when they were married."

Christa flopped backward against the booth. "Well, then, let's just find somebody romantic.

Somebody who'll make a fuss over her, bring her flowers, take her out for a candlelight dinner…" Her eyes got all dreamy.

Emilee brought her back from her fantasy. "Somebody just the opposite of Dad?"

"Exactly."

Matt propped up his chin with one hand. "Where are you going to find somebody like that?"

"We could hang out at flower shops," Christa said as she took another fry.

"Bad idea," Emilee said with a firm shake of her head. "All we'd find are guys who already have wives and girlfriends."

"Yeah, I guess you're right." Christa rested her chin in her hand. "I still think Gabe would be perfect for her."

"Wrong. You heard what she said today. He's the contractor who's working on the basement. Nothing more. She's not interested in him, Christa."

"Then why was she in such a good mood before she went outside to talk to him and in such a rotten mood afterward?"

"Probably because she doesn't like him." Emilee enunciated carefully to make sure Christa understood.

Christa still didn't look convinced, but she didn't

argue. "So, what do we do? I don't know where else to look—not before Valentine's Day."

"Neither do I," Emilee admitted. They all fell silent, and she tried desperately to think. Aretha Franklin belted out a song on the jukebox. Someone in another booth let out a high-pitched squeal.

Matt scratched the side of his neck slowly. "So, if your mom had a date for Valentine's Day, Christa could go to the dance?"

"Sure."

He shifted in his seat to look at Christa. "If I find your mom a date, would you go to the dance with me?"

Christa sat up a little straighter and sent Emilee a triumphant smile. "I'd love to. But who are you going to find?"

"I don't know yet. But one of my friends is bound to know somebody single."

"Oh, no," Emilee said, holding up both hands. "We're not announcing this to the whole school."

"Not the whole school," Matt promised. "I'll just ask a few friends, that's all. *Somebody's* bound to have a neighbor or an uncle or a cousin or a friend who'd be right for your mom."

"Somebody she won't get into an argument with five minutes after she meets him," Christa muttered.

Emilee didn't like the sound of this at all. Too many things could go wrong. "I don't know—"

"Well, what do you suggest?" Christa demanded. "Unless you have some single men stashed away that I don't know about, we're at the end of our list."

"I guess you're right," Emilee conceded reluctantly. "But the more people we tell, the greater the chance Mom will find out what we're doing."

Matt put his arm around Christa again. "She won't find out. Trust me."

"He won't tell everyone," Christa promised for him. "Just guys he can trust—like Adam and Jason, and maybe Byron and Derek."

"It won't work," Emilee insisted.

"Sure it will," Christa said with a scowl. "Especially if Matt swears them to secrecy." She turned her most persuasive smile on Matt. "You *will* swear them to secrecy, won't you?"

"Sure. The guys all like your mom, you know."

Emilee still wasn't convinced. "I don't know… I have a bad feeling about this."

The jukebox changed to a softer song. Christa ticked her tongue against the roof of her mouth. "Do you want to find a guy for Mom, or not?"

"Of course I do."

"Well then?"

Emilee hesitated another minute. "I guess it would be okay," she said slowly.

Christa shared a satisfied grin with Matt and settled into the crook of his arm. "Okay, Matt. You're on."

He grinned like a kid with a new toy, and Emilee allowed herself a tiny smile. Maybe they were right. Maybe this was the solution to their problem. After all, if they only told people they could trust, what could possibly go wrong?

CHAPTER NINE

"ALL RIGHT, spit it out," Adelle demanded.

Sharon stopped with a mouthful of salad halfway to her mouth and glanced across the table at her friend. "Spit what out?"

Adelle waited to answer until their server had refilled their water glasses. She dabbed her mouth with a napkin and scooted her chair a bit closer. "Whatever it is that's been bothering you for the past two weeks. You look as if you've lost your best friend."

Sharon cursed herself silently for being so transparent, but she didn't want to discuss Gabe with Adelle. "I don't know what you're talking about. *You're* my best friend."

Adelle didn't let that distract her. "Is there something wrong with one of the kids?"

"No." At least she didn't have to lie. They'd been behaving normally recently, and she'd been able to put her concerns about Emilee on the back burner.

"Is it work?"

"No."

"A man?"

Sharon tried to laugh, but she had trouble sounding convincing around the mouthful of salad.

"It's a man, isn't it?" Adelle demanded. "You've got that look on your face."

"What look?"

Adelle frowned at her. "That I've-met-a-man look." She wagged her finger in front of Sharon's face. "Don't lie to me. I know that look when I see it. So, who is he?"

Sharon hesitated another minute. But Adelle *was* her best friend. Maybe talking about it would help. "All right," she conceded. "There is someone."

Adelle nearly jumped out of her seat. "I *knew* it. This is perfect. Just in time for Valentine's Day. Who is he?" Without giving Sharon a chance to answer, she started guessing. "The school nurse?"

"Heavens, no."

"That guy you met when you went tubing?"

She shuddered just thinking about Bob. "Of course not. And before you ask, it's not that poor man who owns the office-supply store, either."

"Then who?"

In spite of herself, Sharon laughed. "If you'll let me get a word in, I'll tell you."

Adelle sat back in her chair and made a visible effort to curb her excitement.

"It's Gabe Malone, that contractor you met at my house on New Year's Eve."

Adelle's eyes rounded and her mouth dropped open. "Are you kidding? He's gorgeous."

Even that made Sharon's heart contract. She tried to joke so Adelle wouldn't see how much it hurt. "Does that mean he's too gorgeous for me?"

"No. Of course not." Adelle grinned and slanted forward in her seat. "So, tell me everything."

Sharon sipped ice water and dredged up her flagging courage. "There's not that much to tell. Sometime during the past six weeks, we became friendly."

Slowly, hesitantly at first, Sharon told her everything. The little things he'd done to help her, their growing friendship and, finally, the kiss that had ended it all. Adelle interrupted constantly, laughing, exclaiming with delight and growing increasingly sober as Sharon told her about the last time she saw Gabe.

"So, that's why I'm here today instead of home," Sharon said, pushing away her nearly untouched plate of pasta. "It's just not the same with Gabe's replacement banging around in my basement."

"*That's* why you agreed to meet me for lunch? So you don't have to listen to this other guy working?"

"When you put it that way, it does sound silly."

"Silly? It sounds pathetic." Adelle's face tightened in disapproval. "Forget him."

"I wish it were that simple."

"It is that simple." Adelle waved the pink-tipped nails that matched her suit jacket. "This guy obviously doesn't care for you, so don't waste your time mooning over him."

Hearing Adelle voice her own thoughts and doubts made them even more real. She blinked back a sudden flood of tears.

Adelle looked at her with concern. "The first guy you show any interest in in five years, and he does this to you. I could just kill him."

"He didn't really *do* anything," Sharon reminded her. "It was just one kiss. He doesn't want a serious, committed relationship. He was honest about that right up front. And may I remind you, neither do I."

Adelle made a noise of disbelief. "That's what you keep saying, but I've never believed you. You want a good relationship, you just don't believe they exist."

"Of course I do," Sharon said with a frown. "Look at you and Doug. You have a wonderful marriage. And now, with the baby on the way…" She let her voice trail away wistfully and took a moment to pull herself together. "This is more my fault than his, anyway. Pauline told me he was a playboy, but I convinced myself she was wrong and I let down my guard."

"Another good reason to forget him."

"I suppose you're right. But some good will come from this."

"In what way?"

"It did start me thinking about what I want and what's best for the girls. And I'm seriously considering making a few changes in my life."

Adelle's blue eyes glittered. "That's the best news I've heard in a long time. Don't let Don Juan stop you. Take that decision and apply it to the next man who comes along—the next *decent* man, that is."

"I don't want to date just so I can have a social life. I'm talking about getting out more. Maybe I'll buy season tickets to the symphony, or take a class. I've always wanted to learn about antiques."

Adelle waved her hand again, clearly agitated. "Maybe you've forgotten, but dating is how you figure out if someone's Mr. Right or not. You go out. You have conversations. You spend time together. Maybe you hit it off and maybe you don't, but you *don't* hang around the house waiting for some guy to come knocking on your door and sweep you off your feet."

Sharon nodded slowly. Much as she hated to admit it, Adelle was right. Still, she couldn't completely ignore the unwelcome suspicion that she'd spend the rest of her life comparing every man she met to Gabe. Or the horrible realization that the lifetime alone she'd once thought wouldn't be so bad now filled her with unbelievable loneliness.

AFTERNOON SHADOWS stretched across Sharon's office, warning her she couldn't put off going home indefinitely. Even after two weeks, she hated returning home to find Derry in her basement. But the girls would be there, waiting for her. She couldn't hide behind her work forever.

Maybe she should take her daughters shopping this evening. Or take them out to dinner. Or both. Anything to avoid going home.

A soft knock sounded on her office door, allowing her to put off reality for a few minutes longer. One of her students, a young woman named Liberty Young, opened the door and peered inside. "Can I talk to you for a minute, Mrs. Lawrence?"

"Of course." Sharon motioned for her to come in. "What can I do for you?"

Liberty sashayed into the room and tossed her mane of curly red hair. "I need to talk to you about the final exam last semester."

"We've already discussed it," Sharon reminded her gently. "Several times."

"But it's not *fair*. If you don't let me make up the final, you'll ruin my grade point average."

Sharon shook her head slowly. "I'm sorry, Liberty, but my answer has to be the same as it was before. You're one of my best students, but you still should have made arrangements to make up the final before you left town."

"But—" Liberty slipped her hands into the pockets of her baggy jeans and tossed her hair again. "But that's not fair," she repeated. "I got married at the end of last semester, and I was on my honeymoon during the final. I didn't have time to think about tests and things."

Sharon laced her hands together on her desk and prayed for patience. "I understand how difficult it must have been to have a wedding at the same time as finals, but you knew the schedule when the semester started. Maybe you should have planned the wedding for another time."

Liberty corkscrewed a lock of hair around one finger and pursed her lips again. "Have a heart, Mrs. Lawrence. Willis and I are in love. We wanted to spend the rest of our lives together. Put yourself in my place."

Sharon's heart twisted painfully. She didn't want to imagine herself in Liberty's place. "It's not up to me. I don't make the rules. I couldn't let you make up the final this semester, even if I wanted to. The only thing I can do is urge you to go through the course again and take the final this time."

"But that throws off my whole schedule."

Sharon chewed her lip for a moment, wondering how she could make Liberty understand. Before she could think of a convincing argument, Emilee bounded through the door of her office, with Christa a step or two behind her.

"Guess what, Mom—" Emilee broke off, stepped backward and mumbled, "Sorry. I didn't know you were busy."

"We're through here," Sharon said quickly, hoping it wasn't obvious that she welcomed the interruption. She turned back to Liberty. "If you'd like to discuss it with administration—"

But Liberty cut her off. "I *have*. They won't do anything about it."

"I was afraid of that." Sharon stood and guided the young woman toward the door. "Unfortunately, life isn't fair. I know it's a cliché, but it's true." Before Liberty could offer another argument, she turned her attention to Emilee and Christa. "What brings you here?"

Christa waited for Liberty to leave. "Adam

gave us a ride home, and we heard your message so we asked him to bring us over here."

Christa's friend Adam peered around the door, grinned and ran his fingers through his short, blond hair. "Hey, Mrs. L. How's it goin'?"

His smile was infectious. "Well, Adam, I haven't seen much of you lately."

"I'm on the basketball team this year. I've been practicing a lot." He straightened his shoulders and looked for all the world like a small boy who'd just found a way into the cookie jar.

Sharon tried not to let him see her smile. "Emilee told me you'd made the team. I've been meaning to get to one of your games."

He hooked his thumbs through his belt loops. "Yeah, you should come!" Then he glanced over his shoulder again and motioned someone else forward. A tall, dark-haired man wearing a three-piece pin-striped suit stepped into the doorway behind him. "Have you met my uncle Ed?"

Sharon shook her head quickly and turned a smile in Ed's direction. "No, I haven't."

"Well, here he is. And *this* is Mrs. Lawrence."

Ed let his gaze travel slowly down the length of her. "Mrs. Lawrence."

"Sharon. Please." She stepped behind her desk again and tried not to let him see that he'd disconcerted her.

He stepped into the office and offered a huge hand for her to shake. "Ed Dubois."

"Are you in town visiting?" She looked to Adam for the answer, only to discover that he, Emilee and Christa had wandered out the door and now studied a display case full of trophies.

Ed made himself comfortable in one of her visitor's chairs. "No. I live in Englewood."

"Not far, then."

"Close enough." He raised his eyebrows and widened his smile.

Sharon silently willed the kids to rejoin them. Instead, they moved even farther away. "Are you related to Adam's mother or father?"

"His mother."

"And do you see Adam often?"

"Fairly." Ed cocked an ankle across his knee. "But I think I may come around more often in the future."

She turned her attention to her pencil holder, but she could still see him out of the corner of her eye. He was a nice-looking man, she supposed. And certainly well dressed.

"Well," she said with a polite smile. "I'm sure he'll like that."

Ed tilted his head to one side and gave her another slow, assessing look. "I'm supposed to drop Adam at practice in a few minutes, so

I won't waste time beating around the bush. Would you like to get together sometime?"

Shock froze Sharon in her seat. "Together?"

"Sure. For drinks, or maybe even dinner."

"You mean a date?" The words slipped out before she could stop them.

Ed grinned as if she'd said something utterly charming. "Yes. How about Friday?"

Stalling for time, Sharon glanced at the calendar on her desk blotter. "The twelfth?"

"The twelfth."

It had been twenty years since anyone had asked her on a date, and she didn't know how to respond or even what to think. She let out a stiff laugh. "Well, I…I…" She took another deep breath, managed to stop stammering and ignored the sudden image of Gabe that floated in front of her. Instead she reminded herself of Adelle's advice at lunch. "Yes, thank you. I'd like that."

Ed's grin grew even wider. "Perfect. Can I call you?"

She jotted down her home number on the back of a business card and passed it across the desk to him.

He tucked it into his pocket and flashed another smile. "Until Friday."

Stunned, she watched him lead Adam away

while Emilee and Christa hurried into her office and shut the door behind them.

"What happened?" Christa demanded.

Still reeling, Sharon gripped the edge of the desk for support and whispered, "He asked me on a date."

Emilee let out a yelp. "He did? Did you say yes?"

"Yes."

Emilee squealed in delight. "When are you going?"

"Friday night."

Christa shot a look at Emilee that Sharon couldn't read. "So that means?"

Ignoring her, Emilee rounded the desk and threw her arms around Sharon's neck. Christa joined them a moment later, and both girls babbled about dresses and shoes and hair and makeup for several minutes. Despite Sharon's best efforts, she couldn't work up any matching excitement. Nervousness, yes. And she had plenty of second thoughts. But no excitement.

She waited until the girls exhausted themselves, extricated herself from her chair and retrieved her coat from the rack in the corner. "Let's get out of here."

"We need to go shopping," Emilee said with a firm nod.

"Not tonight," Sharon pleaded. "I'm exhausted."

"But your date's in two days," Christa wailed. "We have to go. There's no telling how long it will take to find the right outfit."

Sharon slipped into her coat and gathered the rest of her things. Maybe they were right. Finding a new outfit might help her work up a little enthusiasm. "We'll go shopping tomorrow after work," she promised. "But only for a few minutes. And I'm not spending a lot of money. It's only drinks."

"Sure." Emilee grabbed Sharon's briefcase and started toward the door. "A few minutes. That's all."

Sharon trailed them out the door, locking it behind them. And she tried not to let the realization that she'd accepted a date with a perfect stranger frighten her. But the truth was, it scared her half to death.

GABE STEPPED OUT of the shower and stood, dripping, in front of the mirror. He felt better now that he'd washed away the dirt and sweat from the temporary job he'd worked all day. Maybe tonight he'd finally be able to sleep.

He studied the faint shadow beneath his eyes, the scowl on his face, the tight lips and creased forehead that spoke of tension and frustration that grew worse with every passing day. Maybe he'd made a mistake by walking out on his father. He certainly hadn't been able to get Sharon out of his mind during the past two weeks. He missed seeing her more than he could have imagined.

No. In spite of the emptiness he felt when he thought of Sharon, leaving Malone Construction hadn't been a mistake. Much as he hated the work he'd been doing for the temporary agency, he couldn't go back to being his father's puppet. Not for anything.

If only he could rid himself of the nightmares that had kept him tossing and turning into the wee hours, he'd be okay. Night after night he watched helplessly as he chased an elusive something he couldn't see. Some nights, he stumbled through a forest. Others, he raced through city streets or even familiar construction sites. Just as he reached for the thing, he'd trip and lose it again.

He'd have to be pretty stupid not to understand what the dream meant. He'd spent more than half of his life chasing the elusive hope that someday he'd take over the family business. That he'd get a chance to prove himself capable. That he'd keep the business running and provide security for his parents. Time after time, he'd let his hopes rise only to have them dashed again. But this time, he'd beat them on the rock himself.

He deepened his scowl and toweled himself dry, keeping one ear tuned to the ten o'clock news on the TV in the other room. His stomach rumbled noisily, momentarily drowning out a story on a house fire in Cherry Hills. He'd skipped dinner—again. He just couldn't seem to make himself eat.

As he looped the towel over the rack, the telephone jarred him. He hurried into the bedroom and grabbed the receiver just before the answering machine picked up. He wedged the phone against his shoulder and rummaged in his drawer for a clean pair of boxers. "Yeah?"

"How soon can you get over here?" his dad asked without preamble.

Gabe's heart stuttered. "Is something wrong? Is Mom sick?"

"I'm at the office." Harold's voice sounded gruff, unyielding. "How soon can you get over here?" he repeated.

"Why?"

"Because I need you here."

Gabe couldn't believe he'd heard those words coming from his father's mouth. He dropped onto the foot of the bed. "What's wrong?"

"Derry Kennedy's been in an accident."

His stomach knotted as if his dad had gut-punched him. "How bad? Was he hurt?"

"His wife says the paramedics took him to the hospital. He's in stable condition, but his leg's broken and he's got a couple of fractured ribs. He's going to be laid up for a while."

Gabe's heart sank for Derry, his wife and their four small children. "Who are you going to bring in to cover for him?"

"I was thinking about Hank Sterne."

"I don't think you'll get him. The last I heard, he was working on that new convention complex downtown. In fact, most of the guys I've worked with in the past are probably on that crew." And his dad wasn't willing to pay enough to tempt them away.

"I'll think of something," Harold said gruffly. "In the meantime, I need you to take over the Lawrence project again."

Gabe froze, half elated, half worried about how Sharon would react to having him around again. "You could always shift Shorty over there."

"Shorty doesn't know enough to finish that project," Harold grumbled. "I need someone I can trust on it. Someone with the skill to do it right."

The unexpected vote of confidence touched Gabe, but he hesitated to give in without discussing the argument that drove him away in the first place.

"You got a problem going back there?" his dad asked.

"No." Gabe reached for the jeans he'd left on the foot of his bed. "I have a problem coming back to work for you until we settle things between us."

"What things? I need you here. I haven't spent twenty years training you to take over just to have you walk out on me."

"I haven't spent twenty years preparing to take over just to have you walk all over me."

"I'm trying to teach you the business."

"If I don't know it after twenty years," Gabe said patiently, "I never will. Dad, I've worked for you since I was seventeen years old. When are you going to let me work *with* you?"

"What are you trying to do, boot me out so you can take over?"

"No. I want you to do as much as you can for as long as you can. But I also want you to be realistic and admit when it's too much."

"I *made* this company. Built it with my own two hands."

"I know, Dad." Gabe summoned every bit of tact he had in reserve. "But some things have slipped past you lately. All I'm asking is that you split some of the responsibility with me. Let's bring in one or two new guys and let me spend some time each week in the office."

A long, uncomfortable silence stretched between them. Finally, just when Gabe thought he'd have to choose between giving in and walking away, his dad let out a heavy sigh. "All right.

We'll talk about it. Now, are you going to take over the Lawrence job again, or not?"

"I'll do it," Gabe said. "Have you told her yet?"

"Her?"

"Mrs. Lawrence. Does she know I'll be there in Derry's place?"

"Does it matter?"

"No. No, it doesn't."

"Good." Harold shuffled some papers near the telephone. "The electrician finished prewiring for the intercom system yesterday, so you can start on the Sheetrock tomorrow."

"Great."

"I want you to head over there first thing. She'll be going over to Beekman's to pick out light fixtures, but she told Derry she'd leave a key with the neighbor to the north."

Disappointment snaked through Gabe at the thought that he wouldn't see her until evening. But he'd waited two weeks already, he could wait a few more hours.

ON ACHING FEET, Sharon trailed Emilee and Christa through the mall's center court for the third time in two hours. Valentine decorations had taken over the entire mall. Hearts and cupids dangled between mannequins in display windows. Everything in sight was either red, white or pink. Plush bears, stuffed devils, boxes of candy. Signs at the jewelry stores urged lovesick young couples to select the diamond that would ensure lasting happiness.

Love was in the air.

Sharon pushed aside a wave of wistfulness, the ridiculous wish that her first date in five years was with Gabe, not Ed. *If wishes were fishes,* she told herself grimly.

Ed seemed nice. She could at least give him a chance. Who knew—maybe Adelle was right. Maybe she'd discover all sorts of wonderful things about him. True, looking into his eyes had done nothing for her, but that didn't mean she might not feel something later. And the annoying fact that Gabe's face, not Ed's, kept drifting into her imagination…well, that meant nothing.

She slowed her step and waited for Emilee and Christa to notice. They'd been in nearly every store that sold women's clothing, but they still hadn't found anything they could agree on. The outfits Emilee and Christa approved were too expensive or revealing. And when Sharon found something she liked, Emilee and Christa vetoed her choice as either old-fashioned or dowdy.

Finally the girls turned back to look for her. "Let's forget about shopping and stop at the food court," she suggested.

Christa frowned. "We can't forget about shopping. Your date's tomorrow night."

They seemed to care more about it than Sharon did. She looked longingly at an empty bench. "At least let's sit down for a few minutes…"

Emilee tugged her forward. "There's one more store I want to try. And even if we find you a dress there, we still have to get shoes and an evening bag."

"I don't know why I need to go to all this bother," Sharon protested. "I'm just having drinks with the man."

Christa rolled her eyes in exasperation. "It's your first date in five years, Mom."

"Maybe so. But I don't see why I can't just wear my black pantsuit."

"Because it's *old*," Emilee said.

"And it's *way* out of style," Christa added.

"Do you have any idea how unattractive you're making me feel?"

Emilee's face fell. "We just want you to look your best."

"Yeah," Christa said. "You're going to look gorgeous by the time we get through with you."

Sharon glanced at her charcoal wool pants and gray silk blouse, both of which she'd owned forever, and smiled at both her daughters. "Are you trying to say I don't look gorgeous now?"

Christa took her other arm. "No. You look

fine. You always do. This isn't the right look for your first date, that's all."

"Trust us, Mom," Emilee said as she led her past the food court.

Sharon sighed softly. "One more store. If we can't find something there, I'll make do with what I already own."

Christa shot a look of such frantic desperation at her sister, Sharon nearly laughed aloud. She allowed the girls to lead her. Too late, she realized Emilee and Christa intended to take her into a trendy store she'd always considered far beyond her budget.

She ground to a halt and shook her head. "Not here. I can't afford it."

Emilee urged her forward. "Relax. It's not as expensive as you think."

Christa tugged on her other arm. "Trust us, Mom."

Against her better judgment, Sharon relented. While Emilee and Christa hurried toward a display of evening dresses, she stopped at a carousel and checked the tag on a pair of silk pants. The price made her gasp aloud. They wanted her to trust them? She could buy a month's groceries for what those pants cost.

She tried to catch their eyes and motion them outside, but Emilee had already pulled two dresses from the rack. One, a long beaded gown. The other a short black dress with thin straps that wouldn't cover much and probably wouldn't come close to reaching her knees.

Shaking her head quickly, Sharon backed a step away as Emilee approached. She'd feel like a fool in the long gown and she didn't have the figure to pull off the short one.

"Try these on," Emilee said, holding them out to her.

"I don't think so."

"Oh, come on, Mom."

Christa came up behind her, cutting off her escape route. "I like the short one. The long one may be too much. But if it looks terrific…"

"It *is* too much," Sharon protested. "And the short one is too short. I can't wear something like that. It doesn't even have any sleeves."

"So?" Emilee held them out to her again. "You have great arms."

"I have flabby arms."

Christa sighed heavily. "Just try it on, okay? If it looks bad, you don't have to buy it."

Sharon hesitated before accepting the gowns from Emilee. She snuck a peek at the price tags, and noted with surprise that the price of both gowns had been marked down by fifty percent. A little pricey, but not outlandish. She still didn't like the long gown. Not for drinks with a man she didn't know. But the girls wouldn't let up on the shorter one until she proved to them how dreadful she looked.

She slipped into the dressing room and changed quickly. To her amazement, the black dress flattered her figure nicely. She turned sideways and checked her profile. The cut of the dress actually made her look slimmer.

Hesitantly, she pulled open the dressing-room door. Emilee saw her first. Her mouth dropped open and her eyes lit with excitement. She grabbed Christa's arm and pulled her around to face Sharon.

Christa beamed with excitement. "That's it. That's the one. You look *wonderful.*"

Sharon glanced at the expanse of leg the dress left exposed. "You don't think it's too short?"

"Not at all," Emilee assured her. "Your legs look great."

"Perfect," Christa said with a nod.

A salesclerk appeared out of nowhere, gave Sharon a once-over, and smiled. "It looks like it was made for you."

Sharon usually dismissed the sales pitch. But she had to admit the dress did look good. Better than she could have ever imagined.

She smiled slowly. "You don't think I'd be making a mistake?"

"The only mistake you'll make with this dress," the clerk said quickly, "is if you don't buy it. At this price—"

"You *have* to get it," Emilee interrupted. "I saw the perfect shoes to go with it earlier."

Christa turned her around to face a full-length mirror. "You'll really impress him in that dress, Mom. Seriously."

Some of Sharon's enthusiasm faded as quickly as it had appeared. The one man she wanted to impress with this dress would probably never see it.

Oh, grow up, she told herself sternly. At least Ed was interested. She worked up a smile. "You've talked me into it. I'll buy the dress. And I want you to show me those shoes. But, please, let's have something to eat first."

A short while later, clutching the bag holding her dress, she led the way toward the food court. Emilee and Christa trailed her, smiling, chattering, laughing, and Sharon knew she'd made the right decision. From this moment forward, she'd stop wishing and start living. And if that meant putting Gabe completely out of her mind, well, that's exactly what she'd do.

CHAPTER TEN

GABE REACHED INTO the high cupboard in his mother's kitchen and lifted down a heavy ceramic serving tray. He'd waited for Sharon to come home until he couldn't stand waiting any longer. Instead of heading home, he'd come here—like a kid with a scratched knee running home to his mother. Not that he wanted to talk about Sharon. He just didn't want to be alone. He didn't want to sit at Milago's and feel sorry for himself. And his mother had a way of making everything seem all right.

"Is this the one you want, Mom?" he asked, looking back at her over his shoulder.

She nodded and added a handful of carrot slices to the salad at her side. "That's the one," she said in the soft voice that always seemed to soothe everything. "Be careful with it. It was my mother's, you know."

Gabe knew. She'd been telling him the same thing as long as he could remember. He placed it carefully on the counter, ran his fingers over the familiar raised pattern. "I've always liked this dish."

His mother laughed and pushed playfully at his arm. "If I left it to you, Gabriel, what would you do with it? Serve hamburgers and French fries?"

He grinned at her, but his heart wasn't in it. "Maybe that's all I'd use it for now anyway," he said, hoping his voice sounded light.

Her smile faltered. She studied him closely for several long seconds, then turned her attention back to the salad. "Tell me what puts that unhappiness in your eyes."

If she'd been anyone else, he might have tried to joke his way out of answering, but he'd never been able to lie to his mother. He sidestepped the question carefully. "Do I look unhappy to you?"

"You have for quite some time, but there's something new."

He reached for a piece of celery from the relish tray and munched it slowly. "You're right about one thing. I'm not completely satisfied with my life."

She glanced at him, then away again. "What would you change?"

"For one thing, I'd bring Tracy back to Denver. I hate having her so far away."

She frowned gently. "I know you do. But you make a mistake in thinking that you can't be close to her anyway."

"I know. I've been trying to make things better between us. I even sent her a pair of jeans just to let her know I'm thinking about her. But every time I try to call, she's out—at least, Helene says she is. I'm afraid I won't ever be close to her as long as she's living with her mother."

His mother placed both hands on the counter and held his gaze. "You won't be close to her until you put Helene out of your mind." She reached for a bowl of thawed frozen peas and added a few to the salad. "You're still giving that woman far too much power over you."

"It's a little difficult to put someone out of your mind after fifteen years of marriage," he argued.

"Just as it's easy to continue blaming her for what's wrong in your life. Tell me when you tried to call Tracy last."

He scowled, wishing he'd gone to Milago's after all. He hadn't expected to be grilled about his life. "Two days ago. She wasn't home."

His mother wiped her hands on her apron and faced him squarely. "Maybe not, but she misses hearing from you."

"How do you know?"

"Because I talk to her every Sunday, and she tells me."

"Maybe I should try calling on Sundays, then."

"Maybe you should."

"I'm always so tired on Sundays, and I want to be upbeat when I talk to her."

His mother shook her head sadly. "You keep yourself too busy. Just like your father."

He didn't like that comparison, and he certainly didn't think it was justified, but chose not to discuss it. "Mom, you just don't understand about Tracy. You've never had to live apart from your children."

"It's true I've never been through divorce. But together or separated, blaming the other person for your unhappiness is always a great temptation. And allowing your own selfishness to keep you from your daughter…" She sent him a look full of reproach.

It knocked some of the wind out of Gabe's sails. "If I lived closer—"

"*If* you lived closer. *If* Helene hadn't moved." She bent to check the roast in the oven. "There's always an *if* for you, Gabriel."

He felt as if she'd slapped him. Hard. "What do you want me to do, leave here and move to Oregon?"

"Of course not." She closed the oven door again and met his gaze. "It's time to stop blaming everyone else and start looking inside. You choose to be unhappy."

"That's not true," he protested, even though

somewhere deep in his core, he recognized the truth in what she said. He didn't like it, but he recognized it.

"When you were a little boy, you used to watch your father go to work before sunlight and come home again long after supper. He was here every night, but he wasn't a part of what went on with us. Do you remember?"

He raked his fingers through his hair and paced to the window. "Yes."

"You were always disappointed when he didn't go to your baseball games. Or when he didn't have time to watch you ride your bike after Uncle Mike taught you to ride it."

He nodded his head slowly. "I remember. I guess I knew he was busy."

"Yes," she said softly, coming to stand behind him. "But did you also know he cared deeply about you and Rosalie? And about me? Do you know that he adores the grandchildren? No one is more sad about Tracy living so far away than your father."

"He doesn't show it."

"He does in his own way." She put her hands on his shoulders. "Your father is doing the best he knows how to do, but you know better."

Gabe paced away from the window, rubbing his face as he walked. "All my life, I swore I wouldn't be like him."

She studied him for a long moment before she spoke again. "Not all of his qualities are bad. You also share some of his best ones. His work ethic and his ambition." She smiled gently. "And that stubborn Malone pride that won't let him admit he's getting older."

Surprised, he turned to face her again. "He *is* getting older, Mom."

"Yes, and so am I."

"I'm worried about him."

His mother's eyes darkened. "I know. He doesn't tell me everything, but I can tell when you two have argued over something at work." She lapsed into silence for a moment. "I'm glad you accepted his apology. Soon, he'll have to admit he can't run the business any longer and he'll need you there when that day comes."

Gabe leaned against the counter. "He doesn't act as if he needs me."

"Your father is afraid of showing what is truly inside him, just as you are. He's afraid of losing you and the business. You—"

He shook his head vehemently.

She ignored him. "You don't want to be unhappy again. You don't want to be hurt. And yet you're guaranteeing both by holding happiness at arm's length." She patted his cheek and tilted his chin until his gaze met hers. "You can tell me I'm wrong if you want to, but I'm not, and you know it. You're running away as fast as you can from the things that could make you happy."

He almost hated to ask. "Like what?"

"Like love."

Gabe forced a laugh and lifted a carrot stick. "Maybe it's skipped your attention, Mom, but I haven't exactly been running away from women since the divorce."

She scowled at him, and he felt all of ten years old again. "Dating casually and love aren't the same things, Gabriel. You know that."

She crossed to him and took his hands in hers. "You're a sensitive man, Gabriel. You always have been. You have a huge heart that gets hurt easily—just like your father. Both so afraid of getting hurt, you lock the world out. Do you know why your father seems so cold?"

"Why?"

"Because the grandfather you never met, the one who started all this Malone nonsense, was a cold and brutal man. Compared to him, your father is a teddy bear."

Gabe couldn't help laughing.

"Your father chose not to be exactly like his father. You have the same choice." Her lips curved into a teasing grin. "And you are lucky. You have me to help you." She gripped his shoulders and turned him toward the door.

"Now get out of here. Go into the living room and watch basketball with your father. I never could get anything done with you underfoot."

Grinning, he snatched an olive from the relish tray and started from the room. But at the door he turned back and watched her for a moment. He looked at her once-dark hair, now almost completely gray. At the wrinkles around her eyes and mouth. At the joints in her fingers that grew larger and more misshapen by the year. And he wondered if his dad knew how lucky he was to have found her.

Before he realized what was happening, he pictured Sharon standing beside her, laughing, talking, sharing secrets in a way that Helene had never been able to. He shook his head to rid himself of the image, but it wouldn't leave.

His heart constricted and he suddenly understood what had been causing his nightmares. He wasn't chasing his father's job. He wanted Sharon. For real. Forever.

If he had half his dad's intelligence, he'd find a way to break through her barriers. Half his stubbornness, he'd keep trying until he succeeded. Half his luck, she'd fall in love with him and stand beside him forever.

LATER THE FOLLOWING EVENING, Gabe pulled to a stop in front of Sharon's house just as a strange car pulled out of the driveway. One of the girls—he couldn't tell which—sat in the front seat with a boy. Hopefully, the other one would be gone, too. He wanted to talk with Sharon to-night. Alone. His mother's words from last night were still with him, and another unsuccessful attempt to reach Tracy earlier this evening had left him more determined than ever to get his life on track.

He cut the engine, pocketed his keys and hefted his toolbox. The sight of the open garage door brought a smile to his lips. He knocked, waited for several minutes with mounting anxi-ety and raised his hand to knock a second time. But before he could, the door opened a crack and one of Sharon's eyes met his through the narrow opening.

The eye widened for an instant, then clouded. "Gabe."

He didn't like that at all. "Is this a bad time?"

Shaking her head, she opened the door slowly until she stood in front of him in her bathrobe. She'd pulled her hair on top of her head with a clip, but tendrils had escaped, sweeping against her shoulders.

Gabe couldn't help staring at her. She was beautiful even in a bathrobe.

"No," she said quickly. "I…I was expecting someone else."

Reluctantly, he tore his gaze away. "Derry had an accident two nights ago. He's in the hospital."

"Is he all right?"

"He will be. I hope you don't mind that I'll be finishing the job."

A smile tweaked her lips and disappeared again. "I thought you'd quit working for your father."

"I did," he said with a shrug. "I changed my mind."

She motioned for him to come in. "I'm sorry about the way I'm dressed. I was just getting ready to leave."

"Like that?"

"I…" Her cheeks burned and she had trouble meeting his gaze. "I have a date tonight."

A date? Who? When? *How?* This wasn't how he'd planned their reunion. He tried consoling himself with the knowledge that it was probably Emilee and Christa's doing, but it didn't help. Sharon hadn't shown any interest in any of the other guys they'd introduced her to. There must be something special about this one. With regret, he abandoned his plan to talk with her. If she'd found someone, he didn't have the right to interfere.

He tried to look only mildly interested. "Someone new?"

"I'm having drinks with the uncle of one of Christa's friends." Her gaze dropped, then rose to meet his again before she turned around to lead him inside.

She stepped aside, as if she expected him to be able to move his feet. "I guess I should leave you a key. I should be home before you leave, but the girls will be out late. They're both at the Valentine's dance."

"Actually—" The word came out scarcely more than a whisper. He cleared his throat, followed her through the door and tried again. "Actually, I'm only planning to stay a couple of hours. I'll be glad to lock up when I leave." To his relief, his voice came out sounding almost normal.

"Great. I'll get the key back again tomorrow." She reached past him to press the button that would lower the garage door.

He nodded dumbly, resisting the urge to catch her arm and pull her into his embrace.

She moved into the kitchen and dug into her saddlebag of a purse, flashed a triumphant smile and held a key toward him. "Here. It will unlock the side door into the garage and the door you just came in."

He tried to say something, but his voice caught in his throat and came out sounding like a growl.

"Now, if you'll excuse me, my…date will be here in a few minutes."

Remembering that her smile was for another man cooled him like a bucket of ice. He slipped the key into his pocket, shifted his toolbox to the other hand and turned toward the stairs. But the ringing of the front doorbell and Sharon's soft cry of dismay stopped him in his tracks.

Her eyes widened and she shot a frantic glance at him. "That must be him. And look at me. I'm not even close to being ready."

Gabe was torn between wanting to help her out of the situation and wanting to open the door and tell the guy to get lost.

"The girls are both out." Sharon let out a resigned sigh and started for the door. "This is certainly going to make a great first impression."

Gabe stepped in front of her. "Why don't you run upstairs and get dressed. I'll let him in—unless you'd rather answer the door yourself."

"No." She shook her head quickly and tugged the robe a bit closer. "No. That would be fine." She pivoted away, then glanced at him from the bottom of the stairs. "Thank you."

"No problem." He left the toolbox on the floor and waited for her to run up a couple of stairs, then crossed to the door and opened it.

The man who stood there made Gabe's stomach knot. Hair slicked back, cheekbones chiseled and a set of straight white teeth that took up half his face as he smiled. Gabe knew immediately, beyond any doubt, that this guy was wrong for Sharon.

Just look at that suit. And the shoes. Gabe could have checked his reflection in them if he'd wanted to—which he didn't.

The jerk's smile faded and half of his teeth disappeared. He glanced into the house over Gabe's shoulder and shifted his weight on his expensive loafers. "I think I have the wrong address."

Gabe battled the temptation to keep his mouth shut and let him think so. But he knew it wouldn't do any good. He'd figure it out soon enough and come back. Still, that didn't mean he had to *volunteer* anything. "Who are you looking for?"

"Sharon Lawrence." Ed took another peek into the house. "Is this the right address?"

"Yes." Unfortunately. Gabe stepped aside and motioned for the man to come in. "She's upstairs getting ready."

Mr. Suave flashed another uncertain glance at him, but this one held a trace of curiosity. "Oh. I see." He took a step inside and waited while Gabe closed the door on the cold night air, then held out a manicured hand. "Ed Dubois."

Gabe shook the hand that had obviously

never done a hard day's work in its life. "Gabe Malone. I'm a friend of Sharon's." He pulled away from the handshake and motioned toward the couch. "Have a seat. She'll be down in a few minutes."

Ed inclined his head a fraction of an inch and took a couple of steps into the room. "Thanks." He looked around slowly, assessing Sharon's possessions. "So you're a friend?"

Gabe trailed him, watching his every move and wondering what on earth Emilee and Christa were thinking. This guy was all wrong for their mother. Even Gabe could see that, and he barely knew her. He resisted the urge to exaggerate his relationship with Sharon. "A friend. I'm finishing her basement."

Ed's smile came back, "I see." He settled himself on the couch and rested both arms on its back as if he owned the damn thing. "So you're working for her."

"I'm a general contractor," Gabe informed him. "Malone Construction." He pulled a business card from his shirt pocket and dropped it onto the coffee table. Not that he wanted Ed's business.

Ed didn't even spare the card a glance. He relaxed a bit more and patted the back of the couch with one hand. "Have you known Sharon long?"

What did that have to do with anything? Whether Gabe had known her a day or a year made no difference. Besides, it was none of Ed's business. "Long enough."

Ed cocked an eyebrow. "I see. She's a beautiful woman."

"Yes, she is."

"My nephew, Adam—do you know Adam?"

Gabe shook his head.

Ed's mouth curved into a satisfied smirk, as if knowing Adam gave him a leg up in some contest. "Adam told me about her. Took me to meet her. And I figured why not, you know?"

Ed's response made Gabe want to drag the jerk to his feet and shove him out the door again.

Before he could do anything, footsteps sounded on the stairs. An instant later, Sharon rounded the corner and came into view. She'd changed into a black dress that he was sure her daughters had chosen for her.

She looked spectacular. Too spectacular. Every instinct in his body told him to take her back up the stairs and tell her to change. But his traitorous feet refused to move.

When Ed caught a glimpse of her, his disagreeable face reddened. He stood quickly and closed the distance between them, taking one of her hands in both of his. "You look remarkable."

Sharon smiled, a shy sort of smile that just made Gabe want to protect her from this guy even more. "Thank you." She turned the smile on Gabe. "Thanks for letting Ed in." She shifted her gaze again, away from Gabe and back to Ed. "I wasn't quite ready when you rang the bell."

The flush crept from Ed's face into his ears. Gabe silently vowed to wipe the floor with him if he hurt Sharon, or if he got pushy or demanding.

She crossed to the closet and pulled a coat from a hanger. Ed took it from her, helped her on with it and brushed his too-smooth hands across her shoulders. She smiled a thank-you at him and turned another glance at Gabe. "I'm sorry to leave you alone like this."

"No problem," Gabe lied, then added loud enough to make sure Ed didn't miss a word, "I have the key. I'll lock up when I leave."

A muscle in Ed's jaw twitched. He put a possessive hand on Sharon's back and guided her toward the door. "I thought we could start with drinks at this little place I know downtown. They serve dinner there, too."

Drinks, Gabe thought. She only agreed to have drinks, not dinner. See? He was right. Ed had *plans.*

Gabe thought furiously, trying to find some

way to warn Sharon, but his mind remained an obstinate blank even after she stepped out into the night and Ed pulled the door shut behind them.

A deep seed of logic told him he was being ridiculous. He couldn't warn her. He didn't have to warn her. She was an adult, not a child. She'd been married before. She knew the score. Besides, with her looks, she'd probably had to deal with more than one man like Ed over the years. But logic had no place in his thoughts. Not tonight.

"IT'S NO USE," Christa moaned, tugging Emilee behind a screen of silk plants in the school gymnasium. "We've tried everything."

Emilee sent her a dark look, but she kept her voice low. Already, couples filled the room, and she didn't want to risk anyone overhearing their conversation. "Quit moaning and let's think of something constructive. We don't have much time. The guys will be back with the punch any minute."

"Fine. Did you see that look on Mom's face when we drove past her and Adam's uncle outside the restaurant?"

"I'm discouraged, too," Emilee whispered. "But I'm not about to give up. It hasn't even been two months."

Christa pulled a tube of lip gloss from her pocket and waited while a couple strolled past. "Okay, Ms. Know-it-all," she whispered back. "What do you have in mind?"

Emilee wished she *had* something in mind. "There has to be *someone* out there Mom will like."

"Well, if there is, *we're* not going to find him."

Emilee scowled a little deeper. "Acting like this isn't helping, you know."

"What do you expect me to do? Mom didn't like Steve's dad. She didn't like Brett or Mr. Taylor or Matt's dad. And it sure didn't look like she was bowled over by Adam's uncle."

"That's only five men," Emilee whispered sharply. "Five, not five hundred. We're just going to have to think harder."

Christa let out a sigh of annoyance, but dance music drowned it out. "I've thought as hard as I can. I've told everyone I can trust. If there's a man out there for Mom, I don't know where he is. And even if we found the perfect man, with the mood she's been in lately, it wouldn't do any good."

Emilee had to raise her voice louder than she wanted in order to make herself heard. "She has been in a pretty bad mood for the past two weeks." There'd been long periods of silence while their mom walked around with the strangest look on her face. Then, before Emilee even knew what happened, she'd start cleaning. *Really* cleaning. Moving furniture and practically scrubbing the surface off anything that didn't move. Even Raoul had steered clear of her.

"Maybe it's PMS," she said.

Christa shook her head. "Even when she does get PMS, it doesn't last this long."

"Menopause?"

"She's not old enough for that." Christa put on a layer of lip gloss and shoved the tube back into her pack. "Maybe Adelle knows what's bugging her. Or maybe something happened at work."

"I don't think so. Stuff happens at work all the time, but she doesn't act like this." Emilee glanced behind her. No sign of the guys yet. Good. "Anyway, we can't ask Adelle. She'd tell Mom."

Christa leaned against the wall and glanced around the crowded gym. "I wish Gabe was still around. Maybe he'd have an idea."

Emilee sent her a look full of disbelief. "You'd ask *him* to help find a boyfriend for Mom?"

"Sure. Why not?"

"Because that's a stupid idea."

"No, it's not. He's nice. He'd help."

"He wouldn't help. Geez, Christa, didn't you ever notice the way he looked at Mom?"

"Yeah, he was always watching her. I don't know why he hasn't been around lately. I thought they were friends."

"They *were* friends," Emilee agreed. Like a bolt, an idea occurred to her. An idea so incredible she almost couldn't believe it. She met Christa's gaze with a smile. "Until a couple of weeks ago."

"So what?"

"Maybe it's no coincidence Mom's been in a bad mood since Gabe left?"

"What—" Christa rubbed her hands. "Oh, I get it. She likes him."

"She *really* likes him."

"So— Now we just figure out some way to get them together, right?"

"Right." Suddenly, Emilee didn't want to stay at the dance. She didn't want to do anything but start to work on this new plan. "Let's do it tonight. After all, Sunday's Valentine's Day. What better gift could we give her?"

"We can't. She's on a date tonight with someone else, remember? Besides, we don't even know how to find Gabe. And what if he already has another girlfriend?"

"Details," Emilee assured her. "We can't let

the small stuff get us down. All we have to do is get home early enough to talk to Derry. He'll know where to find Gabe. After that, it'll all be downhill."

CHAPTER ELEVEN

As ED BROUGHT his car around the curve that led to her house, Sharon's breath caught. There, silhouetted by the moon, sat Gabe's truck. She tried not to show her excitement or her relief. Not that she cared what Ed thought. She'd had a perfectly miserable evening with him and his roaming hands. But as the moment to send him on his way loomed, she liked knowing Gabe was still around.

Not surprisingly, Ed's face tightened into a scowl when he saw Gabe's truck. "Looks like your boyfriend's still here."

She nodded and chose not to set him straight. "Gabe's here nearly every evening." She exaggerated slightly. "And on weekends."

"Sounds cozy." Ed's smirk and tone of voice left nothing to her imagination.

She resented the implication and changed her mind about setting him straight. "Gabe's a friend. Nothing more."

"Really?"

"Really."

"A *friend* who has a key to your house."

What an insufferable jerk. "Whether or not he has a key to my house is none of your concern."

"Tell me," he said, working the car into Park, "why did you need a date with me if you've got lover boy in there waiting for you to come home?"

Sharon leaned a little closer to the door and glared at him. "I didn't *need* a date with you. You asked me out, remember?"

"You didn't want this date with me to make him jealous?"

"No." What a suggestion.

"Because if you did, we could make him really jealous, you know." He cut the engine and shifted in his seat to face her. "If you're having second thoughts about your relationship with him, I could help you make up your mind." He brushed her cheek with the back of one hand.

She jerked away from his hand and fumbled for the door handle. "I don't need any help making up my mind."

He reached for her as if he intended to keep her in the car. "You're a beautiful woman, Sharon. You need a man who'll treat you like the lovely creature you are."

"For your information," she said, slipping

away from him once more and opening the door, "I don't *need* any man."

He slid across the seat, apparently intending to pursue her into the clear black night. "That's where you're wrong. Every woman needs a man."

Sharon managed to get out of the car and gripped the door with both hands. If she had to hurt him with it, she would. "That's where *you're* wrong."

With lightning speed, Ed got out of the car and made another grab for her. "Why are you running away from me?"

She sidestepped him easily, in spite of the stupid heels she wore. "Because I'm not interested."

He laughed. "Right. I don't know what kind of game you're playing—"

"I'm not playing games," she snapped.

He let out an impatient sigh. "Look, sweet-heart—"

"I'm *not* your sweetheart." She turned toward the house but kept one eye on him as she walked. He could easily outpace her in these shoes.

His voice cut through the silence of the night. "Adam told me the whole story about you. I know you've been alone for a long time. It's all well and good to play hard to get—but only to a point. You're taking this too far."

Sharon increased her pace and tried to get to the door before he decided to come after her. She could feel him watching her every step of the way up the driveway, along the sidewalk and onto the porch. Only when she'd let herself into the house and dead-bolted the door behind her did she relax.

She kicked off her shoes, tossed her evening bag onto a chair and waited until she heard Ed's car start and drive away. What a disaster. The whole evening had been a catastrophe, from the moment she'd opened the garage door and realized how much she wished Gabe would try to talk her out of going with Ed, to the moment Ed had finally stopped trying to maul her.

When something brushed against her leg, she jumped and let out a soft scream. Her hands trembled, her heart thudded wildly.

Murff.

She managed a shaky laugh and picked up Raoul. "Hello, boy. Were you waiting for me to come home?"

Murff.

"I thought you were supposed to be a guard cat. Why didn't you come outside and scratch that jerk's eyes out for me?"

He blinked up at her, settled into her arms and upped his purr a notch.

"Why do I need another man in my life when

I have you?" she asked as she padded across the living room. "I'm never doing this again, even if I live to be a hundred. Remind me of that, okay?"

When she reached the kitchen, she heard music drifting up from the basement. It was softer than usual and she couldn't hear any of Gabe's usual noises. No power saw. No electric thingamajig shooting nails into boards. No banging or pounding.

Nothing.

Making a futile effort to argue herself out of it, she put Raoul down, gripped the stair railing, and started down the steps. She moved slowly but steadily. She knew she was being foolish, but she couldn't seem to stop herself.

As she neared the bottom, she caught a whisper of sound. He was probably cleaning up and getting ready to go home. She should turn around and climb the stairs again and leave well enough alone. But all the logic in the world couldn't make headway with her heart.

So she kept going until she reached the bottom of the steps. There, she stood for a moment and watched him work. As usual, just the sight of him made her breath catch.

He stacked a couple of stray boards together and returned a tool or two to the red metal toolbox on the floor. As he reached for the broom and dust pail, he realized she was standing there. He stopped moving and everything about him tensed. A smile flitted across his lips, then disappeared into a slight frown. "You're back."

"Yes."

He attacked the floor with the broom—short, jerky, agitated movements that told her more than his words or expression had—and a flicker of hope grew. Maybe he did care.

He spoke without looking at her. "Did you have a good time?"

"Not really." She took a step toward him, ignoring the shock of cold on her feet.

His sweeping faltered, then started up again, a little less jerky this time. "Well, that's too bad."

She moved closer still, watching him, noting the flush on his cheeks, the grip of his hands on the broom handle. "It was no big loss," she assured him quietly.

This time his glance was filled with uncertainty. "You didn't like him?"

"No, I didn't," she said, unable to take her eyes off his handsome face.

He smiled, only a tight curve of his lips. It was enough. "Are you disappointed?"

"No."

He stopped sweeping and studied her face. He tried to avert his gaze, but he seemed no more able to look away than she could. His grip on the broom handle tightened. His eyes darkened. The pulse in his neck jumped. "Well, that's good. He seemed like a jerk."

Absolute joy filled her, but she held back the delighted laugh that threatened to escape. "He was a jerk. I'd have been happier if I'd stayed here." *With you,* she thought, but she didn't dare say that aloud.

He propped the broom against the wall and watched her for so long she thought he might never move. Finally, after what felt like an eternity, he took a step toward her. "You look incredible tonight."

She battled the urge to move closer and told herself to wait. But the need to feel his arms around her nearly did her in. "So do you."

"Yeah, I'm sure I do." He smiled. "I'm dirty from head to toe. My jeans are old and worn."

"My hair's falling out of this clip," she countered, "and my makeup's half gone."

He closed the distance between them and touched the clip in her hair with one hesitant hand. "You look good this way," he said softly. "But you'd look better with your hair down." When she made no move to stop him, he removed the clip and let the rest of her hair fall.

She resisted the urge to straighten it and waited while he studied her face with such intensity, she thought she might stop breathing. Slowly, gently, he grazed her temple with the backs of two fingers. She didn't move. Didn't make a sound. But when his hand touched her shoulder, she raised her face to his.

He slipped his arm to her waist and pulled her closer. Slowly, he lowered his mouth to hers. Almost hesitantly, he brushed her lips with his.

The touch was featherlight, not at all demanding, but it unlocked something inside her. She slid her arms to his shoulders.

The floor seemed to disappear beneath her feet. The world around them vanished.

Suddenly, from somewhere far away, a noise reached her. She couldn't identify it. She didn't *want* to identify it. She wanted nothing but this moment with Gabe.

Before either of them could react, footsteps pounded down the stairs. Sharon willed them to stop. To go away and leave her in this place she'd never been before. But Gabe started to pull away.

Before he could, Christa reached the bottom and raced into the room. "Derry? We need your help. We need to find—" She broke off suddenly and slid to a stop just as Emilee rounded the corner. *"Mom?"*

Somehow, Sharon managed to make her voice work. "You're home early."

"Yeah," Emilee said slowly. "We, uh, we wanted to see how your date went."

Christa nodded, clearly too dumbfounded to speak.

Sharon moved away from Gabe and tried in vain to pull the tattered edges of her dignity around her. "Ed and I didn't get along."

Emilee looked from Sharon to Gabe and back again. "Apparently not."

Christa leaned against the wall and studied them carefully. "So, are you two going to start dating, or what?"

Sharon peeked at Gabe from the corner of her eye, expecting to see a scowl on his face. Instead, he grinned at the girls and slid his arm around Sharon's shoulders. "Would you mind?"

"Are you *kidding?*" Emilee cried at the same moment as Christa, "Mind? Why would we mind?"

"Come on, Christa." Emilee turned toward the door, tossing them an indulgent smile over her shoulder. "We need to do something upstairs." She didn't give Christa a chance to question or protest, but grabbed her wrist and led her back up the stairs.

Sharon watched them go, comforted by Gabe's arm around her, confused by her daughters' reactions and worried that she'd just stepped over a line she'd never intended to cross again.

Gabe tightened his arm around her and bent down for one more kiss. She pushed everything else out of her mind. There'd be time enough tomorrow to figure out what had just happened. Tonight, she'd just enjoy.

SHARON COULDN'T REMEMBER a Valentine's Day she'd ever enjoyed more. Sunshine promised an early spring. A beautiful bouquet of wildflowers delivered by the florist had warmed her clear through. And an incredible phone call from Gabe shortly after the gift arrived had left her convinced that unlocking her heart was the right decision.

Lost in thoughts of Gabe, she pushed her grocery cart through the aisles of King Sooper's. Emilee and Christa had come with her this morning, but they'd both run off to talk to friends they'd noticed a few minutes earlier. That left Sharon free to relive the comfort of having Gabe's arms around her.

She hadn't slept well—excitement had kept her awake most of the night—but today she didn't feel sleepy. When Gabe phoned, he'd asked if he could stop by later this morning. Of course she'd said yes and had offered to fix him brunch. Now she couldn't wait to get home and start cooking.

She turned down the cereal aisle and spent a few minutes making her selection. Just as she started forward again, Emilee and Christa came around the far end of the aisle. "So, what plans did you make?" she asked when they drew closer.

Emilee looked confused. "Plans?"

"With your friends."

"We're not going anywhere today," Christa said. "We're staying home."

Sharon looked at each of them in turn. "Are you serious?"

"Sure." Emilee hooked her fingers through the wire cart. "Why not?"

"I'd love to have you around all day," Sharon assured them. "It's just that you usually do things with your friends on the weekends."

Christa trailed one hand along the shelf. "Didn't you say Gabe was coming over?"

"Yes, but—"

"So, we want to see him." Christa dropped her hand and walked backward. "He's cool."

Emilee readjusted the cereal in the cart. "Yeah, he is."

"I didn't realize you knew him so well."

"We talk to him a lot," Christa said.

"Yeah, he's a great listener." Emilee held up a

box of her favorite cereal. When Sharon nodded, she dropped it into the cart. "I even helped him pick out a present for his daughter."

Sharon could feel the astonishment on her face. "You did? When?"

Emilee shrugged. "I don't remember, exactly. A few weeks ago."

"You didn't mention it."

"I didn't know it mattered...until last night."

"Of course you didn't." Sharon smiled. "Well, then, if you're going to stay home, you can help me decide what to make for brunch."

"Blueberry muffins," Christa said immediately. "The ones you make are the best."

"Thank you." Sharon gave her a quick hug. "What else?"

"Fresh fruit," Emilee suggested. "And I could make Spanish omelettes."

Sharon's step faltered. "You're offering to cook?"

"Sure. Unless you don't want me to."

"I'd love your help," Sharon said quickly. She pulled paper and a pen from her purse and jotted down the things she'd need to buy. "It just surprises me, that's all. You usually come up with excuses *not* to cook."

"I don't mind today. I really want you to impress Gabe."

"Me, too. I'll set the table," Christa offered.

"We could use the crystal Grandma gave you. And we could put the flowers Gabe sent on the counter."

"That would be lovely." Sharon pushed the cart slowly. "So that's why you're both so eager to help? So I can impress Gabe?"

"You don't mind, do you? It sounds fun."

"More fun than going somewhere with your friends?"

"Sure." Christa fell into step beside her. "We want to make sure Gabe sticks around. It'll be like having a real family." At Emilee's slight frown, she quickly added, "That didn't sound right. I mean—well, you know what I mean… don't you?"

Sharon tried not to show how much that comment hurt. "Yes, sweetheart, I know what you mean." But as she rounded the end of the aisle, she decided she couldn't let the subject drop. "I didn't realize the three of us living on our own bothered you so much."

"It doesn't bother me." Christa glanced at her, then away again. "Not really."

Sharon put a package of pasta into the cart. "What about you, Emilee? Does it upset you?"

"No. It's just that we don't like to see you lonely. We worry about what's going to happen to you when we're not around anymore."

Sharon knew that was inevitable, but she didn't like thinking about it. "Do you miss having your dad around?"

"Sort of." Christa sent her a half smile. "But we talk to him and we see him every summer, so it's not as if he's completely out of our lives."

Maybe not, Sharon thought sadly, but he was far enough removed to make them eager for someone to take his place.

She put a hand on Emilee's shoulder. "Would you like to spend more time with your dad?"

Emilee shrugged lightly. "I wouldn't mind, but it's kind of hard to do that when he lives in St. Louis. Besides, once I start college everything will change, anyway."

"And with Gabe around," Christa added, "we can do all the stuff we used to do with Dad."

"I don't want you to get your hopes up too high," Sharon warned. "Gabe and I have decided to start seeing each other, but there aren't any guarantees that he'll be around forever." In spite of her elation this morning, she still held part of her heart in check.

"Oh, he will be," Emilee said with a bright smile. "He really likes you, Mom."

"And I like him, but—"

"Come on, Mom." Christa scowled at her. "Don't ruin everything, okay?"

"I don't want to ruin anything," Sharon

assured them. But their expectations concerned her, and so did the need she saw in their faces. "Let's just take this one day at a time, okay?"

Emilee shrugged lightly. Christa nodded. "Sure, Mom. Whatever you say."

Sharon pushed the cart slowly and wished she could recapture the euphoria she'd been feeling just a few minutes ago. But it eluded her.

GABE SAT ON the couch, phone on his lap, staring at Sunday-morning cartoons on television. He hadn't watched cartoons since Tracy was small, and then only rarely. He wished now that he'd spent more time with her when he had the chance.

Outside his apartment, a soft breeze stirred the tops of the trees and warm sunlight bathed the still-brown grass on the communal lawn. He picked up the receiver and dialed the first five digits of Tracy's number, but his courage failed him and he hung up quickly.

He sat for a minute, then muted the television and tried again. And he prayed silently that Tracy would answer.

But luck just wasn't in his cards.

Helene answered, and she didn't sound happy to hear his voice. "Gabe. What do you want?"

He tried not to match her tone. "Is Tracy home?"

"Yes. Why?"

"I'd like to speak with her."

"What about?"

He stood and paced toward the window. "I'd like to bring Tracy out for a visit over spring break. That is, if you don't already have plans."

"Why?"

"I've decided you're right. I haven't been much of a father to her lately."

"Really? What brought this on?"

"I've been making a lot of changes in my life," he admitted. "This is one I've been needing to make for a long time. Is she free over spring break?"

"We don't have any plans, but I don't know if she'll want to fly out there. You've hurt her a lot, Gabe."

He closed his eyes for a moment. "I haven't meant to."

"That's the trouble. You do it without meaning to."

"I'm trying to change, Helene."

Helene didn't speak for a long time. Finally, with a resigned sigh, she said, "I'll let her know you're on the phone."

He waited, hoping the worst was behind him. It felt like forever before Tracy picked up the receiver.

When she did, her voice sounded wary. "Dad?"

"It's me, kiddo."

"Mom said you wanted to ask me something."

"I do. What would you say to flying out here for a visit over spring break next month?"

She hesitated too long before she answered. "What would we do?"

"Whatever you like."

"Would you be working all the time?"

He hadn't realized his long hours bothered her. "No. I'll tell Grandpa I need some time off work."

"Yeah?"

"Yeah."

"Where would I sleep?"

"In the extra bedroom in my apartment. Will you come?"

"I don't know."

His heart sank like a stone. He closed his eyes, unable to fight the tears that stung his eyes. "I'd really like to see you, Trace."

"I have things to do here."

He opened his eyes again. "Your mom said you didn't have any plans."

"*We* don't, but I'm just starting to make friends here. I don't want to be gone forever."

"It wouldn't be forever," he argued gently.

"Just a week." Silence fell between them. He held his breath, willing her to agree.

"I don't know," she said again. "Can I think about it?"

"Sure, Trace. Take all the time you need."

He expected her to make an excuse to get off the phone. Instead, she asked, "What about girlfriends? Are you going to be taking off with them all the time?"

Gabe couldn't bring himself to tell her about Sharon. Everything was too new and uncertain, both with Tracy and with Sharon. Instead, he said, "No."

"Could I visit Grandma?"

"Are you kidding? She'd have my hide if I didn't let you spend time with her and Grandpa."

That brought a soft laugh from Tracy. "Okay. I'll think about it."

Relief weakened him. At least she hadn't said no. "Great. When should I call you again?"

She thought for a moment. "I guess you could call next weekend."

He'd rather have her answer sooner, but he'd give her what she asked for. "That sounds good to me. I'll talk to you then."

But when he disconnected a few minutes later, he couldn't shake the feeling that he'd just faced his first real test...and somehow failed.

GRIPPING HIS GYM BAG, Gabe pushed open the door to the health club he and Jesse had joined at the same time years ago, and searched the lobby. Even here, Valentine's Day decorations hung from the ceiling, filled the windows and nearly covered the counter.

He glanced at his watch, hoping Jesse had gotten his message. A second later he noticed his friend on a bench, chatting with a pretty redhead.

Gabe crossed the lobby and took a seat beside Jesse. "Thanks for agreeing to meet me," he said when Jesse stopped talking and looked at him.

"No problem. I was beginning to think you were avoiding me."

Gabe smiled. "As a matter of fact, I was."

Jesse laughed and drew the redhead into the conversation. "Celia, this is my buddy, Gabe. The one I was telling you about. Celia's a friend of mine."

The redhead sent Gabe a smile. "It's nice to meet you."

Once, he might have flirted with her. Now he merely smiled back cautiously. "Nice to meet you, too."

Celia stood and wandered away. Jesse thumped him on the shoulder. "So, what's up?"

"I'm just here to concede defeat."

Jesse's stare deepened for a moment, then he

tilted back his head and brayed a laugh. "I *knew* it. I knew it. You couldn't do it, could you?"

"Nope. You were absolutely right."

"So? Who is she?"

Gabe grinned. "The woman I told you about last month."

"The teacher?"

"Yep."

Jesse grabbed his bag from the floor and stood. "I thought you said she was all wrong for you."

"I thought she was," Gabe admitted. "*I* was wrong." He couldn't remember ever admitting a mistake so easily before.

Jesse led the way toward the men's dressing room. "Does that mean you're seeing her?"

"Yep."

Jesse laughed again. "This win was too easy, buddy. *Way* too easy."

"For you," Gabe said with a laugh. "I had to do some real soul-searching. But I'm a happier man because of it."

"So, are you in love with her?"

"I don't know. Maybe."

"You going to marry her?"

"We've just started seeing each other. Besides, she's not interested in getting married again."

"That's what they all say," Jesse warned, "but they don't mean it."

"This one does," Gabe assured him, a little surprised by the flicker of disappointment the words brought. He chose a locker and dropped onto the bench in front of it. "She hasn't even dated anyone for the past five years."

Jesse scratched his beard thoughtfully. "So, what does Tracy think of all this?"

Gabe looked away and unzipped his gym bag. "I haven't told her yet."

"Why not?"

"I don't know how to. I talked to her this morning and asked her to come out for a visit. She's thinking about it." Gabe changed his shirt and pulled out a pair of sweats. "Things are so touchy between us, I didn't want to rock the boat."

Jesse tugged off his T-shirt and stuffed it into an open locker. "So, when are you going to tell her? When she gets here?"

"No. Later, maybe. She's worried that I'll spend all my time with women while she's here. I think I'd better keep my relationship with Sharon a secret for a while."

"And when she finds out the truth? How are you going to explain that?"

"I'll cross that bridge when I come to it."

Jesse kicked off his shoes and pulled his cross-trainers from his bag. "Didn't you tell me your lady friend has a couple of kids?"

"What does that have to do with Tracy?"

"You get along with them?"

"I get along with them just fine," Gabe assured him.

"Yeah, as long as you're working in their basement. What's gonna happen when the job's finished? How can you be a decent stepfather to them if you can't even make time to have a relationship with your own daughter?"

"Nobody said anything about being a stepfather," Gabe argued. "And I have a relationship with my daughter. Just not a close one."

"And whose fault is that?"

He started to give the answer he always gave, then stopped himself. "Mine, I guess."

"So what are you going to do about it?"

He jerked a towel from his gym bag and stood. "I don't know."

"Well, you've gotta do something. Do you have any idea how Tracy'll feel if you get chummy with those kids when you can't even talk to her?"

Gabe rubbed his face and let out a defeated sigh. "So instead of telling me everything I'm doing wrong, how about offering some suggestions?"

"Be honest with her. Stop trying to make her think you're some knight in shining armor and let her see the real you, rust and all."

"I don't know—"

"Trust her a little bit, man. There's no reason she shouldn't love you in spite of yourself. God knows the rest of us do, though half the time I have no idea why." His smile took away some of the sting.

Gabe pretended to scowl. "You're not going to make this easy on me, are you?"

"Nope." Jesse closed his locker and pocketed the key. "You've got to figure it out on your own."

Coming from Jesse, it sounded simple. But Gabe knew the next conversation he had with his daughter would be the hardest one he'd ever had.

CHAPTER TWELVE

GABE LISTENED TO the sound of music and laughter overhead. Footsteps thundered across the floor—lots of them. Other voices mixed with, and occasionally drowned out, Sharon's, Emilee's and Christa's. The kids—and their mother—were obviously enjoying themselves upstairs. Sharon had told him Emilee and Christa were having a few friends in. She'd even invited him to join them, but the electrician had run into a glitch with the old wiring in the house on Wednesday, and that had thrown Gabe behind schedule again.

The job was just an excuse, he admitted silently. He couldn't relax and let himself enjoy Sharon's company as long as he was hiding the truth from Tracy. He tossed his hammer into his toolbox and tried not to think about the phone call he'd been putting off all day. He had to talk to Tracy—really talk this time—but he honestly didn't know how or where to begin. And he didn't know how she'd react to his clumsy attempts to mend the rift between them or his confession about his relationship with Sharon.

Frowning, he closed the lid on his ratchet set, picked up a couple of wrenches he'd left on the floor and slung his jacket over his shoulder. He'd say goodbye quickly and go home to make his phone call.

But when he stepped onto the landing, he changed his mind. He didn't want to disturb Sharon. She'd been preoccupied all day, anyway. Probably busy planning this party. He'd explain tomorrow and hope she understood.

He let himself out the back door and walked toward his truck, but two cars had boxed him in and he didn't have enough room to pull away from the curb. Frustrated, he locked the toolbox in the truck and turned back to the house. The music and laughter drowned out his first knock. Emilee answered his second.

She blinked out at him in surprise. "What are you doing? I thought you were downstairs."

"I was, but I'm through for the night." He motioned toward the street. "I can't get out. My truck's blocked."

"You're leaving? Why?"

"I have a few calls to make."

"Can't you make them later? We've got pizza."

"This can't wait. Do you know who owns a blue Toyota and a red Ford Escort?"

"Matt and Brittany." She waved him into the kitchen. "Come on, I'll ask them to move."

He trailed her into the dining room, surprised to find that the group was actually much smaller than it had sounded from downstairs. Open boxes of pizza, a stack of paper plates and another of napkins lined the counter.

Christa sat at one end of the table, drawing furiously on a pad of paper. Two boys about her age sat on either side of her, trying to guess what she'd drawn. Sharon sat with her back to Gabe. Her team flanked her and a few stragglers stood beside the table, watching and laughing.

Gabe let himself watch her for a few minutes, realizing she looked as if she belonged with these kids. They seemed to accept her as one of them and she looked relaxed and happy. As if she'd forgotten that she was a mother, that she set the rules, that she had responsibilities. He'd give anything to have Tracy act that way around him.

Emilee waved him toward the pizza on the counter. "Have some while you're waiting. We've got plenty."

"No, thanks. I—"

"You'd better," she warned. "Mom thought you might change your mind and join us, so she ordered extra. Besides, Matt and Brittany are in the middle of a game. You might have to wait awhile."

"Maybe they could interrupt the game for a minute to let me out."

Emilee merely grinned. "Relax. You worry too much. Have some pizza." And without giving him a chance to protest, she grabbed one of her friends by the arm and led her toward the stereo.

Gabe started after her, then thought better of it. He didn't want to embarrass her. Besides, what would another half hour hurt?

He took a slice of pepperoni-and-black-olive pizza and leaned against the counter to eat it. Sheer heaven. He wolfed down the first piece and helped himself to another.

While he watched, the game shifted and Sharon started to draw. She still hadn't noticed him standing there.

Out of curiosity, he stepped closer and watched while she scratched almost indecipherable figures onto the pad. Her teammates guessed wildly. She creased her forehead in concentration and tried again. More guessing, obviously none of them correct. Someone shouted a name Gabe didn't recognize, but the kids all roared with laughter. Sharon smiled up at the girl sitting closest to her and caught sight of him standing there.

Her smile grew warmer and her hand stopped moving for a fraction of a second. Before anyone else noticed the sudden shift in her mood, she pulled herself together and kept going with the game. Finally, just before the time ran out, one of the boys standing behind her shouted the correct answer and she collapsed in her seat, feigning exhaustion.

She glanced up at Gabe again. This time, her smile seemed a little less personal.

Before he could respond, Christa tugged at his elbow. "Take my place. I've got to go."

That was the last thing he felt like doing. He'd never fit in the way Sharon did. He shook his head and backed a step away.

"I've got to *go*." She pushed him toward her chair and raced up the stairs, leaving him facing a dozen expectant faces.

The light of anticipation danced in Sharon's eyes. Her lips curved into a smile and he knew that his response would either keep it there or wipe it away. His conscience pricked when he thought of Tracy, but he told himself to relax. He could call her later. Or even tomorrow.

Lowering himself into Christa's seat, he picked up the pencil and met Sharon's gaze. "What do I do?"

Five voices started in at once. He tried to concentrate on the explanation, but he couldn't make sense of what anyone said. Someone shoved the game box in front of him and pointed at something, but he couldn't tear his gaze away from Sharon's smile.

He wondered if she knew how unlike him this was. How remote the chance that it would happen again. He couldn't remember ever playing games with Tracy and her friends. In his experience, fathers didn't do that. Fathers worked, they brought home the money and they doled out the discipline. Mothers played. Mothers laughed. Mothers loved.

The thought brought him up short. Did he really believe that? He must. He could almost hear his father's voice telling him in one way or another that Malone men didn't let anything come before their work.

Was that why he'd let the rift between himself and Tracy get started? Was that why he'd continually failed at marriage and commitment? And why, deep down, the idea of trying again frightened him?

He thought so, and the realization left him feeling strangely liberated. All these years, he'd been trying to live up to an image. For the first time ever, he understood it was okay to be himself.

GABE SAT ALONE in his apartment. Silence surrounded him for the first time in a long time. It was late. He'd stayed too long at Sharon's. But he hoped Tracy would forgive him. As a little girl, she would have forgiven him anything, but times had changed.

He dialed quickly and waited for someone to answer. Not surprisingly, Helene's voice greeted him.

"Hello, Helene. It's Gabe. Is Tracy still awake?"

"Yes. She's doing homework."

He knew Helene meant that to discourage him from interrupting her. But he didn't let himself toss out an accusation the way he normally would. "I'd like to speak with her. I won't keep her long."

"She's been waiting for you to call all evening."

"I know. And I'm sorry." He didn't offer any excuses as he once would have. He said only, "Can I speak with her, please?"

She hesitated, but at least she didn't argue. "All right. I'll get her."

He took a steadying breath and tried something he hadn't tried in a long time. "Before you do, there's something I want to talk with you about."

"What?"

"For Tracy's sake, I'd like us to try to be civil to each other."

"Are you serious?"

"Very." He leaned back against the couch. "We've been blaming each other for the divorce for a long time. I think it's time we admitted we both had a hand in what happened. Maybe, if we can do that, Tracy won't feel as if she has to choose between us."

"I haven't asked her to choose," Helene said tersely.

He forced his voice to remain steady. "Neither have I—directly. But we have so much unresolved anger between us, I think she feels as if she has to choose."

Helene didn't say anything to that.

"Look," he said gently. "We may always have issues between us, but we can't let them affect Tracy any longer. It's not fair to her."

Another long silence stretched between them before she said, "I suppose you're right. But I sure hate to admit it."

He laughed, and his reaction surprised him. He couldn't remember the last time he'd laughed at something Helene said. "Well, don't worry," he assured her. "I'm sure it won't happen often."

"I hope not." She tried to sound irritated, but he could hear a smile in her voice. "Hold on. I'll let her know you're on the phone."

Tracy picked up a minute later. "Dad?"

"Sorry I'm calling so late—"

"That's okay. I wasn't in bed yet. Do you want to know what I decided?"

"Yes, but I have something to say to you first. I want to apologize."

"What for?"

"For being a lousy dad for the past few years."

"You haven't been a lousy dad."

It was a token protest, and they both knew it. "I've been afraid of losing you, I guess. Afraid that you'd forget all about me out there in Oregon."

"I'd never forget about you. How could I?"

He smiled with relief. "I have this habit—not a good one—of pushing people away. I think it's because I want to keep them from hurting me."

"I wouldn't ever hurt you, Dad."

"I know you wouldn't, Trace. It's not your fault. Having you so far away hurts. Not being able to see you as often as I'd like hurts. Sometimes people do stupid things trying to protect themselves. I'm sorry."

"It's okay," she said softly.

Tears stung his eyes. A lump the size of Alaska burned his throat. "I'd like to start changing things between us. That's one of the reasons I want you to come to visit. But I need to be honest with you before you give me your answer. There's someone I'd like you to meet while you're here."

"A girlfriend?"

"Yes, but this one's different. Her name's Sharon, and she has a couple of daughters about your age."

"Are you getting married again?" She didn't sound happy.

"I don't know. It's too early to think about that yet. We've just started seeing each other."

"So, is this visit *her* idea?"

"No. In fact, she doesn't even know I've asked you to come. This is between you and me, Trace. No one else."

"Promise?"

"Yes, of course."

She paused for several heart-stopping minutes. "I don't think I want to meet her."

Gabe tried not to sound disappointed. "All right. You wouldn't have to meet her this time." There'd be other times, he assured himself.

"Okay, then. I'll come."

Disappointment vanished. "That's great. I'll make reservations and mail you the tickets."

"Does Grandma know I'm coming?"

"Not yet. I didn't want to get her hopes up if

you said no. But I'll call her as soon as we hang up, okay?"

"Okay. And Dad?"

"Yeah, Trace?"

"You'll keep your promise, won't you?"

"Nothing will make me break it." He paused, then added, "I love you, Tracy."

"I love you, too."

His heart soared, and he grinned as he replaced the receiver. Worry flickered when he thought about Sharon and the promise he'd made, but he pushed it aside. She had children of her own. Surely, she'd understand.

BATTLING A HEADACHE, Sharon stirred ground beef for dinner and watched Emilee frowning over an algebra problem at the dining-room table. Christa's music—upbeat and almost frantic— drifted down from the upper level. Downstairs, Gabe's power hammer accompanied the country music playing on his radio.

The hammer popped three times in rapid succession, then stopped. Sharon rubbed her forehead and stirred the ground beef once more. She found herself wishing for some peace and quiet, if only for a few minutes.

In the nearly two weeks since she and Gabe had decided to see each other, Emilee and Christa's easy acceptance of him in their lives had left

Sharon slightly off balance and more than a little worried. With the relationship so new and uncertain, she couldn't let them get too attached to him. They'd had enough heartache.

She glanced at Emilee again and realized with a start she was watching her. "What's wrong, Mom?"

"Nothing a little aspirin wouldn't cure."

Emilee accepted that without question. She made a face and leaned back in her chair. "I hate algebra."

"Are you having trouble?"

"Yes. It's all this stupid stuff about the distributive property. I just don't get it."

Sharon couldn't even remember what the distributive property was, but she forced a confident smile. "Do you want some help?"

"No, it's okay. I know you don't like math."

"That doesn't matter. If we read the instructions, it might jog my memory."

"I've read them," Emilee whined. "And I still don't get it." She pushed away from the table and came to stand behind Sharon. "What are you making?"

"Aunt Dena's casserole."

"The one with the chow mein noodles on top? Cool. Do you want me to do it?"

Sharon scowled at her. "No. I want you to finish your homework."

Emilee sighed and turned away. "Fine. But Gabe says sometimes if you walk away from a problem, it helps clear your mind."

The pounding in Sharon's head climbed another notch. "Gabe doesn't know how often you try to get out of doing your algebra." She started to turn down the burner just as Gabe's footsteps sounded on the stairs.

Instead of worrying about dinner or algebra, she found herself watching the landing. He appeared a second later and, as always, the sight of him wiped everything else out of her mind. "Are you through for tonight?"

He propped one hand on his tool belt and tilted back the brim of his baseball cap to see her better. "No. I just have a couple of questions to ask you about the electrical and phone outlets. If you have a minute, I need you to show me exactly where you want them."

Emilee popped up again. "I'll come with you."

"You've got homework to finish," Sharon said, waving her back into her seat. And to Gabe, "Can it wait a few minutes? Emilee needs some help, and I still need to put the casserole in the oven."

"Sure. Take your time." He perched on a stool and settled in to watch. "Smells good."

"It is good," Emilee assured him. "You

should stay for dinner. There's always more than enough."

Sharon peeled an onion and watched his re-action from beneath lowered lids. Maybe that's why she kept holding back. She knew how he felt about domestic life—her life—and frankly, his attitude worried her. Of course, this new re-lationship was wonderful. More than wonderful. But with such fundamental differences between them, she couldn't help wondering how long it would last.

Gabe stole a glance at Sharon and smiled slowly. "I'd love to stay…if it's okay with your mom. Her cooking always smells good."

"Of course it's okay," she said, positioning the onion on the chopping block. "We'd love to have you."

Something flickered behind his eyes, but she didn't let herself analyze it. "Well, then, I sup-pose the outlets can wait until after dinner. Do you want me to set the table?" He glanced at his hands and grimaced. "After I wash up, of course."

"Not yet. Emilee still has to finish her algebra."

Gabe disappeared into the bathroom and came back a minute later smelling of soap. "Algebra, huh?"

Emilee worked up a pathetic nod. "I hate it. I don't get it, no matter how hard I try."

Sharon waited for boredom or irritation to cross his face. Instead, he moved to the table and sat beside Emilee. "You want some help?"

Emilee's forlorn expression faded. "Are you serious? You know about the distributive property?"

"Sure. Algebra's really not that hard once you learn the tricks."

As quickly as Emilee had turned down Sharon's offer, she shoved the book toward Gabe and propped up her chin with both hands to listen. Sharon pushed down an unexpected flash of envy and told herself not to be ridiculous. She'd never been good at algebra. Emilee knew that; she didn't want Sharon's help.

Concentrating on her own work, she added the remaining ingredients to the casserole. Emilee blossomed under Gabe's attention. And why not? Sharon couldn't remember Nick ever helping the girls with homework. He'd always been too busy. Of course, they'd jump at the chance to have a father's attention.

As if Gabe could feel her thinking about him, he glanced up and his lips curved into a slow, lopsided smile. Her heart skipped a beat. But even that couldn't erase the growing knot of apprehension.

Gabe wasn't the girls' father, she reminded herself. Nor was he likely ever to be their stepfather. No matter how much she loved him, their future together was far from certain.

She dragged her gaze away and tried to pay attention to the vegetables. Once, she caught the hint of a frown on his face, but she didn't let herself meet his gaze. And Emilee's whoop of excitement at calculating a problem on her own dragged his attention away again.

"This is incredible," she said, throwing her arms around Gabe's neck and kissing his cheek. "I actually understand it. Mr. Hatcher will probably think I cheated."

Gabe blushed deeply at the show of affection and his eyes glowed with pleasure. His patience with Emilee touched Sharon deeply at the same time the girl's growing attachment to him frightened her. Didn't he understand the kind of risk he was asking her to take by insinuating himself so fully into their lives?

Later, as they ate together, with the girls obviously enjoying the charade of them as a family, Sharon's uneasiness grew. When Gabe hinted that someone needed to do the dishes—and they eagerly volunteered—Sharon battled another flash of irritation. And when he stopped Emilee from giving Raoul a scrap of meat from the table, she'd had enough.

"Go ahead, Emilee," she said firmly. "A small piece of hamburger isn't going to hurt Raoul."

Emilee looked to Gabe for approval, and Sharon's temper flared. She spooned a piece of hamburger from the casserole and dropped it into Raoul's dish. "We've fed him scraps since he was a kitten."

"You could make him sick," Gabe said.

"We never feed him anything but meat and an occasional spoonful of ice cream," she informed him, hunkering down beside Raoul's dish and trying to maintain some control over the tension that seemed to be taking control of her.

"You can't be this upset over the cat," Gabe said. "What's wrong?"

"I'm not upset," she lied. "I'm just not going to stop feeding Raoul a piece of hamburger now and then just because you don't approve."

Behind her, one of the girls clanked a dish too hard on the counter. The water shut off suddenly. Even Raoul obviously sensed something amiss. Keeping his tail close, he skittered from the room and up the stairs.

Gabe's eyes darkened. "You're mad at me for that?"

"I'm not mad," she snapped, but even she could hear the lie in her answer. She wrapped her arms tightly around herself and turned away. "It's not the cat."

"Then, what is it?"

She glanced at Emilee and Christa, who pretended to be fascinated with the dishes. "Maybe we should go into the other room."

Gabe followed her into the living room and waited, silently, while she took a moment to pull herself together.

Strangely, that helped restore some of her common sense. Nick had hated waiting for her to sort through her emotions, and his snide comments had usually resulted in a screaming match. "I'm sorry," she said at last. "I guess I'm just tense. Bad day."

Gabe closed the distance between them and took her gently by the shoulders. "You weren't tense a little while ago. Obviously, I did something to upset you. I'd like to know what it was."

She didn't know how to respond to that. Nick would have accepted her apology and dropped it there. "It's not anything you did. Not really. But that whole thing with the homework and then dinner…" It wasn't coming out right, but she didn't know how to explain.

"You didn't want me to help Emilee?"

"I *did*. I can't even begin to tell you how much I appreciated it. Seeing her so pleased meant the world to me."

"But?"

"But…" She took a deep breath and made herself go on. "But I don't understand what's happening. I thought you didn't like this kind of life, yet here you are having dinner with the family, doing homework with the kids, assigning chores… If you're trying to win over the kids, you can stop. They already adore you."

His eyes darkened with concern. "Is that what you think I'm doing?"

"I don't know." She rubbed her arms briskly and put a little distance between them. She couldn't think with him standing so close. "Sometimes I wonder if you're just amusing yourself by playing house for a little while."

"I'm not playing, Sharon. I'm trying to change."

She listened for the first hint of anger. Surprisingly, she didn't hear it. "Why?"

"Because I want to give this thing between us a fair shake, and I wish you would, too."

"You don't think I am?"

"I think you're too afraid to give it a chance." He moved closer and pulled her close.

Strength and comfort radiated from him, but Sharon resisted it. "I don't want you to change for me. That would be asking for trouble."

Gabe pressed a soft kiss to her forehead and another to her cheek. "I'm not doing it for you. I'm doing it for us."

Us. Did he really mean there was an "us"? Or was she allowing her own hopes to color her interpretation?

Gabe studied her face for what felt like forever. His eyes bored into her. "I said something else wrong, didn't I?"

"I just don't want to rush into anything."

"And you think I'm rushing?"

"I feel like I'm on a runaway train and there's nothing I can do to stop it."

He traced one finger along her cheek. "You can stop it anytime you want to, Sharon. I know it must be frightening to get involved with someone after being on your own for so long. If you think I'm moving too quickly, just say so."

Relief made her feel weak. She sent him a grateful smile. "Really?"

"Absolutely. Just don't run away from me."

"I'm not running," she whispered. "I'm just walking fast."

"Then I'll slow down." He brushed another kiss to her forehead and moved away as if he intended to leave. "I'll call you tomorrow."

"Yes. Please."

With one last smile, he left the room. She curled into the corner of the couch and listened to him say goodbye to the girls. Only when she heard the door shut behind him, did she dare to analyze her feelings. He was going to call her

tomorrow. Part of her was filled with anticipation, but part—perhaps the larger part—was
warning her that things *were* moving too fast.
The bottom line was she didn't trust her own
judgment when it came to men. Gabe seemed
almost perfect, but she'd been fooled before.

CHAPTER THIRTEEN

STARTLED BY A KNOCK on her office door, Sharon set aside the stale sandwich she'd been munching while she graded term papers and tried to blink her eyes back into focus. "Yes? Who is it?"

The door opened and Liberty Young peered inside. She looked exhausted. Dark circles shadowed her red eyes and her usually fiery hair looked limp and lifeless. "Do you have a minute?"

"Yes, of course." Sharon motioned the girl toward an empty chair. "What can I do for you?"

"It's about the article I wrote for our last assignment." Liberty perched on the edge of the chair and twisted her hands in her lap. "I didn't do so well, did I?"

"It wasn't one of your best efforts," Sharon admitted. "In fact, I've been surprised by your grades all semester. You used to be one of my top students."

"I've already done all this stuff once," Liberty

reminded her. "It's not fair that I have to do it again."

Sharon didn't want to get into that discussion again. "I understand your frustration, but I'd expect your performance to be just the opposite. You should be able to ace the course since you've already been through it once."

"I know, but I don't have *time* to do it this semester, Mrs. Lawrence. I'm married now. I've got a house to clean and meals to fix and—"

"And you're going to school and working part-time," Sharon cut in. "Doesn't your husband do his share of things around the house?"

Liberty flicked a wounded glance at her. "Not really. He works really hard, and he goes to school, so he's tired when he comes home."

"You work, too. And with your schoolwork, I'm sure you come home tired."

"Sure, I do. But…" Liberty lowered her gaze and studied her hands. "It's not just that, Mrs. Lawrence. It's everything. I never get any time to myself. From the minute David walks in the door, he wants me right there with him. And if I try to do something else—like study—he pouts." She lifted her gaze again. "It's driving me crazy."

Sharon fought the familiar tide of panic when she thought of her own changing life. She told herself that wouldn't happen to her. She and

Gabe were older, and hopefully wiser, than Liberty and her husband. "Surely, he understands that you need to study," she said, hoping she sounded more confident than she felt.

"He says he does, but he doesn't like me to do it. I've tried doing my homework before he gets home, but then dinner's so late we're both starving and in bad moods by the time I finally get it on the table. Besides, money's so tight, I need to get a full-time job. We can't really afford for me to stay in school right now."

Sharon warned herself not to get involved in the girl's private life. She wasn't a marriage counselor, and she had no business offering advice. Still, she hated to watch a young woman with promise fall by the wayside. "But you can't really afford to toss aside your own future, can you?" she asked cautiously.

Liberty lifted her chin and met Sharon's gaze. "There'll be time for me to finish school after we've made some money."

"I said the same thing once," Sharon told her. "I let my ex-husband talk me into leaving school, but I didn't go back until after we got divorced."

"That won't happen to me."

Sharon chewed her bottom lip and told herself again to pull back before she got in too deep.

"You're one of my best students. You could have a brilliant future."

"I *will* have," Liberty insisted. "Just not right away. David and I have already agreed that I'm coming back as soon as he graduates. I'm a wife now, Mrs. Lawrence. I can't just think about myself anymore."

"I'm not suggesting that you should think only of yourself," Sharon assured her. "But you can't forget about yourself, either. Unless you have your own life and follow your own interests, you'll have very little to offer your husband or your children, if you decide to start a family later."

Liberty's eyes flashed. "I know what you're trying to say, but that's not going to happen to me. I won't let it." She gathered her things and stood. "You watch. I'll be back in a couple of years."

Sharon tried to smile. "I hope so."

Liberty crossed to the door, then turned back to face her. "Things are different than they used to be, Mrs. Lawrence. Women don't give up everything like they used to."

Didn't they? Wasn't that exactly what Liberty was doing? Sharon recognized all the signs. She'd done exactly the same thing for Nick.

Nick's betrayal had hurt her, but she'd survived. She wasn't at all sure she'd be able to survive another one. And everything she knew about Gabe warned her that she could be exposing herself to just that.

JUGGLING AN ARMFUL of books, Emilee dodged students on their way to lunch. She couldn't take time to eat, no matter how hungry she was. She and Christa had plans for their lunch hour. Gabe was still worried that their mom would find out about the Man Plan. He'd talked to Emilee again last night and she'd had to promise that she and Christa would sort everything out. They'd find everyone who knew about the plan and call the whole thing off before lunch ended.

Smiling, she hugged her books tighter. She liked knowing that Gabe worried about their mom's feelings. And she really liked seeing her mother so happy. Who would have guessed that her mom would fall for someone like Gabe? Or that he'd fall in love back?

In fact, Emilee couldn't wait for Gabe to pop the question. She knew he would one of these days. She just hoped he'd do it soon.

She drew to a stop in front of Christa's locker and checked the crowded hallway. No sign of Christa yet. But she caught a glimpse of her friend Derek making his way toward the opposite end of the corridor.

Clutching her books tightly, she hurried after

him and caught up just before he turned the corner. "Derek? Do you have a minute?"

"For you? Anytime." He slung his letter jacket over his shoulder and gave her a once-over. "What's up?"

Emilee suddenly wished she'd taken time to check her hair and makeup. "You remember when Matt asked you to help Christa and me find a boyfriend for our mom?"

"Sure. But I haven't been able to come up with anybody yet. The only single guy I know is about ninety-five years old."

"It doesn't matter," Emilee assured him. "We don't need you to look anymore."

"Are you serious? Somebody found her a guy already?"

"She found one on her own."

"Cool." Derek fished a pair of sunglasses from his T-shirt pocket and settled them over his eyes. "But that's going to disappoint a lot of people who are hoping to win the contest."

Emilee's smile faded. "Contest? What contest?"

"You know...whoever finds a guy for your mom gets a date with you or Christa for the Spring Fling."

Emilee stared at him, openmouthed. "Who told you that?"

"Matt."

Derek must have misunderstood. "Not that it matters now, but there wasn't any contest. Matt just wanted to take Christa to the Valentine's dance, and we told him he could if he found Mom a date, too."

"Okay. If you say so." Derek shrugged casually and checked his watch. "Look, I've gotta go. Some of the guys are waiting for me in the parking lot. We're going to McDonald's for lunch. Do you wanna come along?"

"I can't. Christa and I promised my mom's boyfriend that we'd tell everyone today. I still have to find Christa and tell a few other people."

"Okay." Derek moved his jacket to the other shoulder. "You want me to tell the guys I see?"

"No. There are only a few people who know about it, anyway. I'm sure Christa and I can find them all."

Derek pulled down his sunglasses and peered over the tops at her. "You're kidding, right?"

"No. I really need to stay here—"

"Not that," he said, cutting her off. "I mean about only a few people knowing. *Everybody* knows about it."

Emilee gaped at him. "But we only told a few people. It was supposed to be a secret."

"Some secret," Derek snorted. "It's probably the worst-kept secret I've ever heard. Some of the guys were talking about it at practice yesterday."

Emilee thought she might be sick. "Basketball practice?"

He nodded. "And Kelley Hill said he heard about it at the swim meet the other day."

"But—" Emilee *knew* she was going to be sick. "How did everybody find out?"

"Are you kidding? The winner gets a date with one of the Lawrence sisters. That's big news."

"That was never the deal," Emilee insisted.

"No? Well, that's what everybody thinks."

Emilee's stomach lurched. "You've got to help me straighten this out."

"Me? Why me?"

"Because you can go into the boys' locker room, and I can't."

Derek didn't look at all concerned. "Okay, I guess. I'll do what I can. But I don't know how much good it will do." He put a hand on her shoulder. "If you really want to call it off, maybe you ought to make an announcement on the PA system. It'd be a whole lot quicker."

Feeling slightly nauseated, Emilee watched him leave, then started searching for Christa. They had to fix this *now*.

GABE FINISHED SHAVING, checked his reflection in the mirror and decided he looked presentable.

He had a plan for tonight, and in a few minutes he'd put it into action. He'd expected his relationship with Sharon to grow over the past three weeks. Instead, she seemed to be pulling away. Could she be having second thoughts?

Tonight, he intended to find out. He'd asked her to have dinner with him, and once they were alone—without kids, assignments, test papers, dishes, housework, contracts, electrical outlets, light fixtures and the cat to come between them—he'd draw her out.

He pulled on his new shirt, checked his reflection once more and grabbed his keys and the single white rose he'd picked up on his way home. He pulled the door closed behind him, ignoring the blinking light on his answering machine. Nothing was going to delay him tonight.

Whistling softly, he drove across town and smiled when he realized he had the jitters, just like a kid on the way to pick up his first date. He'd never felt this way about any woman. Nor had he ever been so willing, even eager, to change.

When he reached Sharon's house, he parked in the driveway for the first time and jogged up the walk to the front door. No garage-door entrance for him tonight.

Emilee answered and gave a yelp of surprise

when she saw him standing there. "You look *good*. Christa, come here, quick. Look at Gabe."

Grinning, he held out his arms and turned around slowly for Christa. "Do I pass inspection?"

"Are you kidding?" she said with a laugh. "You're a total hunk. Mom's gonna flip."

He certainly hoped so. "Where is she?"

"Upstairs getting ready." Emilee grabbed his arm and tugged him into the living room. "I'll tell her you're here."

Not surprisingly, Christa hurried off to help. He could imagine them sitting on Sharon's bed while she dressed, brushed her hair or sprayed perfume behind her ears. He bent to scratch Raoul, then settled into one of the wingback chairs to wait. He ran through his plans for the evening one more time. Dinner and dancing, candlelight and wine. He'd never known them to fail.

Within minutes, Emilee came back alone. Some of her excitement had faded. "She'll be down in a few minutes."

Gabe studied her slight frown and the clouds in her eyes. "Is something wrong?"

"No." She shook her head quickly and dropped into a corner of the couch. "I don't know." She glanced at him. "You haven't done anything to upset her, have you? Like maybe telling her about the plan we had to find her a man?"

"Me?" He shook his head quickly. "No."

"Are you sure? She's acting weird."

Disappointment flickered in his chest. He thought back over their earlier conversation, but he couldn't think of any mistakes he'd made. "I'm sure."

Emilee gave that some thought. "I just don't understand her sometimes. She—" She broke off and glanced over her shoulder at the sound of approaching voices. "Shh— Here she comes."

Suddenly nervous, Gabe stood and watched the door. Sharon came into the room slowly, almost hesitantly, and he could see by the set of her face what Emilee meant. Other than the wariness, she looked beautiful in a silky flowered dress. Soft dark curls cascaded to her shoulders. Her eyes caught the muted glow of the lamp.

Somehow, he managed to speak. "You look beautiful."

A shy smile curved her lips, but she didn't meet his gaze. "Thank you." She let her eyes light on him for a moment, then looked away again. "You look very nice."

"Almost respectable, huh?"

That earned another smile, this one slightly

more relaxed than the first. "Almost," she teased.

Some of his confidence returned. He offered her the rose, and when she lifted it to inhale its scent, his heart leaped. But when she looked at him again, the shutter had dropped in front of her eyes.

He motioned for Emilee and Christa to leave them alone, then asked, "Is something wrong?"

She took so long to answer, his heart began to thud in his throat. "No," she said at last. "I guess not."

She *guessed?* That didn't sound very promising.

Sharon breathed in the rose's scent again and lifted her eyes to meet his. "Actually, I'm glad we're going to have a chance to be alone tonight…"

Yes!

"…because we need to talk."

No!

Yes, he wanted to draw her out about their relationship, but the words sounded ominous coming from her.

He stole another look at the resolute line of her jaw, the stiff set of her shoulders, the dark light in her eyes and decided he didn't want to know. Unfortunately, once a woman announced the need to *talk,* no man could escape. Gabe had learned that the hard way. So he'd listen to whatever she had to say. But he wouldn't let even bad news discourage him. One way or another, he intended to win her over.

GABE FOLLOWED SHARON and the restaurant's hostess through the crowded tables of the Blue Iguana to a corner booth. He waited for Sharon to choose her side of the booth, then slid onto the seat opposite her. So far, so good. He sat back in his seat and smiled at her. "I hope you're hungry."

She tried to smile, but it didn't make it all the way to her eyes. "Yes," she said softly. "I am." She linked her hands together on the table. "Gabe, I want to talk to you about the girls. I'm worried about them and I know Emilee and Christa talk to you sometimes. Do you have any idea what they're up to?"

If that's all she wanted to talk about, he could still salvage the evening. Maybe he should tell her about the girls' scheme. And maybe he should just shoot himself in the foot and get it over with. He tried to look confused. "Up to? You think they're up to something?"

Sharon's eyebrows knit and she tilted her head to one side. "They're behaving strangely again as if they're hiding something from me."

Gabe wedged a tortilla chip into his mouth and chewed thoughtfully. "Is your birthday coming up? Maybe they're planning a surprise."

She shook her head. "No. My birthday's not until August."

"Mother's Day?"

"That's two months away."

"Saint Patrick's Day is in a couple of weeks…"

"Yes," she said slowly. "But we're not Irish, and they don't plan surprises for Saint Patrick's Day."

"It's probably nothing," he assured her. "Maybe one of them has a new boyfriend they don't want to tell you about."

Sharon took a chip, but she didn't eat it right away. "I don't think so. They always tell me about the guys they meet."

Scratch that. He didn't want to upset her further. "It's probably nothing," he said again. "They seem fine to me."

"Then they haven't said anything to you?"

Gabe gave her a look of wide-eyed innocence and ate another chip. "Relax, Sharon. You've got great kids. But let's talk about us now. This is the first chance I've had to get you alone. I'd rather talk about—" he broke off and smiled up into the face of a dark-haired waitress wearing a frilly Mexican folk dress "—what you want for dinner. Are you having the cheese enchiladas again?"

Sharon gave the menu a cursory glance and handed it to the waitress. "That sounds good."

"Give her three of them," Gabe said, "so she can have leftovers." That might earn a favorable mark or two. At this point, he'd take anything he could get. "And I'll have the large combination plate." He handed both menus to the waitress. "And bring us two Tecatas."

Sharon held up a hand. "I'm not sure I should have anything to drink—" She paused, sent him her first genuine smile of the evening, and shrugged. "On the other hand, maybe I should. Maybe then everything will make sense again."

Gabe doubted that, unless the Tecata made her a mind reader. "So is that what you wanted to talk about? The kids?"

Sharon nodded slowly. "Yes. But not just about my kids. Let's talk about your daughter."

"About Tracy?" Gabe leaned back in his chair. "What do you want to know?"

"It seems to me that you know everything about me and about my daughters, but I know next to nothing about yours."

"I guess I haven't really talked about her much, have I? But you're wrong about me knowing all about you. There are a million things I don't know."

She adjusted her napkin on her lap. "So, tell me about Tracy. She's fifteen?"

"Yes. The sad thing is, I don't feel as if I know much about her anymore. When she lived with me, she was quiet and fairly shy. She didn't have many friends. But the last time I talked to her, she mentioned her friends. In fact, she hesitated to come and visit me over spring break *because* of her friends."

"Does she look like you?"

"A little, but she looks more like her mother."

"Do you have a picture with you?"

He pulled his wallet from his back pocket, opened it to the most recent picture he had and handed it to Sharon.

She studied it for a minute, then gave it back to him. "She's very pretty."

"Thank you." Pride warmed him clear through. "I think so, too."

Sharon smiled softly. "She's coming to see you over spring break, then? You must be looking forward to that."

Gabe nodded. "Yes, I am. But I'm a little anxious, too."

That seemed to surprise Sharon. "Why?"

"Because I haven't seen her in so long, and things are kind of touchy between us."

"I have trouble believing that. You're great with Emilee and Christa. I'm sure they'd love to meet her while she's here." Sharon sipped water and set the glass back on the table, running her fingers over the condensation for a second before she added, "I would, too."

Gabe stiffened, realizing a moment of truth had arrived. "I—" He broke off and tried again. "It may be some time before she's ready to meet you all."

Hurt filled Sharon's eyes. "Why?"

Gabe smiled, hoping to soften the sting a little. "It's been so long since she and I have seen each other. I think she's really nervous about being with me. And she has to visit with her grandparents. I kind of promised her we'd wait before I introduce her to you."

"Well, I can't say I'm not disappointed, but I do understand," Sharon said.

"Thank you," Gabe said and then tried again to change the subject. "I don't want to talk about the kids all night. I'd like to know more about you."

Sharon's eyes softened. "Okay. What would you like to know?"

He settled on something insignificant. "What kinds of movies do you like?"

"Romantic movies are my favorites, but I like almost everything except horror. What about you?"

"Adventure, mostly. Stuff with lots of action." He let a moment of silence pass, then thought of another question. "Do you like to travel?"

"Very much. Do you?"

Gabe nodded and dunked a tortilla chip into salsa. "Where's your favorite place?"

She gave that some thought. He watched the way her eyes shifted to one side as her hair caught the light. Her beauty overwhelmed him sometimes.

She shifted her gaze back to his and smiled. "I loved New England. The atmosphere is so… charming. The air even feels different. The huge rivers, the small towns with their town squares and white churches. The coast with its tiny fishing villages… I loved the confusion of Boston, and the almost reverent feeling I got when we went someplace historical. It was as if those people were all still there, wanting us to understand what life was like for them and what they'd dreamed of for us." She let out a wistful sigh. "What's your favorite place?"

"Alaska."

"Why?"

"Because it's huge and raw and bigger than life."

Sharon smiled. "I've never been there."

"Everyone should visit Alaska at least once in their life." And he'd love to be the one to take her there.

"Maybe someday." She toyed with her napkin for a moment, but some of the tension seemed to leave her. "My turn. What do you do when you're not working?"

"There's a bar close to my house. Milago's. I usually drop in there after work for a few minutes." Never before had that sounded as pathetic as it did to him now. "What do you do?"

"I'm usually at home doing laundry or cooking dinner or cleaning something." She brushed a strand of hair away from her face and let her gaze travel toward the front windows. "But sometimes I wonder what I'd do if the girls didn't live with me."

"What do you think you'd do?"

She shrugged. "I've been a mother for almost half my life. It's hard to imagine anything else."

"Maybe you should. After all, they're not going to be around forever. One of these days, you're going to be on your own."

Her eyes filled with panic. "That thought scares me. Isn't that horrible?"

He put a hand over hers and rubbed his thumb across her palm. "Not at all. I think it's probably normal."

"Sometimes I think I've been a mother for so long, I've forgotten who *I* am." She smiled wryly. "I'll probably turn into one of those over-bearing mothers who can't let their kids live their own lives."

"I don't think that will happen," he assured her.

"I wish I could be that certain. Sometimes—" She broke off and her eyes filled with doubt. "Sometimes, especially lately, I worry that I'm already doing it."

"You worry that you're interfering in your kids' lives?"

Sharon shook her head slowly. "Not that, exactly. But I do wonder if I'm living my life through them."

Gabe sandwiched her hand between both of his, surprised to find it felt exactly right. "You don't have to do that, you know."

She started to say something more, but broke off and waited while the waitress came to check on them. When they were alone again, she said, "I've always admired people who take risks, but I've always taken the safe route."

He scowled at her. "I don't believe that."

"It's true. I married the first man who came along and had two children almost immediately. And I've spent my life hiding behind them."

"But you got a divorce," he argued. "And you

went back to school and struck out on your own. Those were all risks."

She shook her head. "No, they weren't. Not really. If Nick hadn't left me, I'd probably still be with him. Miserable, but still there. And going back to school… Well, that was a necessity."

"No, it wasn't. You could have made other choices."

She looked doubtful.

"You could have taken another job that didn't require an education. There are plenty of them out there. Or you could have jumped into marriage again and let some man support you."

"I'd never get married just for security."

"That proves what I'm saying, doesn't it? There are half a dozen easy choices you could have made, but you didn't. You took a risk instead."

Her lips curved softly. "Maybe you're right."

"I know I'm right." He sent her a playful scowl. "I'm not sure I like this honest self-analysis. It makes you sad. Besides, if you're going to do it, I'll have to do it, too."

She laughed. "Well, that would be terrible."

Gabe's smile grew. "I have a plan for after dinner that will just about guarantee we won't have any more soul-searching conversations."

She laughed again, and he liked knowing he'd

made her happy, if only for a moment. "What do you have in mind?"

"Dancing."

"Dancing?" Her eyes widened and her smile faltered. "If you think dancing will keep me from soul-searching, you're wrong. But I did say I wanted to start taking chances, so I might as well start tonight. After all, I'm here with you, aren't I? I've already taken one."

"Are you saying that coming here with me tonight is a risk?"

She held his gaze steadily. "Isn't it? It's taking our relationship in a different direction...out of the safe zone of kids and work—"

Yes, he admitted silently, it was a risk—for both of them. He'd never had a relationship that scared him half as much as this one did. Nor one that made it so difficult to keep his mind and heart detached. But this—

He drew a steadying breath and stared into Sharon's eyes. He'd only kissed her a couple of times. Yet he felt a stronger attachment to her than he'd ever felt to any woman in his life. And he knew, suddenly and without question, that he wouldn't be able to pull back this time. Even if he'd stood up and walked out of the restaurant right that minute, he'd have to come back to her eventually. He no longer had a choice.

He was in love for the first time in his life.

CHAPTER FOURTEEN

WITH GROWING RESIGNATION, Sharon watched
the emotions playing on Gabe's face. His eyes
lit for a moment, then darkened again. That lopsided smile toyed with his lips. She'd accepted
his invitation to dinner, thinking that this might
be their first and last real date. In all the discus-
sions she'd had with herself, she'd concluded that
she had to put an end to their relationship before
it went any further. But the sight of him holding
that single white rose had been her undoing.

She loved him. No matter how hard she resisted, she couldn't change that. Wise or foolish, she longed for his company, for the sound
of his voice and the deep rumble of his laugh.
But all her longing didn't change the facts. He'd
be a great diversion, but he wasn't made to be
permanent.

To Sharon's relief, the waitress chose that
moment to bring their food. They both began
eating, breaking the silence only to comment on
their meals, the strolling mariachi band or some
other inane subject. Her mind skipped ahead to

the time when he'd hold her in his arms on the dance floor, then careened toward the inevitable end of their relationship. An end that would hurt her and destroy the girls.

After Gabe paid the bill, he led her toward his truck. She walked slowly, breathing in his scent as they walked, savoring the feel of him beside her. He opened her door and waited while she settled herself inside, and she tried to still her trembling hands when he slid onto the seat beside her.

He put the key into the ignition, then turned to look at her. He searched her face with his eyes, robbing her of breath. She felt as if her heart had vaulted into her throat.

Slowly, he released the key and reached for her. Ignoring the warning bells, she ran one hand to his shoulder and left it there as he leaned in to kiss her.

"This is pretty sad, isn't it? I feel like a teenager kissing you in my car," he said.

The mention of teenagers brought reality crashing down around her again. She pulled back and tried to remain rational. "I think I'd better forget the dancing and go home," she forced herself to say.

He stiffened and disappointment filled his eyes. "Are you sure?"

She nodded, battling the tears she didn't want

him to see. "It's a bad idea. I think we both know that. The kids will be wondering where I am, anyway."

"Yeah." He ground the key in the ignition. "We wouldn't want to worry them."

Sharon closed her eyes, willing the tears to go away. He'd gotten the message loud and clear, and she'd lost him. She could hear it in his voice and see it in his posture as he drove. From what she'd been told about him, Gabe Malone was not used to being rejected. By this time next year, he probably wouldn't even remember her name.

SHARON PUSHED THE BUTTON to open the garage door and waited impatiently for it to lift so she could drive the car inside. She'd been in a foul mood all day—even she couldn't deny that—and now that she was home, her mood took a downswing.

Since Saturday, she'd tried to put Gabe out of her mind. She'd worked hard, graded exam papers, she'd even spent her lunch hour researching a new textbook, but even while she'd carried on conversations with other people, the memory of that night had tormented her. As she'd lectured her classes, the look on his face had danced through her mind.

She pulled into the garage, shut off the car and started to gather her things from the seat beside her. Before she could get out of the car, the door to the house opened and Emilee stepped into the garage—barefoot.

"You're home early," Emilee called as she took mincing steps toward the car.

Sharon nodded and climbed out to face her. "Am I?"

"A little." Emilee brushed a kiss to her cheek and reached for her briefcase. "I would have started dinner, but I didn't know what you'd planned to cook."

For the first time in a long time, Sharon hadn't planned anything. In fact, she hadn't given it a thought. She worked up a smile and pulled a suggestion out of thin air. "That's because I thought we'd go out for dinner. How does that sound?"

She expected Emilee to look excited. Instead, her eyes narrowed and her smile faded. "You want to go out?"

"I thought we would." She took a long look at Emilee's expression. "Don't you want to?"

"But…" Emilee looked away for a second, but when she turned back, she wore a smile. "But won't Gabe be here tonight?"

"I don't know."

"Didn't he call you last night?"

"No, he didn't." She hadn't expected him to—

she knew he'd had family plans—but his silence still hurt.

"Why not?"

Sharon stalled by pulling her purse from the car. But in the end, she decided it made sense to tell the girls the truth. "I don't think Gabe and I will be seeing each other anymore."

Emilee gaped at her. "Why not?"

"Things just didn't work out," Sharon said, stepping into the house. Music pounded from the living room, scattering her thoughts like petals in the wind.

"Mom—" Emilee trailed her. "You can't say something like that and then walk away. What happened?"

Sharon set her things on the kitchen counter and turned to face her. "We're too different, Emilee. It wouldn't have lasted, anyway." She walked into the living room and lowered the volume on the stereo.

"Mom and Gabe broke up," Emilee said to Christa before Sharon could get a word out.

The look of horror on Christa's face matched Emilee's. "No way."

Sharon stared from one to the other. "For heaven's sake, you two. We weren't ever *together*. We had one date."

Emilee ticked her tongue in irritation. "Yeah?

Well, that doesn't matter. He's crazy about you anyway."

"Besides," Christa said, "you're perfect for each other."

"We're not perfect for each other," Sharon argued. "We're too different."

"Yeah, but—" Emilee didn't finish her thought. A knock on the back door cut her off. Her head jerked up and she shared an elated smile with Christa. "It's him."

Sharon's heart immediately shot into overdrive and her hands, traitors that they were, began to tremble. She chided herself silently and stayed right where she was, even though every instinct she had urged her to at least move into the kitchen so she could see him.

Christa looked at her as if she expected her to do something. When Sharon didn't move, she bolted to her feet and raced from the room with Emilee hot on her heels.

Sharon heard Emilee open the door and Gabe's voice drifting through the house toward her. She forced aside the childish longing and curled up in the chair to keep herself from giving in to her urges.

To her dismay, she heard his footsteps moving through the house, growing steadily closer.

She closed her eyes and willed herself to be strong. But she knew what would happen. She'd see his face and hear his voice and she'd throw caution and intelligence and common sense right out the window.

He filled the doorway. She could see him from the corner of her eye. He took a step toward her, and the soft scent of roses filled the air. Before she could stop herself, she glanced toward him. He held a vase with a dozen roses in one hand, and something remarkably close to embarrassment colored his face.

The gesture touched her more than she wanted to admit.

He held the vase toward her uncertainly. "These are for you."

"Thank you." She took the vase and tried to keep her heart steady when their fingers brushed. Such relief washed over his face, she couldn't help smiling. She turned away so he wouldn't see it. "I'm surprised to see you."

His eyes widened. "Why?"

"Because… Because I—"

He hunkered down in front of her and took her free hand in his. To her amazement, he looked as nervous and uncertain as she felt. "Things felt like they were moving too fast. Am I right?"

She managed a hesitant nod.

"Oh, Sharon." He brushed her hand with his thumb, just the way he had the other night.

Softly. Tenderly. "Then let's slow everything down."

Her heart skipped a beat. Two. "Do you mean that?"

"Of course I mean it." He leaned up and kissed her gently. "I guess it's time I told you the truth."

Her heart stilled completely.

"I realized it on Saturday, but I was afraid to tell you."

Her hand trembled so violently, she thought she'd drop the vase.

"I love you, Sharon. I'm head over heels in love with you. And I want to make you happy. We can take this as slowly as you need to."

She buried her face in the roses and inhaled their fragrance. "Thank you."

"So? Are we friends again?"

She lifted her head and met his gaze. She knew the time had come to do what she feared most in the world. She had to let down the walls and open the gates to her heart. "Yes, of course," she whispered. "I love you, too."

SHARON SAT ON THE COUCH and watched Gabe with the girls. They were all on the floor, digging through the entertainment center, arguing good-naturedly about which movie they should watch. True to his word, he'd been moving slower over the past week, but it still felt too good to be true.

She forced that thought aside. She wouldn't let anything ruin this evening.

As if he sensed her thinking about him, Gabe rolled onto his back and grinned up at her. "Help me out, here. It's two against one."

"Which movies are you voting on?" she asked.

"The Green Zone." He held up the DVD and wriggled his eyebrows, then switched to the second one with a curl of his lip. "Or a chick flick."

Outraged, Emilee tried to snatch the DVDs away. "You're trying to influence her."

Sharon laughed aloud. "Don't worry about it, sweetheart. I think I can figure out which movie *he* wants on my own."

"So?" Christa leaned back on her hands. "Which do you vote for. And don't vote for *The Green Zone* just because he's your boyfriend."

"You can't honestly believe I'd do that," Sharon protested.

"I think you *should* do it," Gabe argued with a teasing scowl. "I think there should be one or two perks that go along with the job."

She studied his face closely, decided she didn't see any hidden agenda in his eyes and tried again to relax. "I'll bet you can all figure out which movie I'd rather see."

Gabe let out a groan and fell back to the floor. "Not another chick flick. Am I going to lose every vote we ever take?"

"Not every one," Sharon reminded him. "I voted with you for Chinese food."

Christa made a face. "And I ate it, even if I don't like whatever that stuff was you ordered."

Gabe got to his feet and started across the living room toward Sharon. "It was lo mein."

"It was soggy noodles," Christa teased. "I like the crisp ones."

Gabe mussed her hair affectionately. "Well, you're going to have to learn to like the soggy ones, aren't you?"

Sharon's heart stuttered as it always did when he hinted at a future together. Did she even want that?

Yes, she had to admit that she did. When she could put aside her fears, she knew that losing Gabe would hurt worse than anything she could imagine.

Christa's broad grin and the teasing face Emilee made at him told her the girls wanted that future, too. Sharon had run from it long enough.

He dropped onto the couch and draped an arm

loosely around her shoulders. "All right. I'll give in this time. But next time, I get to choose the movie." He hugged her close to him.

Emilee crawled across the floor and leaned against Sharon's legs. She sighed with contentment and beamed up at them. "This is perfect, isn't it?"

Gabe smiled into Sharon's eyes. "Yes, it is."

Sharon couldn't disagree. She didn't even try. She lost herself in the movie, and the slow lazy pattern Gabe traced along her shoulder with his thumb. She didn't even realize the doorbell rang until Emilee started to answer it.

She started to her feet, but when she saw a boy about Christa's age on the front porch, she relaxed against Gabe again. The boy motioned a man of about forty to stand beside him and peered over Emilee's shoulder into the house. "Hey, Emilee. Is that your mom?"

Gabe stiffened. Christa shot to her feet and raced to the door. Emilee tried to block the boy's line of vision.

Sharon's relaxed mood evaporated. "Is something wrong?"

"No," Emilee said quickly. Too quickly.

Sharon glanced at Gabe. A muscle in his jaw jumped and he drew his arm away slowly.

The boy stood on tiptoe to see inside. "I'm

Nathan Hawkes, and this is my mom's cousin, Pete."

Confused, Sharon acknowledged the introduction. Cousin Pete smiled, but he didn't say a word. Gabe made an odd noise in his throat.

Embarrassed by Emilee and Christa's bizarre behavior, Sharon stood quickly. "Please, come in. Are you a friend of Emilee's?"

Nathan flushed a deep red. "Not really."

"Oh, then you're Christa's friend."

"No." He sent a longing glance at Emilee that spoke volumes. "But we do go to the same school."

Emilee let out a sharp laugh and sent a meaningful look at her sister. "Why don't we talk outside, Christa?"

Christa started toward the door.

Nathan's face fell. "But we came to see your mom."

"Me?" Sharon tried to take a step closer, but Gabe took her arm and held her back.

"We need to talk."

His reaction confused her as much as Emilee and Christa's behavior did. "Not now."

"Yes." He held her gaze steadily. "*Now.* And I think the girls should join us."

Convinced that everyone had taken leave of their senses, Sharon looked from one to the other. Emilee was almost frantic, Christa strangely subdued and Gabe upset. "What's going on here?"

"We'll explain everything," Gabe assured her. "In the kitchen. If you gentlemen will excuse us for a minute…"

"But, we're here for the contest," Nathan protested.

"Contest?" Sharon looked at her daughters. "What contest?"

Neither of them said a word. But Nathan supplied the answer eagerly.

"You know. The one to find you a boyfriend."

Sharon stared at Gabe and her daughters in dismay. Emilee let out a cry of distress. Christa groaned. Gabe looked as if he wished he were somewhere else.

"What is he talking about?" Sharon asked.

"There isn't any contest," Emilee assured her.

Nathan's eager smile faltered. "But I heard—"

"Well, you heard wrong," Christa said quickly.

Gabe tried once more to pull Sharon from the room. "It's not as bad as you think. Come with me. We'll get this straightened out."

Sharon pulled her arm away. *"What contest?"*

"Everybody's talking about it," Nathan told her. "The guy who finds you a boyfriend gets a date with Emilee or Christa to the Spring Fling."

Christa clamped her hand over her mouth. Emilee dropped her head and groaned. And Gabe's shoulders slumped in defeat, but not before Sharon caught a hint of a smile.

"You've been trying to find me a boyfriend?" Sharon asked.

"Well, yes, but there wasn't ever a contest," Christa said sheepishly.

"Then why does Nathan think there is?"

"Because…" Emilee let out a heavy sigh. "Because we told some kids at school about it— we didn't want you to be alone for Valentine's Day—and they…well, they blew it all out of proportion."

"I see." Sharon turned to Gabe. "And you knew about this?"

Christa took a step toward her. "Don't blame him. It was all Emilee and me."

Emilee nodded eagerly. "That's right. He didn't do anything. Christa and I got the idea on New Year's Eve."

"You've been at this for over two months?" Sharon shook her head as if that might restore some order to her thoughts. When she realized that Nathan and cousin Pete were still waiting, she apologized and saw them to the door. When she'd closed it between them, she turned around with a disbelieving laugh. "You've been so worried about me that you'd go to those lengths to make sure I wasn't alone?"

Christa gave her a hopeful smile. "Well... yeah."

Gabe put his hands on her shoulders. "They really meant well."

"I know they did," Sharon said, turning to face him. "But they're not the only ones who have some explaining to do. Tell me, how did you find out about it? You and the girls must be closer than I realized."

"I overheard them planning it while I was measuring the basement on New Year's Eve. They weren't exactly pleased to find out I was down there."

Emilee dropped onto the couch with a sigh. "We were worried because we heard what Adelle said."

Sharon sat beside her. "What did Adelle say?"

Christa curled up on Sharon's other side. "Don't you remember? She said you were going to wind up alone forever."

"We didn't want that to happen," Emilee said softly. "We want you to be happy."

"I *am* happy," Sharon assured them.

"Yeah," Christa said. "You are now because of Gabe."

Sharon glanced up at him. "Please tell me that's not why you decided to get involved with me."

"No." He leaned down and traced a fingertip down her cheek. "Of course not. I got involved with you because you got under my skin."

Emilee let out a heavy sigh and rested her chin on her hands. "We're really sorry, Mom. We were only trying to help."

"I know that, but I didn't need help. I was doing just fine." Sharon rubbed the back of her neck and tried not to think about the difference Gabe had made in her life. "Just fill me in on everything so I know. Who did you have in mind?"

"Well, we thought about Steve's dad," Christa admitted after a moment.

"And Mr. Taylor," Emilee added sheepishly.

"The school nurse?" Sharon laughed in amazement. "*That's* why you faked the sprained ankle?"

Emilee nodded slowly. "And Matt's dad. And Brett at the bookstore."

"And Adam's uncle," Christa added.

"Ed the Egomaniac?" Sharon shook her head slowly. "You've certainly been busy, I'll grant you that. Any others?"

"Not that we know of."

Sharon lifted her eyebrows pointedly. "Not that you know of? What does that mean?"

"Well…" Christa glanced at Emilee, took a deep breath and spoke quickly. "Like we told you, the whole thing got out of hand. We told a few friends about it, but we couldn't seem to find the right guy, so we told a few more…" She lowered her gaze to the carpet. "And now everybody knows about it."

"We tried to stop it after you and Gabe got together," Emilee explained. "But we couldn't. Not without taking out an ad in the school paper."

Sharon could feel her face growing warm. "So the entire student body has been playing matchmaker?" She could quite cheerfully kill her daughters—and Gabe.

Christa sent her a sidelong glance. "Are you mad?"

"I'm not sure how I feel," Sharon said honestly.

"Just remember they were trying to do something nice," Gabe said softly. "It's a case of doing the wrong thing for the right reason."

She didn't need him to tell her that. She knew her daughters better than anyone. "Don't think you're off the hook," she said to him. "I'm still wondering why you didn't tell me."

"I didn't even know you at the time," he reminded her.

"Maybe not on New Year's Eve, but what about later? You could have told me when we started becoming friends. Or when you kissed me for the first time. Or after that disastrous date with Ed. And you certainly could have told me when we were out for dinner the other night."

He held up both hands to stop her. "I know. You're absolutely right. I don't have a good reason for not telling you, except that I'd promised the girls that I wouldn't, and I didn't want to break that promise."

She couldn't fault him for that, she supposed. In fact, she liked knowing he felt so strongly about keeping his word.

She turned toward her daughters again and fixed them with her sternest gaze. "I'm not angry," she said, "but you need to find some way to stop it before it goes any further—short of taking out an ad in the school paper. Please… no more men."

Her daughters both spoke at once, offering assurances, making promises, tendering one last set of apologies.

"Let's forget about it and finish the movie," Sharon said when they showed no signs of letting up. There hadn't been any *real* harm done. And if it had happened to someone else, she might even find the situation humorous.

The girls vacated the couch eagerly and

Gabe took his place beside her, wrapping an arm around her shoulders. She settled back into his embrace, relieved to finally understand why Christa and Emilee had behaved so strangely, and glad that Gabe was the one beside her and not one of the men her daughters had tried to set her up with.

Having Gabe here, a part of the family, felt right. And for this one night, Sharon wouldn't let herself worry about what tomorrow would bring.

CHAPTER FIFTEEN

HERE IT WAS, Gabe thought as he led Sharon and the girls downstairs, the moment of truth. He'd let them watch the basement take shape slowly until last week; then he'd banned them from coming downstairs until he could finish.

He was prouder of the work he'd done here than anything he'd ever done—probably because he'd long ago ceased to think of it as a job and looked at it instead as a labor of love. And now, in spite of the problems he'd run into working on this old house, his dad, Tracy and all his other commitments, he'd finally finished.

When he'd come across Sharon staring wistfully at an ad for ceiling fans, he'd purchased two with his own money. When he realized how much she loved to read, he installed the bookshelves at his own expense. Now, he couldn't wait to see the look on her face.

He reached the basement landing and turned to face them. "Are you ready?"

Emilee and Christa clamored for a peek, but Sharon held back.

He reached out a hand toward her. "You first, Sharon."

The teenagers made token noises of protest, but they stepped aside to let her pass. When she reached the bottom landing, he wrapped an arm around her shoulders, squeezed gently and led her into the family room. Her gasp of delight when she looked at the bookshelves and brass fans warmed him clear through.

Emilee let out a yelp of pleasure, moved into the center of the room and spun around to look at everything. Christa ran from window to fireplace to bookshelf, exclaiming with delight over everything.

Gabe kept his gaze riveted on Sharon's face.

"It's beautiful," she whispered, and he thought he saw the glimmer of tears in her eyes.

"You like it?"

"I love it."

"Wait until you see the bedroom." He grabbed her hand and urged her down the short hallway. "I think you'll like it even better."

He leaned against the door frame, arms folded, and watched her circle the room. Contentment spread clear through him.

"Oh, Gabe, this is truly wonderful. This is nicer than *my* room."

He wrapped his arms around her waist from

behind. "Maybe you should move into this one, then. It would give you more privacy."

Sharon turned to face him. "I've already put up with enough bickering over this room, I'm not going to start another round. Besides, this is Emilee's room. It'll be perfect for her when she starts college in the fall."

Emilee froze with one hand on the closet door, the other on a shelf. "It's an incredible room. Really. But I've been thinking maybe Christa should have it after all."

Sharon laughed without humor. "Oh, no. No. We're not going to start this all over again."

"I'm serious, Mom." Emilee shifted her weight nervously and glanced over her shoulder at Christa. "See, the thing is, I've been thinking about going away to college."

Sharon tensed visibly. "When did you start thinking about that?"

Emilee shrugged casually. "A few weeks ago. I was thinking, you know, that since the University of Utah has such a great nursing school…." She let her voice trail away, no doubt hoping Sharon would dive right in with her approval.

She didn't, of course. "I thought you'd decided against leaving home right away."

"I had," Emilee assured her. "But then, well, Gabe and I were talking about it and—" She shrugged again and sent him a silent plea for help.

The light in Sharon's eyes died. She stared at him for what felt like forever while he tried to decide how to respond. "We had a conversation weeks ago—"

"You helped her make a decision like that without talking to me?"

"It wasn't like that," he explained. "She mentioned that she wanted to go away. I had no idea she'd actually listen to me."

"I see." Sharon turned slowly to face Emilee. "Don't you think that's a decision *we* should have made?"

Emilee's face crumpled. "But I—but you—"

Gabe's heart went out to her. He tried to smooth things over. "Look, Sharon, I'm sorry, but don't be too hard on her. She's just a kid."

Sharon held up a hand to stop him. "Girls, would you go upstairs for a few minutes? I need to talk to Gabe alone." When they didn't leave immediately, she split a glance between them. *"Please."*

Emilee hurried toward the door with Christa only a step behind.

"I'll talk to you later," Sharon called after her. When they were alone again, she put some distance between them and turned to face him. "You can't do things like that, Gabe."

"Like what? We had a harmless conversation."

"Harmless? You've managed to work your way into their hearts. They're totally taken with you."

He didn't even try to mask his confusion. "And you're upset about that?"

"Exactly."

"I thought you wanted me to get along with them."

"Get along, yes. Take over their lives, no. Do you have any idea what you're doing to them?"

The unfair accusation roused his anger. He tried to keep it under control. "You're upset because she made a decision without talking to you. I can understand that—"

"I'm upset," Sharon snapped, "because you've gone too far. You had no right to help her make a decision like that."

"I had one conversation with her."

"I don't want Emilee and Christa growing so attached to you. And I don't want them relying on you."

His anger flared again. "I think you're skirting the real issue."

"Do you?" She rubbed her forehead with her fingertips. "Maybe I am. Gabe, this whole thing has been a mistake."

His stomach knotted. "You can't be serious."

"Can't I? What guarantee do those girls have that you'll still be around in a month?"

"Is that what's upsetting you? You're afraid I'm going to bail out on you?"

"It's not about me," she argued. "Don't you see what's happening? You're stepping into a father's role with Emilee and Christa."

He clenched his hands to keep from reaching out for her. He couldn't fix this with his usual techniques. "Aren't you happy that the girls have accepted me?" He took a tentative step toward her. "We have something pretty good. At least, I thought we did. I think you're afraid I'm getting too close, and you're using the girls as an excuse to pull away."

She backed away. "You're not listening to me. It's not about *us*. I can't risk the girls being disappointed when you decide you've had enough."

Gabe studied her for a long time. His gaze flicked over her eyes, her lips. "If you're that convinced I'm going to leave eventually, you don't trust me. And if you don't trust me, what kind of relationship do we have?"

"Can you honestly say you trust me?"

"Yes."

"Then why won't you let me meet Tracy when she comes?"

"I want you to," he assured her. "Like I said, she just needs a little time to adjust—"

"But Emilee and Christa don't? Why don't you admit it, Gabe? You don't want to introduce us to Tracy because you're not sure you're going to stick around. Why rock the boat if it's not necessary?"

His jaw tightened and anger curled like a ball in his chest. "Is that what you really think of me?"

The look on her face said it all.

Pain and frustration combined to push him over the edge. "If you're trying to get rid of me, at least be honest about why. Don't keep using your daughters as your excuses."

Her face reddened dangerously. "I do not use my daughters," she shouted, then made an effort to pull herself together. "This conversation is over."

He battled the urge to put his fist through her new wall. "You're right. It's pointless." He looked around at the bedroom he'd built for her and let out an acid laugh. "I've got to hand it to you. Your timing is perfect."

Seething, he stormed from the room and pounded up the stairs. When he let himself into the garage, he slammed the door behind him. But it didn't relieve the blind fury that thundered through his veins. And it sure didn't heal the gaping wound where his heart had been only minutes before.

"CALL HIM," ADELLE MUMBLED around a mouthful of barbecued Thai pork.

Sharon shoved her Oriental noodles and shredded vegetables around with her chopsticks and shook her head quickly. "No."

"Look," Adelle said, frowning deeply. "I understand your concerns, but I think you're overreacting a little."

"Well, I don't," Sharon snapped. Usually, she enjoyed eating at this restaurant, but today the scents of fish, pork and spices mixed with the strong smell of dishwashing soap made her slightly nauseated. She pushed away her bowl and took a sip of diet soda. "Can we not talk about this? All I want to do is forget about him and get on with my life."

"It's been two months," Adelle said, as if Sharon needed a reminder. "*Have* you forgotten about him?"

"I could if you'd stop talking about him all the time," Sharon lied. She hadn't been able to put Gabe out of her mind for a single moment, but she had no intention of admitting that to Adelle. She took another drink of soda, but it landed in her stomach like a rock. "Why don't we talk about the baby instead?"

Adelle ran her hand over her softly rounded stomach. "Because the baby's fine and so am I. You're not."

"I need to get back to work," Sharon said, desperate to change the subject. "Are you finished with your lunch?"

Adelle glanced at her bowl. "We just got our food." As if to make her point, she took another bite and gestured toward Sharon's. "You're not eating again?"

"I'm not hungry."

"If you'd get rid of some of that stubborn pride of yours and talk to him, you'd get your appetite back."

"If I don't, maybe I'll lose a couple of pounds." She brushed a lock of hair over her shoulder. "I'm serious, Adelle. I just want to forget about the whole thing." She would forget about him, she'd be able to sleep again and she'd get her appetite back—eventually.

Adelle took another bite of her lunch and shook her head while she chewed. "I've never known anybody so determined to be unhappy."

"I'm not determined to be unhappy." Sharon tried to keep her voice low so they wouldn't disturb the other diners. "Maybe it's escaped your notice, but I'm trying to keep from being unhappy."

Adelle lowered her chopsticks to the table. "And maybe it's escaped *your* notice, but you've gone to such great lengths to keep yourself from being unhappy that you've made yourself exactly that." She dropped her voice and went on. "You think that by avoiding Gabe, by locking yourself away, you're going to prevent heartache. But don't you see—" she reached for Sharon's hand "—whether or not you're with him, you'll still feel everything. I guarantee that there'll be times when you laugh and times when you cry. Days when you're happy and others when you're miserable. You can't hide from the emotions, Sharon. So if you have to feel them all anyway, wouldn't you rather do it with the man you love than because you're lonely?"

The truth of that hit Sharon squarely. Her hand began to tremble and her heart thudded dangerously in her chest.

Adelle looked as if she might say something more, then apparently changed her mind. She stirred her pork and noodles thoughtfully. "How are the girls?"

"They're fine." It was another lie, but she didn't want to admit how much Gabe's absence hurt them.

"And the college thing?"

"Emilee's put in applications to both Denver University and the University of Utah. We've agreed to see where she gets accepted and then go from there."

"Are they still dating as much as ever?"

"Of course. That's the one constant in my life."

Adelle leaned an elbow on the table and propped her chin in her hand. "With those two around, it's no wonder you don't think *you* need a life."

Sharon rolled her eyes. "Adelle—"

"Just listen to me for once. You know what you should do?"

"No, but I'm sure you'll tell me."

Adelle placed her napkin on the table. "I think you're right. You *should* put Gabe completely out of your mind and get involved with someone else."

"Not interested." Sharon folded her own napkin, left it beside her nearly full bowl and slipped a tip for their server onto the table. "And I meant what I said earlier. I don't want to talk about it anymore."

Adelle shrugged and pushed to her feet. "Fine. Have it your way. Be alone forever if that's what you want."

Sharon tugged the strap of her purse onto her shoulder and led the way toward the cashier.

Adelle made it sound so simple, but it wasn't simple. Not by a long shot.

She pulled in a deep breath of fresh, clean air mixed with exhaust fumes and tar from some nearby road-construction project.

Adelle followed her outside and snagged her arm. "Thanks for meeting me, even though I know your heart wasn't in it."

Sharon managed a thin smile. "I'll be all right, Adelle. Don't worry about me."

"I do worry, though. I can't help it." Adelle pushed her bangs out of her face again. "I'm serious about what I said in there. You should start seeing other guys."

Sharon sighed softly and let her gaze travel over the parking lot. The truth was, she didn't want to see other men. She hadn't stopped loving Gabe yet. And she didn't know if she ever would.

GABE KEPT HIS BACK toward the dancing couples and waited while Ringo placed a platter holding a garlic burger and a sizzling mound of fries on the bar in front of him. He ordered another beer and pounded ketchup from the bottle onto his plate.

It had been two months since his argument with Sharon. Two of the longest months of his life. The only good thing that had happened had been Tracy's all-too-brief visit over spring break. Gabe had been pleased with the way he and his daughter had finally gotten to know each other. But then Tracy had left and Gabe had been lonelier than ever. He'd picked up the phone to call Sharon several times, but he'd managed to talk himself out of actually calling every time. She'd made herself perfectly clear. It was over. He just wished she'd been honest with herself about the reason.

The band started a new song, something with a Caribbean flavor. Gabe sighed, irritated with the upbeat music, and took a bite of his burger. Behind him, the outside door swished open. He took a long drink and glanced over his shoulder. Late-afternoon sunlight spilled into the smoke-filled room and Jesse strode inside.

Good old Jesse. A true friend. He'd never end their friendship over some imaginary problem.

Jesse crossed to the bar and hitched himself onto a stool beside Gabe's. "You're here again? What is this now, eight weeks in a row?"

Gabe cocked an eyebrow at him. "You counting?"

"Nope." Jesse placed his order and dragged a bowl of peanuts closer. "You can do whatever you want. Makes no difference to me."

"Good."

Jesse munched for a few minutes, bobbing his

head in time to the music. "Isn't Tracy coming for the summer?"

Gabe nodded. "Yeah. Why?"

"Curiosity, buddy. Sheesh, you're getting worse by the day."

"Wrong," Gabe snapped. "I'm getting my head on straight again for the first time in years."

Jesse bit back a smile. "Of course you are. I can tell."

"Tracy and I got to know each other when she visited over spring break. Now I want to concentrate on making the summer great for her. Dad and I had a long conversation and he's going to let me take over more of the business end of things. I'm going to start working out regularly at the gym. I've got plenty to do."

Jesse glanced at him. "Sounds like you've got everything under control."

"I do," Gabe insisted.

"Since you feel that way, maybe I should have Celia introduce you to a friend of hers I met the other night."

Gabe deepened his scowl. "Don't bother. I'm through with women."

Jesse laughed. "Where have I heard that before?"

"I mean it this time," Gabe informed him.

Jesse shifted on his stool and studied him for a second. "She really got to you, didn't she?"

Far more than Gabe wanted to admit, even to himself. "You couldn't be more wrong," he lied.

"Oh. Sorry. I forgot. You're always this cheerful."

"I'm tired, that's all."

"Tired like you were after Helene kicked you out of the house."

Gabe shoved away his plate and fixed Jesse with a pointed glare. "If you can't drop the subject—"

Jesse didn't let him finish. "No, I can't. And you know why? Because I'm tired of watching you throw your life away and feel sorry for yourself. You're so lovesick, anybody can see it. Why can't you just admit that the woman broke your heart? Why can't you swallow some of that stupid pride of yours and talk to her?"

Gabe opened his mouth to protest, but Jesse was on a roll. He didn't let Gabe get a word in edgewise.

"You know what your problem is? You keep waiting for the perfect woman to show up. Somebody who'll never make a mistake, but who'll turn a blind eye to all of yours."

"*She's* the one who told *me* to leave," Gabe growled.

"Yeah? Because she's worried about you walking out on her. Her husband cheated on her, didn't he? If you were any kind of man at all, you'd try to understand what's bothering her." Jesse shoved away the empty peanut bowl and met his gaze. "Instead, you decided to prove her right. If you love her, and I know you do, you'll get over there and prove that you're not going to abandon her when the going gets rough. If you're not willing to do that, then maybe she was right to send you packing."

Gabe didn't want to listen. The words hit too close to home. He balled his fists and clenched his jaw and let his anger override his common sense. "What are you, a relationship expert now? I don't see you having any better luck with women than I have."

"Luck," Jesse said dryly, "has nothing to do with it. I've been seeing Celia for a while now, and I'm trying to learn from my mistakes. Not repeat them. So, stay here and cry into your beer if you want to. I'm having dinner with Celia." He tossed a bill on the counter and crossed the bar again, leaving Gabe alone with nothing but his thoughts for company.

CHAPTER SIXTEEN

"WHAT ARE WE GOING to do about it?" Emilee asked from the side of the pool. She kicked her feet gently in the cool water and let the sun kiss her face and shoulders.

Christa stood inside the pool, up to her neck in water. She glanced over her shoulder to make sure their mom was still swimming laps and couldn't hear them. "We're not going to do anything about it. Think, Em. We nearly screwed everything up. Besides, he'll come back."

Emilee couldn't share her sister's optimism. "When? It's already been ages."

"It doesn't matter when," Christa said, tipping her head back to wet her hair again. "If they love each other, he'll come back. It's fate."

"I can't wait for fate," Emilee argued. She kicked her legs a little harder, trying to work off some of the frustration she felt whenever she thought about Gabe walking out on their mother. "It doesn't matter that Mom's the one who sent him away. If he was any kind of man at all, he'd come back to her."

"You know what?" Christa pulled herself out of the pool and sat, dripping wet, next to Emilee. "I think you feel guilty."

"Why should *I* feel guilty?"

"Because they got into that stupid argument over you and college."

Emilee checked Sharon's progress across the pool and ducked when some jerk decided to jump into the water over her head. "Okay, maybe I do. I never should have talked to him about it."

Christa mopped her face with her towel. "You know what, Em? If it hadn't been that, it would have been something else. Mom wasn't ready."

"Of course she was."

"No, she wasn't. She still had a bunch of stuff to work through. And maybe he did, too."

"I still think we should try to find him. I'll bet we could talk him into coming back."

"Yeah." Christa snorted in derision. "And just think how that would make Mom feel." She lowered her towel and stared into Emilee's eyes. "We're not doing anything. Nothing. Zip. Nada. We're going to let fate take it from here."

"But—"

"But nothing. I'm serious, Emilee. If you start interfering, you'll ruin it for them."

"What if he doesn't come back?" Just the thought made her sick to her stomach.

"He will." Christa slid back into the water. "He will."

WHILE HE WAITED for Sharon to answer the door, Gabe clasped his hands together in front of him, unclasped them nervously and latched them behind his back. Dusk had already fallen, and shadows clustered in the corners of the porch and pooled on the sidewalk. Not too far away, someone's dog barked. A kid shouted. Normal sounds for a summer's evening in a subdivision, he supposed. But every noise made his nerves jump.

He didn't know what to expect. Sharon might easily turn him away, and he wouldn't blame her. He'd let nerves keep him from making a commitment to anyone for too long.

He raised his hand to ring the bell again, but before he could push the button, Emilee opened the door. The look of shock on her face didn't surprise him. What did surprise him was the width of her smile.

Christa's greeting was even warmer. She came up behind Emilee and let out a shriek of delight. "I knew it. I knew you'd come back." She reached past Emilee and tugged him through the door. "Come on in. I'll get Mom."

Emilee didn't move. She just stared at him, grinning, until Sharon appeared what felt like an eternity later.

He'd expected a reserved coolness from Sharon. Anger, even. But he saw neither. Instead, she smiled tentatively and her expression mended his heart and told him he'd done the right thing by swallowing his pride.

She sent Emilee and Christa into the other room, then gestured toward the living room. "This is a surprise. Please come in and have a seat."

He caught her gaze and held it. "How have you been?"

She smiled. "Is that why you came?"

He shook his head quickly. "No. Not exactly." He crossed to the couch and sat at one end, foolishly hoping she'd sit on the other. She didn't. Instead, she chose that wingback chair that closed in around her like a protective wall. "I came to talk to you. I'm sorry—"

"I'm so glad you came," she said, holding up both hands to stop him. "I've been trying to get up the courage to call you for days."

He rocked back in his seat and stared at her. "You have?"

"I'm the one who's sorry, Gabe. I let fear and

other people's opinions convince me you'd eventually get tired of me and leave."

"I'd never get tired of you," he assured her quietly.

"How can you be sure?"

"Because you're an incredible woman. You've helped me be more honest about my feelings than I've ever been in my life." He pushed to his feet and took a tentative step closer. "I fell head over heels in love with you, and that frightened me."

"Not as much as my loving you frightened me," she said with a laugh. "That's why I needed you to go away."

"You wanted me to leave because you *love* me?" His laugh faded to a chuckle. "I swear, I'll never understand women."

"I don't want you to understand women," she said with a teasing smile. "But I hope you'll try to understand me." Her smile faded and her eyes darkened. "You scared me, Gabe. After Nick left, I vowed I'd never let another man get that close to me again."

"I'm not sure that's the most flattering thing I've ever heard, but it's probably true. And I didn't think I could give you what you needed from a man. After you sent me away, I decided it would be kinder in the long run to just stay out of your life."

To his amazement, her smile returned. "So, what are we going to do? Spend the entire evening arguing about which of us is most dysfunctional?"

"No. I love you. I need to spend the rest of my life with you. And I'll do whatever it takes to make that happen."

She let out a pleased sigh. "Let me just say one thing first. I know the idea of home and family frightens you. But if you think I want to sit home night after night and never do anything, you're sadly mistaken. And if you think I want you hovering around all the time bugging me, or that I'll never want a moment alone, you don't know me very well." She touched his hand softly, hesitantly, but the touch held the promise of a lifetime. "Home and family is important to me, Gabe. But it's not a prison. I'm not so needy or insecure that I can't let you out of my sight once in a while. And I'm not so boring that I won't want to join you from time to time."

"You're willing to give me a second chance?" He gripped her hand and held on, and his voice came out choked with emotion.

"I'm willing to give *us* a second chance. I love you. I don't have much choice." She glanced toward the dining-room door and her lips twitched. "Besides, if I send you away again, those two might start trying to find the perfect man for me again, which will be pretty hard since I already found him."

"I'm not perfect—"

Sharon touched his lips with her fingers to stop him. "I didn't say you were perfect. I said you were the perfect man for me. There's a difference."

He grinned and looked toward the dining room just in time to see two blond heads duck out of sight. "Do you think they'll mind?"

"Why don't you ask them? You may just fit their man-for-mom plan."

He laughed softly and turned back to Sharon. Slowly, he got down on one knee and took her hand in his. "Before I do that, I want to ask *you* something. Sharon Lawrence, will you marry me? Please?"

In answer, she leaned forward and pressed her lips to his. Through the pounding of his pulse in his ears, he heard whispers from the dining room.

"She didn't say yes."

"She *has* to say yes."

"What are they doing now?"

"Kissing."

"Do you think that means yes?"

Sharon pulled away from him reluctantly and called over her shoulder, "It means yes."

Emilee and Christa didn't need anything

more. They bounded into the room, threw their arms around Gabe and sent him tumbling to the floor. Almost immediately, they released him and launched themselves at Sharon. Excited chatter filled the air with everyone talking at once.

"When are you getting married?" Emilee asked.

Christa let Sharon go and grabbed Gabe's arm. "Before the end of the year. It has to be before the end of the year."

"I know!" Emilee cried. "New Year's Eve. Before midnight!"

Sharon laughed and met Gabe's gaze in silent question. He grinned and nodded in agreement. To be honest, he didn't care when or where they did it, as long as they were together every day for the rest of their lives.

He'd found the peace and contentment he'd been looking for forever. Strangely, he'd found it in the one place he'd never thought to look.

At home.

EPILOGUE

"ALL RIGHT, try it now."

Sharon smiled at the muffled voice of Gabe's father whose head was hidden by the sink and whose legs stuck out into the middle of her kitchen floor. She turned on the faucet and let it run for a second, then shut it off again quickly. "Is it still leaking?"

Harold pushed out from beneath the sink and grinned triumphantly. "Looks like we got it. There's not even a drop."

Sharon held out a hand and helped him to his feet. "Thanks, Dad. I don't know what we'd do without you."

"Nonsense." Her father-in-law's voice sounded gruff, but he sent her an affectionate glance. "Sometimes I wonder if you intentionally break things, just to make me feel useful now that I've retired."

"Honestly, Harold." Gabe's mother looked up from the salad she was making, but she sent Sharon a grateful smile when her husband looked away to put the wrench back in his toolbox. "How could you accuse Sharon of something like that? This is an old house, and heaven only knows Gabriel's too busy to keep everything in working order."

Sharon smiled softly. She'd been part of their family for only six months, but she felt as if she'd been one of them forever. She turned her attention to Tracy, who stirred a pitcher of lemonade at the end of the counter. "Would you mind asking your dad if he's ready to start grilling?"

Though their initial meeting late last summer had been a little strained, they'd discovered so many things in common the uneasiness had disappeared almost immediately. And Gabe's twice-a-week phone calls between visits had helped to remove the rest of the barriers between them, as well.

"I don't know," Tracy said skeptically. "He might never want to start cooking. He's been playing with Taylor all afternoon."

Gabe's attachment to Adelle's son, already nearly a year old, never ceased to warm Sharon's heart, and she wondered how she'd ever let herself doubt his ability to commit to their family. She'd never seen a more devoted father or husband.

As if on cue, Gabe appeared in the patio door holding Taylor. "Are you ready for me to start the burgers? I suppose I could let this little guy sit with his mother for a while."

Harold closed the toolbox and hefted it. "Why don't you let me cook this time? Looks like you've got your hands full."

"Sure, if you want to." Gabe shrugged casually and chucked Taylor under his chin. "I'd like to run a couple of things past you, anyway. We got that contract for the store in that new strip mall, and I'd like your input."

Harold's quick smile confirmed what Gabe had told Sharon. Seeking his father's advice helped make the transition smoother for all of them. She let her gaze linger on her husband for a moment, marveling at her good fortune as she often did.

"You've made him happy," her mother-in-law said softly.

Sharon turned to face her. "He's made me happy, too."

"I can see that." Gabe's mom positioned tomato wedges on the salad and glanced outside. "Why don't you spend a few minutes with the girls. I'll finish up in here."

Sharon accepted the offer gratefully. Emilee would only be around a few more days before she headed back to college for summer quarter, and Christa would be leaving at the same time for an extended visit with Nick.

She stepped onto the patio, relishing the warmth of the early summer day. Emilee and Christa played badminton with Gabe's nieces on the far edge of the lawn while Rosalie and Jack looked on. Adelle and Doug sat in the shade of the old oak tree, heads together, probably discussing Adelle's hopes to give Taylor a brother or sister by next year.

Sighing with contentment, Sharon caught Gabe's eye. They shared a smile, filled with the joy of the moment and the promise of forever.

Together.

* * * * *

BESTSELLING AUTHOR COLLECTION

In our Bestselling Author Collection, Harlequin Books is proud to offer classic novels from today's superstars of women's fiction. These authors have captured the hearts of millions of readers around the world, and earned their place on the *New York Times, USA TODAY* and other bestseller lists with every release.

As a bonus, each volume also includes a full-length novel from a rising star of series romance. Bestselling authors in their own right, these talented writers have captured the qualities Harlequin is famous for—heart-racing passion, edge-of-your-seat entertainment and a satisfying happily-ever-after.

Don't miss any of the books in the collection!